Christmas
in the
Little Irish
Village

BOOKS BY MICHELLE VERNAL

Michelle Vernal

Christmas
in the
Little Irish
Village

Bookouture

Published by Bookouture in 2022

An imprint of Storyfire Ltd.
Carmelite House
50 Victoria Embankment
London EC4Y 0DZ

www.bookouture.com

ISBN: 978-1-80314-845-8
eBook ISBN: 978-1-80314-844-1

For Paul and our boys, family and friends near and far and my beautiful Mum and Dad. We miss you.

FOUR DAYS UNTIL CHRISTMAS

May peace and plenty be the first
To lift the latch at your door
And happiness be guided to your home
By the candle of Christmas.
God's blessings and peace be yours throughout
This New Year.

— *IRISH CHRISTMAS BLESSING*

1

It was four days until Christmas, and Shannon Kelly was leaving home. She took one last, lingering walk around the upmarket apartment in the centre of Galway where she'd resided over the previous two years. Beside the front door were two suitcases stuffed with her worldly belongings, her boots, a cat climbing tree, and a pet carrier containing Napoleon, the tortoiseshell Persian cat Julien had left her with sole custody of. Napoleon was currently voicing his discontent over the indignity of being pushed head first into the carrier.

As she padded toward the kitchen, the carpet beneath her stockinged feet was soft, with a deep pile you literally sank into. She'd made it a house rule that shoes were to be left by the door, and even now, as she was about to go, she couldn't break it. If she hadn't felt so miserable, she'd have smiled as the memory of a comment her little sister Hannah had made the first time she'd called around to see her 'big sister's swanky love nest' popped into her head.

'It's the sorta carpet that makes you want to throw your clothes off and roll around naked on it. I hope it's sustainable.'

Shannon had been awestruck by all the shiny fixtures and

fittings when she and Julien first came to view the apartment. The floor-to-ceiling view over the River Corrib and stone's-throw location from the city's lively cobbled streets had sold her the moment she'd walked through the door. But she'd known her public health nurse's salary would find the monthly rent a stretch.

Julien, however, had declared the fully furnished apartment *idéal*. It hadn't mattered to him that she'd have to drive over an hour a day to the medical centre where she was based because his job as a software designer meant he worked from home.

As a Parisian, she could hardly blame him for preferring to live in buzzy Galway rather than the quieter Kilticaneel where she worked, or her home village of Emerald Bay. And because she just wanted him to be happy, they'd signed the lease that same afternoon.

Shannon wouldn't have cared where they lived so long as they were together. She wasn't a girl for whom 'things' mattered. All she wanted was a simple, happy and honest life with the man she loved, like the life her mam shared with her dad. It hadn't seemed much to ask for in the grand scheme of things.

It was surprising how quickly you took luxury for granted, she thought as she reached the kitchen and trailed her hand over the white Italian marble worktop. It was smooth and cold to the touch. How often had she perched on the stool here watching Julien demonstrate his culinary prowess in the kitchen? She closed her eyes and pictured herself nursing a glass of red in one of those ridiculous fishbowl wine glasses he'd loved.

A wave of pain crashed over her, and she bit her lip to stop herself from audibly moaning over the injustice of it all. It had been cruel that he'd given her no warning and no chance to fix whatever was wrong. Determined to torture herself further, she let her eyes flit across the open-plan floor space to the enormous leather sofa angled for the best view of the river beyond. Oh, the bliss of sprawling across that sofa, eyes half-closed, while Julien gave her a foot rub. Foot rubs had usually progressed to the bedroom.

'Do not go there, Shannon Marie Kelly.' Her voice wobbled, and she broke off as the pocket of the denim jacket she'd slung over her polo neck began vibrating. Glad of the diversion, she dug her phone out and glanced at the screen before sliding the green icon across.

'Mam, I'm leaving in half an hour at the most.'

'Grand, I'll make your favourite for dinner,' Nora Kelly said.

At fifty-six, her mam was what Shannon's dad described as a fine figure of a woman, and he was prone to serenading her with Van Morrison's 'Brown Eyed Girl' when he'd had a few too many pints. Nora, however, was apt to lament the loss of her waist in recent years. Her chestnut hair was kept steadfastly at shoulder length since she'd passed fifty, and the roots were zealously maintained. Her rich brown eyes were a gift she'd passed on to three of her girls, but it was her smile that made her beautiful. It lit up her face, giving those around her a warm glow. Shannon no longer minded being labelled her mam's mini-me, although she'd hated it when she was a teenager, desperate to form her own identity.

She frowned at the mention of favourite dinners, having heard this talk before when going home. She'd walk in, expecting to be greeted by the rich aroma of the hearty pot pie she loved. But, oh, the disappointment when she found Mam had got muddled as to whose favourite dinner was whose. Instead of pot pie, it was the fish pie Imogen loved, or the corned beef and cabbage Ava was partial to. She supposed it must be hard to keep track of the whims of five daughters.

'Guinness, beef and onion pot pie?' She clutched the phone tighter seeking confirmation, because in her fragile state she'd not be able to take the disappointment if it was boxty, colcannon or the like.

'One and the same, and your nan's making brown bread for afternoon tea too.'

Heartbroken she might be, but the thought of biting into a round of Nan's soda bread with its soft middle and crunchy crust made her stomach growl. Kitty Kelly's soda bread was the stuff of legends.

'And will she make enough so I can toast some in the morning?' Her knuckles were now white from all that clutching. The only thing more comforting than a steaming dish of Guinness, beef and onion pot pie for your dinner was a piece of Nan's bread toasted and slathered in butter and jam with your morning cuppa. There was no point trying to lose the pounds she'd slapped on since Julien left, not over the festive season, and why should she even bother? She was off men and planned to become a disagreeable old spinster in her dotage.

'Who's "she", the cat's mother?' her nan's voice sang out in the background.

For a little woman, she had a big voice, Shannon thought. In her mind's eye, she could see her beloved nan waving the whisk she was using to mix the flour, salt and soda before adding the buttermilk to the bread mix. She always said the key to a good loaf was in opening a fresh packet of baking soda. No doubt she'd had the pinny gifted to her by one of the guests who'd stayed in the B&B above the family pub, the Shamrock Inn, knotted around her middle. It was a firm favourite with its *I don't need a recipe, I'm Irish* slogan. Her mane of once deep-red curls was kept short these days, a faded copper halo around a face with wily blue eyes that didn't miss much. The Kelly girls might have pulled the wool over their mam's and dad's eyes once or twice in their teenage years, but they'd never managed to get anything past Nan!

'Sorry, Nan. Mam, stop putting me on speakerphone.'

'Shannon, I'll have to run. Your father needs a hand behind the bar. We'll see you soon, love. Drive safe.'

Shannon disconnected the call and her eyes swept the space she was standing in. Her chest tightened as the memories swamped her and the phone was like a hot potato in her hand. She turned her gaze to the screen. Should she torture herself just a little bit more? *Too late.* She'd opened her Instagram account and tapped in Julien's name.

Voila, there he was, and more to the point, there she was too. The new girlfriend.

The familiar queasiness settled in her stomach. It had only been three months since they'd broken up and Julien had left her high and dry. How could he have moved on so fast? In her darker moments, she wondered if he'd ever loved her at all.

'Angular Audrey,' Shannon muttered, scowling at the glamorous French woman as she flicked through the grid of images. It was agony seeing all the happy and in-love shots. Then, enlarging the latest picture of Audrey stuffing a flaky croissant in her face, she decided she'd no right to be that thin.

What was wrong with her? As her fashionista younger sister Imogen would say, Shannon's cream polo neck and red plaid miniskirt were on-trend. Plaid was all the go this winter. Irish girls were stylish too. 'Not stylish enough, Napoleon.'

'Shannon, I hope you're not doing what I think you're doing.'

She pirouetted around, red-faced at having been caught out.

'Sorry, but the door was open.' Her neighbour, Aidan, who'd promised to help her cart her worldly goods down to the car park, pushed his black-rimmed glasses back up onto the bridge of his nose. He looked anything but sorry as he stood in the doorway, aware of Shannon's shoes-off rule. 'You promised us you'd delete your Instagram account.' His voice sounded school teacherly despite his perpetual rumpled student look. 'Stalking your ex is not healthy.'

'I'm not stalking him. I'm...' Shannon cast about for the word.

'Stalking him.'

She pulled a face. 'Anyway, I made that promise under the influence.'

When Julien announced he didn't see his future with Shannon in Ireland after all, she'd been left in disbelief that he'd gone. She'd not told anyone at first. Not even her family. Especially not her family. They'd have had far too much to say on the subject, and she wasn't ready to hear it, not when she was certain he'd come back. Sure, any minute he'd come barrelling back in the door, weighed down by roses and apologies for having been a fool, she'd told herself. Except he hadn't.

Her prediction regarding her family had proved correct, with the terms 'arse', 'eejit' and 'French gobshite' (from her father) being bandied about. Poor Mam had almost been as heartbroken as she'd been upon hearing her dream of free accommodation in the City of Love was crushed.

Aidan and his partner, Paulo, in the apartment opposite hers had saved her from many a Bridget Jones moment since the split, insisting she come over and squish in with them on their sofa every Friday night. They'd even let her bring Napoleon – well, once. Napoleon had expressed his upset at Julien abandoning him by spraying the curtains. She wasn't the only one hurting.

The lads had topped up her wine and listened to her rant about how Julien had left her with three months to run on a lease for an apartment she could ill afford. And how she was sick of the sight of beans on toast for dinner now her credit cards were maxed. They'd plied her with bags of Tayto crisps and turned the volume down on *The Late Late* as the weeks went by and she'd pestered them as to what she could have done differently, championing her when she asked what was wrong with her.

'Look at that beautiful hair of yours. I'd kill for hair so shiny,' Paulo had said, referring to the hair that drove Shannon mad because it was neither straight nor curly. If she let it grow past her shoulders, it got very thick at the bottom, and she wound up looking like she'd asked for the 'triangle, please' on her last visit to the hairdressers.

'And when you use mascara and do a bold red lip, you've got a look of Leighton Meester about you,' Aidan added.

She'd deigned to share the crisps with the boys that night.

Worst of all, though, was the day she'd woken up and dragged herself out of bed to find the colour had leached from her world. Her footsteps as she waded through her days were as heavy as her heart.

'It's the five stages of grief, Shannon,' Aidan had informed her as she'd waved the crisps away apathetically one Friday night. Somewhere along the line, they'd lost their magic comfort powers. 'Denial, Anger, Bargaining, Grief.' He ticked them off on his fingers.

'That's only four,' she'd replied.

'I saved the best for last. Acceptance. You're nearly there, girlfriend.'

Was she? Shannon wondered, stuffing her phone in her pocket guiltily. She wasn't convinced because it was very, very hard to accept she wouldn't be spending Christmas in Paris, meeting Julien's family. In anticipation, two weeks' leave at Christmas had been booked early. Nor would she be receiving the proposal with the Eifel Tower backdrop she'd been gunning for. Nope, instead, she was moving home to Emerald Bay to lick her wounds and regroup financially and emotionally for an indeterminate amount of time. Oh, and to eat Nan's brown bread too.

'Paulo's sorry he can't be here to see you off,' Aidan offered up.

'I know. He told me he'd an urgent meeting. What he's

really going to miss is being next door to nursing care for his ingrown toenail, runny nose or whatever else is ailing him on any given day.'

Aidan grinned, knowing his partner had hypochondriac tendencies, then ran a hand through his unruly mop. 'We'll miss you and Napoleon, Shannon.' He crouched down beside the pet carrier and began making kissy noises.

'Don't stick your finger in there, Aidan. He's not impressed with his current situation, and you know what sharp little teeth he has.'

Aidan's hand shot back. 'Take care of your mammy, Napoleon.'

A frantic mewing and scrabbling sounded as Aidan straightened.

'We'll miss you too.' Shannon sniffed. 'I don't know how I would have made it through these last few months without you and Paulo.'

'No more tears. New beginnings, remember? And you're moving back to Emerald Bay, not the ends of the earth.'

Shannon thought he might look like a student, but he'd a professor's wisdom, blinking furiously as she nodded.

'I packed you a survival kit.' Aidan held out the carrier bag in his hand.

She gave him a watery smile and moved toward the door, taking the bag to peek inside. 'Wine, cheese and onion crisps, a Lion bar.' She looked up. 'Thanks so much.' Her hand patted around in the bag, settling on something stringy. 'Hang on, what's this?' A split second later, she was dangling a realistic toy mouse by its tail.

'For Napoleon.' Aidan shrugged. 'To show him there are no hard feelings. You know, for the curtain-spraying thing.'

Her bottom lip trembled. 'Aidan, I really do think I'm going to cry.'

'No, you're not.' He was all brusque and businesslike as he

took hold of her cases. 'I'll take these down to the car park. It's time to get this show on the road.'

Shannon patted the front pocket of her jacket to check the keys were there, having decided she'd drop them off at the estate agent's on the way out of the city. The lift pinged, and she shoved her feet into her boots before picking up the pet carrier and dragging the cat climbing tree behind. 'Hold the lift, Aidan, we're coming!' she called out as the door closed with a click behind her. She didn't know if she was sad or relieved to be leaving the apartment. Either way, it was the end of a chapter, she thought, not looking back as she stepped into the lift.

2

Shannon wound her way through the boggy, rust-coloured fields peppered with limewashed-stone farm cottages. She'd tossed the empty Lion chocolate bar wrapper from Aidan and Paulo's survival kit onto the passenger seat of her car and hoped she'd not got chocolate down her front.

Big Bird or BB, her car, was a sunshine-yellow blip on otherwise empty roads. The tinsel and fairy-light strewn streets of Galway were behind her now with the occasional nod to Christmas in the windows of the cottages she was driving past. The only sign of life was the spiralling smoke from their chimneys. It was as if this pocket of the west was hibernating, and the barrenness of the landscape suited her empty mood, as did the heavy grey sky.

Her dad had talked her into buying the yellow Honda Jazz, and he'd been the one to christen the car Big Bird.

'Yellow's the most visible car colour on the road in bad conditions, Shannon,' Liam Kelly had stated knowledgeably in the yard of the second-hand dealership. He'd been standing with his hands thrust in the pockets of his jeans, a paunch showing through his sweater. His thick crop of hair, once a vibrant red inherited from his mam, Kitty, had faded to copper these days and his blue eyes were canny. Like Kitty's, they didn't miss much. He drove a pee-coloured Hilux and Nora said the ridiculously big vehicle was an extension of his unmentionables. His daughters were convinced he'd put the big monster truck tyres on it if he thought he could get away with it.

'It's a fact that is,' the oily salesman with euro signs lighting his eyes had agreed with Liam wholeheartedly before giving Shannon's bust an admiring glance.

'But, Dad, it's hurting my eyes,' she'd said. Unlike her sisters, she didn't enjoy being the centre of attention and a car that bright was attention-grabbing. She also valued her privacy, something that wasn't easy growing up in a village the size of Emerald Bay, and everybody would know her whereabouts in that thing, she'd moaned. But it was a foregone conclusion she'd end up with the car, because Shannon was one of life's pleasers.

Shannon Kelly did not like rocking the boat or breaking the rules.

This trait was something Imogen found infuriating because it was Shannon's duty as the oldest sibling to defy their parents. The no-make-up-to-school, no-stopping-out-past-ten-on-a-weeknight and no-lads-upstairs rules when they were teenagers should have been rebelled against, thus carving a far easier path for her younger siblings when their time came.

'Sure, your job has you out driving in all kinds of weather, Shannon. Who'll have to tell your poor mammy who loves you that you've had an accident when the farmer on the tractor doesn't see you in that silver yoke you've your eye on over there?'

The salesman had shaken his head sadly at Liam's scenario. His eyes firmly fixed on Shannon's bosom as he murmured, 'Poor, poor Mammy.'

It was two against one, so yellow it had been. Besides, her dad had a point. Shannon's home visits did take her all over the countryside on roads where there were more potholes than tar. So, an eyesore BB might be, but she was also a reliable vehicle and easy to park. Visibility aside, another bonus of having a vivid-coloured car was never worrying about remembering where she'd parked at Tesco's. BB stood out in a white, black, blue, and grey sea of cars. Her patients loved the neon car because they always knew who it was who'd come calling without having to squint through the front door's peephole. Best of all, though, was the adjustable driver's seat. Shannon felt like she wasn't peering over the steering wheel for the first time in her driving career. She was sitting pretty.

A splatter of raindrops hit the windscreen, and she turned the wipers on, feeling the car get buffeted by the wind. Still and all, she was toasty with the heater blasting and the radio tuned to a local easy-listening station. Her choice in music was something her family, Julien included, poked fun at her for.

'Here she is, the Celine Dion queen,' her sisters would laugh.

So what if she loved filling her lungs and singing her heart out to 'The Power of Love'?

'Sure, when I was your age, it was The Cure I was into, not Barry Manilow,' her dad would say.

In her opinion, Barry did write the songs that make the whole world sing.

'Michael Bubble's a grand voice, Shannon,' her mam would add.

'Bublé, Mam, not bubble, as you well know.'

'Heathens the lot of them, my girl. They wouldn't know good music if it jumped up and bit them on the arse. The state of your father when he was young with his hair dyed black and more hairspray in it than Nessie Doyle uses in a month – and her a hairdresser. Poor Father Angus, God rest his soul, didn't know what to make of him with all that attitude, and when he started borrowing my best lipstick, it nearly pushed him over the edge.'

Shannon thought you could always count on Nan to speak her mind as the newsreader finished the one o'clock update by giving a long-range forecast for a white Christmas. It was where Hannah got her propensity for blurting whatever was on her mind.

'Wishful thinking, Napoleon,' she tossed over her shoulder, listening for a meowed response. When none was forthcoming, she decided he must have given up on trying to break free and gone to sleep at last.

Snow was predicted most years and never came to more than an icing sugar dusting. She rolled her eyes, knowing whether or not they were in for a dumping would be a hot topic of conversation around the village. The consensus of those who weren't in the farming game fretting for their sheep was that if it was going to be cold, it might as well be pretty and give the tourists their picture-postcard photographs to take home with them.

Her fingers began to tap out the distinctive opening beat of Tom Jones's hit 'Delilah' and, despite herself, she smiled.

'Eat your heart out, Nan.'

Shannon wasn't the only easy-listening music devotee in the Kelly clan. Kitty Kelly was an ardent Tom fan, with Engelbert Humperdinck a close second. She'd even seen Tom play in Cork a year or two back with her pals, Eileen Carroll and Rita Quigley. There had been fierce debate in the Shamrock Inn that night as to whether or not there'd be knicker-throwing going on at the concert. Ollie Quigley had piped up it would be like the parachutes dropping for the D-Day landings if Kitty, Eileen and Rita were to toss their bloomers on stage.

Shannon rounded a bend, and even though she knew what was coming, her breath still snagged at her first glimpse of the thrashing Atlantic with the ruins of Kilticaneel Castle keeping guard over the expanse of Emerald Bay. It was a sight that always humbled her because she felt so insignificant against the sea's might. Life's problems were nothing more than the ocean's flotsam and jetsam. The sea was a great equaliser.

'Nearly there now, Napoleon.' She glanced into the rear-view mirror, seeing the cat climbing tree Aidan had slid in on top of her cases and the pet carrier on the back seat. She hoped Napoleon would settle into his new home. He'd been a house cat in Galway City, but at the Shamrock Inn, under her eagle eye, Shannon would let him have the run of the beer garden now and again. It would be a better life for him. For her, however, there was a sense of failure.

'Fecking Julien!' She banged her hand on the steering wheel, and this time there was a startled meow from the back seat.

'Sorry, Napoleon, it's all right. Mammy's being silly, that's all.' She retrieved a mint from the open packet in the drinks holder and popped it in her mouth. Then Shannon did what she always did when she was low, eating aside; she thought about her grandad and what he would have said to her if he was sitting alongside her right now.

'Shannon girl, there's nothing wrong with going home. Sure, what's a home if it's not somewhere you're always welcome? It's where you find the people who love you most.'

'And judgement, Grandad,' she said aloud, thinking about the wagging tongues and clacking knitting needles over tea and cake in the Silver Spoon cafe when news of her homecoming spread. 'Mam and Dad had been married thirteen years by the time they were my age. Going home a single woman once again is not where I saw myself in my thirties.'

'A good retreat is better than a bad stand, Shannon.' She remembered her grandad's sayings so clearly. Finbar Kelly had a wise old Irish proverb for everything.

'I miss you, Grandad.' Even now, nearly twenty years since

he'd passed, Shannon's brown eyes filled with tears. She blinked them away furiously. He'd been too young to die of the heart attack that had taken him from them all with no warning. Well, no warning was a loose term, she thought, sucking hard on her mint to get to the soft middle bit.

Grandad had had a penchant for an extra helping of his wife's cooking most nights, followed by a pint or two to keep the customers, who were like family, company as he worked the bar. There'd been so much comfort in the aroma of his favourite, Peterson's Old Dublin tobacco, as he puffed on the clay pipe dipped in whiskey for added flavour. The pipe had belonged to his grandfather, and it was a smell that transported Shannon to toasting marshmallows around a campfire when she'd been in the Ladybirds, a precursor to the Girl Guides. She'd loved to sit at his knee and listen to the stories he had to tell, especially the ones about the selkies. His tales of the seals who, once on land, shed their skin to take on human form had seen her hiding behind the rocks surrounding Emerald Bay for hours on end in the hope of seeing a selkie for herself.

She wondered if he'd have run out of stories if he'd lived longer.

Emerald Bay had been glorious the Saturday morning he passed. The sky hadn't so much as a cloud, and the sun was beating down. Shannon could remember thinking later that it was a day where nothing awful should have happened. Her science homework was to find what she thought might be a limestone rock to bring into school on Monday. Ms Foley had an experiment planned that would demonstrate whether it was limestone. Science wasn't Shannon's favourite subject, but Ms Foley wore cool clothes and was all right for a teacher, so she was determined to hunt out a prime rock specimen. She could remember thinking it beat the whispered-about frog dissection planned for later in the year.

Grandad had been getting under Nan's feet, and she'd

flapped him off with the tea towel and promises of a fresh scone when he returned if he accompanied Shannon on her quest. So, they'd been trooping companionably along the well-trod coastal path that led them away from the fishing harbour towards the ruins of Kilticaneel Castle and then down to the crescent-shaped bay.

Shannon could remember Grandad had been wheezing heavily and that they'd rested on the bench seat in the shade of the castle on the pretext of admiring the sea while he tried to catch his breath. The sounds of that morning were still razor-sharp in her mind. The crash of the waves and the squeals of children in the distance. Her sisters were already at the bay, and she was eager to get going so she, too, could strip down to her swimsuit and plunge into the icy water before beginning her hunt for the perfect rock specimen. She'd only been half listening to Grandad talking about how when he was a boy, he and the other lads had used the castle as a lookout to keep an eye out for invading Vikings. She'd heard it all before, and it was a game still popular with the youngsters of Emerald Bay. However, that morning, the ruins were deserted in favour of a swim.

She'd asked him if he was feeling all right, noticing his waxy pallor and the beads of sweat on his forehead. He'd announced he was raring to go, but upon standing up, Finbar Kelly had fixed his gaze on Shannon, panic flickering in his eyes before he'd pitched forward.

The sickening thud as he'd hit the path had stayed with Shannon for the longest time, as had her inability to move. Her feet seemed to have taken root, but she'd screamed for help at some point. Then, dropping to her knees, she'd rolled him over onto his back. She'd received her first-aid badge the previous year when she'd still been in the Guides and had instinctively begun CPR. Her small hands, one on top of the other, had pumped his chest as hard as possible. Finally, Mr Geraghty, who'd heard her cries from the beach, steamed up the path and took over from her. Never in all her life had she been so relieved to see an adult. By the time Doctor Fairlie arrived and pronounced her grandad dead, they'd been doing CPR for thirty minutes between them.

Shannon knew this trauma had shaped her decision to become a nurse. She was driven by a need to save people, which didn't always present itself in the black-and-white sense. Her role as a public health nurse servicing the Galway region, including Emerald Bay, had taught her loneliness was a silent killer. A cup of tea and a chat were as essential as changing a dressing or checking medication. It was a job that brought her joy and sadness in equal measure. No two days were ever the same. She might assist with a home birth on Monday and tend to a terminally ill patient on Tuesday. Shannon loved feeling she was doing something worthwhile, although she wasn't so enamoured with the screeds of paperwork that were also part and parcel of her job. It took valuable time away from her patients.

The next bend loomed, and the last of the mint dissolved on her tongue as she rounded it.

'Look, Grandad's sent me a rainbow, Napoleon.' She admired the vibrant colours as they arced over land and sea. 'He always sends me them when I need them.'

And then there it was. Her home. Emerald Bay.

3

With its stretch of sand and rockpools, the cove was where Shannon had had so many of her firsts. First kiss, first cigarette and, ugh, first illicit sampling of a cocktail of vodka, gin and, mostly, blue curaçao pinched from behind the bar because of its pretty colour, all hastily mixed in a jam-jar. To this day, the thought of blue curaçao made her feel queasy.

The water lapping into the sandy cove was aqua on a sunny day. In the villagers' opinion, it could rival any Mediterranean beach, never mind the disparity between the frigid Atlantic and the tepid Med! On a day like today, though, grey water churned angrily up the sand leaving behind bubbling froth and the odd piece of driftwood. Shannon wasn't sure which she preferred because there was a majesty to the sea when it was angry, and when it was calm, she found the gently lapping water soothing.

She slowed her speed as the road began to snake toward the village and the harbour. The red, blue and white boats bobbing in the water were a splash of colour on a dull day. Rory Egan and two of his sons, Michael and Conor, had been out on their boats despite the inclement weather. Shane would be behind the counter of the family's fishmongers in the village. They matched BB in their yellow wet weather gear and, waving out of the window, she received a raised hand in return from Rory. Michael and Conor glanced up from unloading their catch but didn't acknowledge her. Surely they weren't still out of sorts with the Kelly girls for Ava having ended things with Shane?

The three brothers were fiercely loyal, and Shane was the youngest Egan. Her sister had tried when she'd moved to London, but it wasn't easy to maintain a long-distance relationship, especially not with someone with a jealous streak like Shane had. Shannon sighed. There were times when Emerald Bay didn't just feel small with its population of seven hundred and fifty-three at last count, but positively tiny. She didn't blame Ava for opting to see more of the world than the village where she'd grown up one bit at all.

She drove past the impressive but austere stone Benmore House that had been in the Leslie family for generations. The days of the big houses in Ireland might be gone, but the Leslies still held themselves aloof from the rest of the village as if they were in the nineteenth century, not the twenty-first. Shannon was only young when Mrs Leslie Senior died. However, she could still remember being goggle-eyed on the rare occasion the elderly woman had swept into town swathed in couture like a dowager duchess. They'd all lined the streets hoping for a glimpse of the fur-clad vision like it was a visit from the Pope himself.

'Oof, sorry, Napoleon. I'd have thought those potholes would have been filled by now.' She bounced past the cluster of thatch-roofed wattle and daub cottages on the edge of the village. Two were used as holiday lets these days, with only the third one being occupied by a resident of Emerald Bay, Maeve Doolin.

It was common to see tour buses pulled off the road here so their passengers could clamber down to take a picture. It was especially photogenic when the heather blossomed on the surrounding bogs during springtime.

The lights twinkled invitingly from Maeve's front windows. Shannon might officially be on her holidays, but Maeve was one of her favourite patients, and she knew the poor woman was lonely since being widowed a year or so back. A holly wreath festooned her red front door and a lantern with a candle in it was placed on the stoop. The cottage reminded Shannon of a Christmas tree decoration she'd seen for sale in Isla's Irish Shop there in Emerald Bay one year. She glanced at the clock on the dashboard. She'd made good time and was gasping for a cuppa, and the apple-cheeked little woman always had rich, buttery shortbread in her biscuit tin, but it was the fact she might be the only person Maeve saw all day that made up her mind. Shannon slowed to a stop and then reversed back to park out the front of her cottage.

'You can come in with me, Napoleon,' she said, pulling the carrier out and holding it firm as the Persian scrambled to peer out the mesh door.

In spring, the path she was walking up was a riot of daffodils, but weeds were now rearing their head. She could smell peat burning and, looking up, saw telltale, thick smoke twirling out the chimney. Maeve would have her fire roaring with the sods of turf the late Ivo Doolin had stockpiled in the shed out the back for her. A nostalgic pang hit her. It was rapidly becoming an outlawed fuel in Ireland because of climate change, and the days of seeing sods of turf stacked into small stooks to dry for the winter around these parts were all but gone. Still and all that sweet, smoky aromatic scent was hard to beat. It was the smell of home. She'd like to see Maeve's tree too. She always decorated it beautifully.

Shannon rapped on the door with its paint beginning to flake, knowing Mr Doolin would turn in his grave if he could see the cracks in the limewashed walls and spider webs in the

eaves. She'd been his palliative care nurse, and he'd been a
subscriber to a man's home being his castle. So he'd seen to the
upkeep of the exterior while Maeve kept the inside shining.
Without his input, though, the place was beginning to look
tired.

Maeve had confided that her son, Fergus, a blustering, red-
faced man Shannon had only seen once when he'd come to visit
from where he'd made his home in England to say goodbye to
his father, was on at her to move into a retirement village in
nearby Kilticaneel. She didn't want to leave her home, though,
and clasping Shannon's hand, Maeve had told her it was where
she felt close to Ivo. Perhaps a working party could be organised
in the spring, Shannon thought, recalling her promise to Ivo to
keep an eye on his wife when he was gone. It was clear Fergus
wasn't going to, which was no doubt why he was eager for his
mam to move into a retirement village where she'd be someone
else's responsibility.

'You're grand, Napoleon,' Shannon soothed in response to
his mewling. She didn't bother to knock again as she waited
patiently for the door to open. Maeve would need a few
minutes to reach it if she was settled in her usual spot in the
kitchen-cum-living-room at the back of the cottage. The poor
woman was riddled with arthritis, and it plagued her worse in
winter.

A reedy voice called out, 'I'm coming.'

'It's me – Shannon. I hope you've got that kettle on, Maeve.'

A feline howl erupted as the door was opened. Maeve's face
lit up seeing Shannon there as she leaned heavily on her
walking stick. She was well rugged up in a green sweater and
matching pleated skirt with slippers on her feet. Her fluffy
white hair curled becomingly, and she'd a pink lipstick on,
which gave her an optimistic air she'd not had the last time
Shannon had dropped by. There was something else too, but
Shannon couldn't put her finger on it.

'Shannon! You're my second visitor today. What a lovely surprise. Now, who's this you've brought to see me?' Her inquisitive blue eyes danced.

'My cat, Napoleon. It's proving to be a traumatic day for him, Maeve. We've moved out of the apartment in Galway, and we're on our way home.'

'Well, now come in, the pair of you, and tell me all about it. The fire's roaring, and I've a wee notion for a cup of tea and a piece of shortbread. I might even find a little something for you, young fellow,' she said, stooping to peek into the carrier Shannon was holding up for inspection. 'Do you like tuna, Napoleon?'

Meoooooooow!

Not wanting to let the damp air inside, Shannon hurried over the threshold to wait in the narrow passage beneath the faded Sacred Heart of Jesus picture. Maeve closed the door and waved her hand in the direction of the kitchen.

'You know the way.'

It was as warm as toast inside the little cottage, and Shannon did a quick, surreptitious sweep to see how Maeve was managing. To the left was her bedroom. The door was open to let the heat in, revealing the neatly made bed with not so much as a ripple in the colourful handstitched quilt spread over it. On her right was the formal dining room. The polished mahogany table was laid with the best china as though someone was coming for tea. The good room was a tradition Maeve held on to. Shannon wondered if she did so in the hope Fergus might surprise her by packing up his wife and children and crossing the water to see his old mammy. Fergus was the Doolins' only child, more's the pity.

As Shannon passed by the crucifix and the picture of John F. Kennedy, along with the photograph of Pope John Paul II's visit in the seventies, she smiled, thinking about many identical images hung in the passageways of the homes she visited on her rounds. Finally, she stepped into the welcoming hub of the cottage. In the stone-cut fireplace flames hissed and spit, and the room glowed red. The Christmas tree she knew her dad had delivered to Maeve in Ivo's absence dominated the corner, drawing Shannon over to it. She breathed in the pine scent and admired the colourful decorations dripping from its boughs, many of which looked handmade, before setting the cat carrier down on the rug.

'How are you managing with your chair, Maeve?' Shannon gestured to the ergonomic arthritis chair she'd arranged for Maeve to have. It resembled an office chair, and while not aesthetically in keeping with the rest of the furnishings, it was a practical must. The wheels meant she could move about the cottage and sit at the kitchen worktop when it was too painful to stand for long periods. Little things like that would ensure Maeve could manage here on her own for as long as possible.

'Oh, it's grand. I race about the place in it, so I do.'

Shannon laughed, delighted the little woman was in excellent spirits today. Moving over to the oak dresser, she admired the thimbles on display. Maeve had quite the collection, thanks to the more adventurous souls of Emerald Bay. No doubt a couple of them were from villagers hoping to curry favour with the widow because it was whispered that she was sitting on a sizeable nest egg.

'Any new ones?'

'I have a lovely one from the Algarve there somewhere. Nessie Doyle's young apprentice, Tara, gave it to me when she got back from her holidays. She calls every Wednesday to give me a shampoo and set.' Maeve fluffed her hair. 'She does a grand job. Better than Nessie, between you and me. I always look like a poodle when she's had a go at me with the rollers.'

Shannon laughed, fully understanding Maeve's sentiment because she wouldn't let Nessie near her hair either. She and her sisters had received far too many hatchet haircuts as children. Dad used to say they looked like the Von Trapp sisters after their six-weekly trim, and would they be running through the village holding hands, singing about the hills being alive too?

'I see it,' she said, spotting the thimble. 'The blue and yellow's a pretty combination.' A sudden yearning for white sands and turquoise sea washed over her, but then, realising Maeve was still standing, Shannon added, 'Why don't you sit down and get to know Napoleon while I make us both a cup of tea.' She waited until the older woman was settled in her chair, and while she was tempted to drape the rug across her knees she knew she'd get her hand slapped for fussing.

'Will you let him out, Shannon?' Maeve looked at her hopefully. 'I'd love to meet him properly, and he doesn't sound very happy. Perhaps if we shut the doors to the kitchen, he could have a wander about?'

So long as that was all he did, Shannon thought, moving to close the door to the passage and the door off the kitchen to the room that would have been Fergus's once upon a time.

'Why not,' she said, satisfied he wouldn't be going anywhere. 'He's been cooped up in there far too long.' And, squatting down, she opened the hatch, pulling the disgruntled Persian out. She cuddled him to her. 'Say hello to Maeve, Napoleon.' He obliged with a meow before beginning to squirm, so Shannon put him down, watching as he stalked about the room sniffing here and there before eyeing the fire warily. Then, to Maeve's delight, he jumped into her lap and curled up, waiting to be petted once he'd finished his inspection.

'You've made a friend there,' Shannon said as she wandered past the table, which was far too big for one to sit at alone, and flicked the kettle on. She cast a wary eye up at the electric box over the back door. The wiring in the old place left a thing or two to be desired. It was like a complicated string puzzle, and every time she popped the kettle on, she half expected it to go bang. Maeve, however, was insistent there was no need to fix what wasn't broken.

'Don't forget the tuna, Shannon. You'll find it in the top cupboard over the cooker,' Maeve called out. 'And remember to warm the pot first. The shortbread's in the biscuit tin.'

Shannon, obliging, filled the teapot with hot water and left it to stand while she located the tin of fish and a can opener. She scraped out its contents onto a saucer and was about to set it down on the lino when she heard a soft thud. Napoleon swiftly followed it. 'You'd think you were half-starved.' She laughed, leaving him to his treat while she finished making the tea.

'He's loving that, thanks, Maeve.' Shannon carried in two cups and saucers with a slice of shortbread on the side. 'Here we go, with a dash of milk and half a teaspoon of sugar, just how you like it.' She set Maeve's down on the coaster on top of the cabinet alongside the radio, then, balancing hers, sat on the rose-patterned sofa with its comfortable sag in the middle. Family photographs decorated the walls and her eyes settled on a picture of Ivo and Maeve standing either side of Fergus. How sad it was that an only son should make so little effort where the two people who'd been devoted to him were concerned. Despite her smiles, she thought there was an aura of sadness about Maeve in the pictures.

Catching sight of Maeve wincing as she reached for her tea, Shannon turned away from the photos. 'Where's your hot-water bottle?' she asked, already half out of her seat, intending to fill it and prop it behind the old lady's back to see if it helped ease her aches.

'It has a leak in it, Shannon. Don't fuss. I'm grand.'

She did seem very chipper, and there was a rosiness to her cheeks that would have Shannon suspecting she'd been at the sherry if she didn't know better.

'Now, tell me about yourself. How are you faring?'

'Grand,' Shannon replied, automatically making a note to

pick up a hot-water bottle from Heneghan's Pharmacy tomorrow; her patients didn't want to hear her woes, not when they'd plenty of their own. But then again, she considered Maeve to be a friend. 'Actually, Maeve, not so good.'

'He broke your heart good and proper, didn't he, that Frenchman?'

'He did.'

'It will heal,' Maeve said gently. 'There are some hurts you think will never heal, but then one day, when you least expect it, they do.'

Something in her tone suggested she wasn't just talking about the state of Shannon's trampled heart, and she looked at her sharply, but Maeve's face offered no clues. She wondered if it was Ivo she was referring to.

The older woman smiled at her. 'You might not believe it now, but you'll think you had a lucky escape one of these days, Shannon. Mark my words. And in the meantime, while you're waiting for it to mend, get that biscuit down you.'

Shannon gave her a weak smile as she bit into the crisp shortbread. 'I wish you'd let me have the recipe,' she mumbled.

'Ah, now a woman's got to have some secrets to hold on to.'

'I'll get it from you one of these days.' Shannon laughed. Sitting back on the sofa, she sipped her tea, enjoying the warmth of the fire. A sated Napoleon strolled in, licking his chops before clambering up on Maeve's lap. There was no sound other than his purring and the crackle of the fire. The two women sat in silence for a few seconds before Shannon asked, 'And what about you, Maeve? How are you faring? Any word from your Fergus about Christmas?' She immediately regretted having asked as the woman's bony shoulders slumped.

'No, sure, the children would be bored silly here for a week with no Wi-Fi or the like. They're better off at home with all their things around them.'

Shannon would have liked to give Fergus Doolin a kick up the backside for the way he treated his lovely old mam.

'You'll be coming to us at the pub for your Christmas dinner then.'

'That would be grand. Nobody does stuffing like Kitty Kelly, and I wondered if there might be room for one more around the table?'

Shannon grinned. It was true. Her nan's stuffing was the best. 'That's very cryptic, Maeve. Who's your plus one?'

'Well, something unexpected has happened.'

'What's that then?'

'The visitor I mentioned earlier says he's a relative.' Maeve lowered her eyes, feigning great interest in Napoleon's tortoise-shell coat.

'A cousin or the like?' Shannon was curious.

Maeve shook her head. 'I need to be sure before I talk about it. Besides, what was it I was just after saying, about a woman having to have some secrets.' She tapped the side of her nose. 'All in good time, Shannon.'

4

Shannon drummed the steering wheel as she closed the distance between Maeve's cottage and the village. She was perturbed by her friend's refusal to elaborate on the relative coming to see her. Maeve had remained tight-lipped despite Shannon pressing her further on the subject.

'Don't you think it's odd, Napoleon? I mean this person showing up out of the blue, like.'

Napoleon stayed silent because he was sulking. Shannon guessed he'd been hoping Maeve Doolin's cottage was his and Shannon's new abode and had a feeling he'd be back to his usual dry biscuits come dinner time.

'I think what's bothering me is this money she has squirrelled away. I don't know for sure she has a nest egg, but everybody in the village seems to think she does and a decent-sized one at that. So there must be something in it. What if this so-called relative has heard about it too somehow? Scammers prey on the vulnerable. You read about it all the time.'

A sudden smell engulfed the car.

'Napoleon! That's the last time you have tuna.'

The rows of houses on either side of the road as Shannon

neared the village's aptly named Main Street were painted like
the rainbow she'd seen earlier. She was distracted from Maeve's
mysterious visitor by the holly wreaths decorating the doors and
the enormous blow-up Santa on display in the Brady family's
window. The Riordans opposite had a reindeer in theirs, not to
be outdone, while a Jesus figurine looked on serenely from the
Kildares' window. In the kitchen cupboards of every house, a
whiskey-soaked plum pudding would be curing in anticipation
of the main event: Christmas dinner.

Christmas was usually Shannon's favourite time, and she'd
revelled in seeing Galway transformed into a winter wonderland in previous years. You'd know the yuletide season was
upon you simply by inhaling the warm, spicy scents of
cinnamon and cloves from the mulled wine stalls filling the
streets. If that didn't give enough of a clue, the city was illuminated by lights and strung with over-the-top decorations. Santa's
Express vintage train was loaded with weary shoppers, and the
Ferris wheel provided a glowing landmark as it presided over
the Christmas market. The festive spirit was bountiful.

It was just as well she was organised and had done her
Christmas shopping in the June sales, she mulled, because she'd
been in no mood to tackle the crowds this year and, more to the
point, she had no money either. As a result, her festive spirit
was in short supply.

'I feel very Grinch-like, Napoleon. I'd be happy to head off
to the hills with you and at least a month's worth of chocolate
until the silly season's over.'

As much as she'd like to forget about the twenty-fifth of
December this year, there was no mistaking that Christmas was
nearly upon them, she thought, peering up at the enormous red
bow she was about to pass under. It marked the entrance to
Emerald Bay's Main Street. The Tidy Towns committee had
excelled themselves this year, and as BB crawled past the shops,
she saw they'd been made even more colourful with cheery

bunting strewn from one to the other. Everything from snowflakes, angels and holy symbols sparkled overhead. It was only early afternoon in the village, but the lights were on in all the shops, giving them a welcoming glow.

She brightened as she glimpsed Freya Devlin with her mane of blue hair, chatting to a customer inside Mermaids. Her old school pal had been determined to inject some culture into Emerald Bay and had opened an art gallery which also served as a studio for her handmade Celtic jewellery. Hopefully, once she'd settled Napoleon in and said hello to her family, she'd be able to call in on her. She could always rely on Freya to make her laugh.

Emerald Bay's only pharmacy, Heneghan's, had a traffic-stopping Christmas window. 'Ooh-la-la, Napoleon, Nuala McCarthy's gone to town.' The pharmacy's long-serving – or suffering, whichever way you wanted to look at it – shop assistant's usual offering of baubles and sedate lavender and rose gift-set smellies was nowhere to be seen. Instead, there was a life-size cut-out of a supermodel in a slinky black dress advertising a perfume called Seduce Me. Of course, Nuala had added creative touches like a Santa hat and tinsel scarf to yer exotic goddess woman. A giant bottle of the perfume itself was nestled among colourful gift-wrapped parcels.

What was Paddy McNamara doing? she thought, squinting at him in his tattered old trench coat as he swayed in front of the shop window. She could make out the brown paper bag in his hand. There'd be a bottle of takeout in that, no doubt, she thought. It looked like he was talking to yer supermodel wan. She shook her head, poor old Paddy.

'I tell you what, Nuala will have them all talking with that. I wonder if she's trying to tell Mr Heneghan something.' The pharmacist had been widowed for eight years now. He was the only one in the village blind to his shop assistant, Nuala, being besotted with him. 'Either that or the Irish Countrywomen's

Guild are sick of receiving rose-scented hand cream and soaps from their husbands and have asked her to spice things up a bit — Jaysus!' Shannon's foot slammed down on the brake.

Mrs Tattersall, buttoned up in a brown coat with her head-scarf firmly knotted under her chin, had stepped out onto the street without a glance to her left or right. Her wheeled shopping trolley bag bounced behind her, and she'd come to a standstill in front of BB holding her hand up in the universal sign for stop.

Shannon twisted in her seat to check Napoleon's carrier hadn't slid forward with her sudden braking. It hadn't, but then she'd hardly been speeding; in fact, any slower, and she'd not have been moving. Mrs Tattersall was well known for her disagreeable nature and, seeing the woman glaring at her, she slid down in her seat. 'G'won, get on your way,' Shannon muttered, already knowing she wouldn't get off that lightly.

She watched as Mrs Tattersall stalked around to the driver's side with lips pressed together and eyes narrowed. She rapped on the window, and Shannon reluctantly pushed the button for it to slide down.

'Shannon Kelly, is that you?' she asked, squinting in. 'I thought it was one of those hooligans from Kilticaneel trying to mow me down.'

'Yes, it's me, Mrs Tattersall, and I wasn't trying to knock you down.' There was no point in mentioning she'd been driving below the speed limit. The hooligans Mrs Tattersall had referred to consisted of one Bobby O'Shea, who'd sped through the village honking his horn and waving his Ireland scarf out the window four years ago. He'd been celebrating the country's historic win against the All Blacks. Sergeant Badger had made sure he was suitably punished with a fine and early Saturday morning starts on the litter collection about town. Mrs Tattersall, however, was a woman with a memory like an elephant.

Her best course of action, Shannon decided, was a charm

offensive. 'How're ye keeping? You're looking very well, so you are. The brown's fetching on you. And how're Mr Tattersall's knees these days?' She was gratified to see the older woman's expression soften as much as it could when you'd a nose and chin on you that could crack a walnut.

'We can't complain.' Mrs Tattersall took a deep breath, preparing to do just that. 'Although I have the gout in me leg and a pain in me shoulder. The mister's knees are playing up again and all, since you asked. Sure, why it is that quack who calls himself a doctor over in Kilticaneel can't put us right is beyond me. And him with all that training and study too.' She made a clucking sound with her tongue, uncaring that the 'quack' of a doctor was Shannon's boss.

'I'm sorry to hear that, Mrs Tattersall. I'll light a candle for you, so I will.' Shannon had heard her mam trot this out to the old bag over the years to appease her. 'I'd best be on my way. They're expecting me.' She gestured vaguely down the road in the direction of the Shamrock Inn before shutting the window on the woman's disgruntled face. Then, taking her foot off the brake, she moved slowly onwards.

An enormous Christmas tree took centre stage in the village square. It was festooned with fairy lights which Shannon hoped had been updated in recent times. She could still recall the great turning on of the lights the first year Dermot Molloy of Dermot Molloy's Quality Meats had sponsored the tree. They'd all been gathered, stomping their feet against the cold as they waited breathlessly for the magic moment, which had lasted all of thirty seconds before they'd sparked, fizzed and flickered off, shorting the village's power supply with them.

'I hope it wasn't your grandad who put that star up there, Napoleon.' Shannon shook her head. She could see her dad pooh-poohing all the safety recommendations as he leaned a ladder against the tree and clambered up it. 'Who's that?' She narrowed her eyes to get a better look at the man admiring the tree. He wasn't from around here, not in all that expensive Gore-Tex gear and with hiking boots. Any God-fearing Emerald Bay man wouldn't be seen dead in anything other than an Aran sweater, well-worn jeans and wellies, brogues for good. He looked to be around her age and was probably waiting for his wife to finish buying up all the Celtic Cross embossed goods at Isla's Irish Shop to take back to family in wherever they hailed from, Shannon deduced as he turned around at the sound of her car idling past. Damp sandy-brown curls stuck to his forehead. He was good-looking, she vaguely registered, but his eyes grabbed her and pulled her in. She wasn't close enough to make out their colour, but they were arresting nonetheless. He held a hand up in greeting.

Shannon's face flamed at being caught like a yokel unused to out-of-towners, and she fixed her eyes on the street ahead, keeping both hands firmly on the steering wheel. 'Just because I'm Irish doesn't mean I'm friendly,' she said through gritted teeth. 'Bah fecking humbug.'

5

Shannon pulled into the gravelled car park next to the pub's beer garden, coming to a halt alongside her dad's handwritten reserved sign. She'd parked next to a coach filled with sleepy-looking passengers. A lunchtime pint or two would do that to you, and she waved over, recognising Ned behind the wheel. He raised his hand in return before beginning to reverse slowly out.

The coach driver always called into the Shamrock Inn on his Dublin-to-Galway run. Liam Kelly turned on the charm and gave his overseas travellers a good time with his pitter-patter about how it took precisely one hundred and nineteen seconds to pour a pint of Guinness.

The wee-wee-coloured monster truck was parked up, and her sister Hannah's battered old Ford was next to it, Shannon saw once the coach had inched out of the parking space. It was easily recognisable with its myriad of stickers for the various causes her crusading sister supported. She shook her head, recalling how Hannah had given them one card between them last Christmas, which informed the Kelly clan they'd gifted a pig to a family in need. They'd all agreed that it was a lovely

idea until she'd asked them to chip in a tenner each for it. She'd
used next month's rent money to pay for the pig and had given
them a sanctimonious speech about how working for a non-
profit organisation entailed making sacrifices like being permanently broke.

Shannon felt a guilty flash as she cast her mind back a
month or so to when Hannah had called. She'd been excited
over her new role at the Cork city branch of Feed the World
with Bees, and Shannon had rained on her parade with her
lacklustre response. She'd remedy that over Christmas.

There was no sign of Imogen's racy red coupé as yet.
Imogen insisted her interior-design business demanded she
drive a statement car, given her dealings with Dublin's movers
and shakers. Would they trust her to re-design their houses if
she pulled up in a clapped-out old banger like Hannah's? That
her sister was yet to put in an appearance was good, Shannon
thought. Having the bedroom to herself meant peace and quiet
while settling Napoleon in. Besides, the less time spent
listening to Imogen prattling on about her Insta-perfect life in
Dublin, the better. Grace and Ava had flown in from London
yesterday and would cadge a lift home with Imogen whenever
she deigned to show up.

Shannon checked her phone, but there were no new
messages, and then, shoving it in her bag, clambered out of the
car. It felt good to be upright and she raised her hands over her
head to stretch, waiting for the satisfying click before letting
them fall back to her sides. She opened the back door and
picked up the cat carrier.

'Home sweet home, Napoleon.' It was just as well he was
light, she thought, holding the carrier up so he could see the
empty beer garden with its four picnic tables and empty wine
barrels that overflowed with pansies and gardenia in spring to
the misty field beyond. Someone had been using one of the
barrels as an ashtray, and she made a note to put the butts in the

bin later. 'This is your kingdom now, Napoleon. You can frolic in the beer garden when I'm with you, but you're not to venture into those fields because of your coat. It could get all in a tangle, and it's not good for your breathing to be outside all the time.'

The scrabbling started up again along with the meowing, and Shannon realised that the poor fellow was probably desperate to do his business. She initially planned to set the litter tray up in her bedroom wardrobe, and his food and water bowls could go on a sheet of old newspaper under the window. Another reason it was good Imogen wasn't home yet! But it would only be for a few days until he got used to his new home, then she'd move all his paraphernalia into the laundry annexe. Out of sight, out of mind.

'C'mon then, Napoleon. In we go.' Shannon pulled open the door to the rear entrance of the pub and stepped inside, feeling the warmth of the fire roaring in the grate wash over her. The Christmas tree was resplendent in its usual spot near the windows, and in years gone by, it would have been all hands to the deck decorating it, but nowadays with the Kelly girls scattered, it fell to her mam. Dad must be changing a barrel down in the cellar, or perhaps he was out the back, she thought, surveying the scene with an impartial eye for a moment.

The Shamrock Inn had been in the Kelly family for two generations and was an ode to polished timber with its dark wooden panelled walls, floor and ceiling. Above the dado line, the walls were painted forest green and littered with framed higgledy-piggledy photographs of Emerald Bay's glory days, including a picture of Dermot Molloy standing proudly in front of the square's Christmas tree that fateful year. There, too, was Liam Kelly immortalised on Christmas Eve 2003 as Father Christmas handing out sweets to the village children, a tradition he'd started when Grace and Ava were just tots. The barstools lined up beside the bar top were wooden with green leather seats, and behind the bar, in between the glasses and bottles, was a Smithswick Stout sign, a Guinness mirror and a decade's worth of keepsakes and bric-a-brac. The Shamrock Inn was as traditional as an Irish pub got.

The recently vacated tables needed clearing, and if she hadn't had Napoleon with her, Shannon would have automatically begun tidying away the empty glasses.

'Hannah, lass, 'tis good to see you,' Enda Dunne said, peeking out from under his tweed cap to give her a gappy grin. He raised his glass in her direction from over on his barstool pew.

'It's Shannon, Mr Dunne, and it's good to see you too.'

'What's that you've got there then?'

'My cat, Napoleon, Mr Dunne.'

'A ferret, you say. That's an odd sort of a pet. You want to watch it doesn't get out. One ran up me auld da's trouser leg once when he was trimming the hedgerow.' He winced at the memory.

'A cat, Mr Dunne. C-A-T.' A couple warming their toes by the fire swivelled in her direction. He was still refusing to wear the fancy hearing aids he'd had fitted, Shannon thought, and how he got ferret from cat was a mystery indeed.

'There's no need to shout at me, young Grace. I'm not deaf. If Kitty's out the back, you could tell her, her pretty smile would make this lonely farmer's day.'

Grace? Shannon shook her head. She could understand Enda calling her after Hannah. They were both dark-haired after all, but Grace was a redhead. He clearly still had designs on Nan too. She gave him a weary smile, and her eyes flitted past him to the couple huddling in the snug that overlooked Main Street. The woman was flicking through pictures on the phone her partner was holding up. A half-drunk pint of Guinness was in front of him and an empty wine glass in front of her. A pang shot through Shannon, picturing herself and Julien sitting there doing the same thing when she'd brought him home to meet her parents last winter.

She wondered if the couple had etched their names in the soft timber tabletop as she and Julien had. It was a tradition at the Shamrock Inn, after all. Shannon remembered how determined she'd been that Julien only WhatsApp his mother the very best shots of her family and had been deleting those that didn't make the grade. So, it had been a big fat finger pressing down on the rubbish bin icon when she'd come across her dad looking like he'd be more at home in the American wilderness strumming a banjo than playing the uillean pipes in the Irish pub he presided over.

'Would you fetch your da, lass,' Enda Dunne said, draining his glass and placing it on the bar with a satisfied 'Aah,' before wiping his mouth with his hand. 'Tell him he's a customer in desperate need of a drop of the black stuff and a kind word from a good woman.'

She dragged her eyes away from the snug and told Enda she'd send him through pronto. She was making no promises where her nan was concerned. Then, pushing open the door beside the bar marked private with her spare hand, she stepped into the family hub, the kitchen. A heated discussion was going on around the table.

'I'm home,' she sang out, interrupting the debate between her mam, dad and Hannah as she mustered up a smile and turned her attention to her nan. 'Hello, Nan. I see Enda's still carrying a torch for you.'

Kitty Kelly bobbed back up from where she'd been peeping in the door of the Aga. Her cheeks were flushed from the heat and, seeing her eldest granddaughter, she beamed before wiping her hands on the pinny she'd knotted about her waist to give Shannon a quick squeeze. 'Don't talk to me about that man. It's the drink and his dog he loves.'

Shannon's mouth watered at the savoury aroma of slow-cooking beef and Guinness mingling with a fresh loaf or, even better, two.

'Is it the bread you were checking on, Nan?' she asked hopefully. 'Because I'm desperate altogether for a piece.'

'It was, and I'll butter you a slice as soon as it's done.' Kitty winked at her before turning her attention to the cat carrier. 'Hello there, Napoleon. Jaysus wept. Would you look at the poor little flat face on him?'

'Close your ears, Napoleon. He's regal-looking, Nan.'

'Is that what you call it!'

'What about me, Nan?' Hannah piped up. 'Can I have some bread too?'

'There's no show without punch, is there?' Kitty shook her head, but her eyes were twinkling.

'And me, I am your firstborn son, Mam,' Liam added. Then his eyes skated over Shannon. 'Sure, is it the Scottish dancing you're into these days, Shannon?' he asked, referencing her red plaid skirt.

'Plaid's in this winter, Dad.'

'I hope it's made with hemp,' said Hannah, who was looking like she'd spent the last few months living in a Rastafarian-based commune, giving her the once-over.

'Shannon, love!' Nora Kelly pushed her chair back from the scrubbed pine table and, getting up, also subjected her to a quick head-to-toe. 'That hair could do with a trim, my girl.' She announced that the ends looked like a goat had been chewing on them before suggesting, 'Why don't you call in on Nessie? She'll squeeze you in. She always did you girls a lovely cut when you were young.'

Shannon was pulled into a hug, and she rolled her eyes over her mam's shoulder for Hannah's benefit, receiving a smirk in return. She breathed in the comforting scent of the coconut shampoo Mam had used forever and a day before remembering she was on a mission. She didn't want Napoleon getting off on the wrong foot with everyone.

Her mam held her at arm's length and asked, 'And how's that mad cat?'

'Grand, Mammy. I've got to sort him out before he has an accident.' Shannon broke free and took quick stock of her sister. If Mam had had something to say about the state of her split ends, she'd like to have been a fly on the wall when Hannah got home. Her sister had best lock the door of the bedroom she shared with Ava and Grace at night, lest their mam decide to sneak in and snip her dreadlocks off.

'If that cat craps—'

She held a pacifying hand up. 'Dad, he's house-trained, don't be worrying.'

Liam Kelly followed up with a harrumphing sound, saying, 'I'll bring your cases up for you when I've finished my tea.' A chocolate Hobnob was halfway to his mouth.

'I thought Mam had you both on a diet,' Hannah said, deliberately stirring.

'I do.' Nora frowned at him. 'But some of us find it harder to stick to than others. The doctor's after telling us we need to lose a stone and a half each. I told your dad he could have Christmas Day off, and it's not Christmas Day yet, is it, Liam? And, Kitty, you're not to be giving him any of that bread either.'

Kitty bristled, commenting under her breath about her bossy daughter-in-law thinking she knew best. The two women tussled for the top-dog position in the Kelly household regularly, but it was water off a duck's back to them both, and when push came to shove, they always presented a united front.

Nora barely drew breath, swinging her attention back to Hannah. 'And don't think I don't know your game, madam. Telling tales on your dad won't win you any points. It's still a no to the beehives. Can you believe she's after wanting us to put hives in the beer garden, Shannon?'

'I'm Switzerland,' Shannon said, heading for the narrow hallway that led to the stairs. There were two other rooms and a toilet downstairs. A tiny bedroom which was never let but in which the bed was always made up 'just in case', and a cosy living room. A quick glimpse in the living room door on her way past revealed Mam had got new throw cushions for the squishy sofa they somehow all fit on. She halted at the bottom of the stairs and backtracked to poke her head around the kitchen door. 'I nearly forgot, Dad. Enda's after dying of thirst out there.'

'Dying of thirst, my arse,' Liam muttered, reluctantly returning the biscuit to the plate as he got up to tend to his customer. 'Sure, a man can't grab a moment's peace without someone mithering at him.' His pointed stare was directed at Hannah. She scowled back at him.

'No bees, Dad, no food.'

'Sure, I'm virtually nil by mouth, thanks to your mammy. So it won't make a jot of difference to me.'

Shannon left them to it and set off up the stairs. Mam had hung a photograph in a chunky wooden frame on the wall at the top of the landing. It depicted Nora and Liam Kelly standing proudly outside the pub's blue door. The sisters joked she'd hung it there to remind them who was in charge.

On her left was the bathroom and toilet, Nan's room was next door, and Room 5, used as a guestroom, overlooked Main Street. The room she'd shared with Imogen was on her right at the end of the passage, and she padded past Hannah and the twins' room. The floorboards squeaked beneath the well-trodden carpet as she passed by her mam and dad's bedroom to find the door open to her and Imogen's old room. She hurried in, deciding there would be time for an inspection later. Right now, she needed to get that tray set up. She put the carrier down on the rag-rug Nan had made and reassured Napoleon she'd be right back before haring off down the stairs.

As she raced back through the pub juggling the bag with his food and bowls, a white tray and a three-quarter full sack of gritty clay mix, she heard her dad say, 'I tell you, Enda, there'll be hell to pay when Imogen gets home tomorrow and finds there's a cat in their bedroom.'

'Why's young Ava got a ferret in her room?' Enda asked with his frothy-topped pint glass halfway to his mouth.

6

Napoleon was in the wardrobe, indisposed; his food and water bowls were laid out by the window alongside his climbing tree. Meanwhile, Shannon was sitting on the end of her bed, letting it sink in that she would be camping out in her old bedroom for the foreseeable future.

These days the room she and Imogen had draped a sheet down the middle of denoting whose side was whose as teenagers was let as a double twin during the busy summer months. The sheet had been Imogen's idea. She was tidy, whereas Shannon was not, and when her mess had begun to spread to her side Imogen demanded the room be split in two. It had been like living in a miniature East and West Germany during the Cold War with staunch border control. The sheet/wall had only come down when Shannon left to do her Bachelor of Nursing Science degree at St Angela's College in Sligo.

Mam had gone to town with the nautical theme here, Shannon thought, seeing it through different eyes now she wasn't just staying for a few nights. The blue and white colours she'd picked out were very Cape Cod. A simple black-framed watercolour of the red and blue fishing boats bobbing in Emerald Bay's harbour hung over her bed where once it had been Justin Timberlake blu-tacked there. A table with a drawer next to her bed was home to a lamp and a piece of driftwood.

Imogen's side of the room mirrored her own apart from the painting over her bed, which depicted the village's Main Street in a montage of red, pink and yellow buildings.

The pink drapes and fairy dado rail were long gone, replaced with crisp white tiebacks and matching walls, while over by the window, their old toy box had been recovered and repurposed as a seat or blanket box.

'Thirty-four years old, Napoleon, and I'm back to sleeping in a single bed. How sad is that?' She sighed before adding. 'And Julien Riviere's an arse. An arsey arse, arse.'

A pair of yellow eyes peered cautiously out of the wardrobe. Napoleon had heard it all before over the last few months, and unlike her father, who'd appeared in the doorway, he didn't answer back.

'You won't hear me arguing with yer.' Liam Kelly staggered cowboy-like into the room with its sloped ceiling, ducking from years of habit as he deposited Shannon's suitcases at the foot of the bed. 'Jaysus, girl, what've you got in these?' He straightened, rubbing his arms, then frowning as he sniffed. 'Christ on a bike, what have you been feeding that cat?'

'Tuna.'

'Well, you'd better get rid of whatever he's after doing in the wardrobe. Flick it over the fence.' He waved in the direction of the window to the boggy fields beyond the beer garden out back. 'How long do you plan on holding him captive in here, anyway? There'll be murder when Imogen arrives if she walks in here to a whiff like that, and we have an English couple arriving later today. Fully booked, we are.'

That wasn't hard, Shannon thought, given there was only Room 5 going spare with the whole family coming home for

Christmas. So it was just as well her parents had seen fit to reno-
vate. A builder had added a small en suite to the guestroom
along with her parents' and Nan's bedrooms. Otherwise, there'd
be a battle for the bathroom each morning with all the sisters
under one roof. It would be just like old times!

'Only a day or two, and he's not usually smelly. The tuna
didn't agree with him. I'll put the window on the latch.'
Shannon stood up. 'And close the door, Daddy. I don't want
him getting out.' She moved quickly to the window opening it a
crack to glance out at the stretch of waterlogged green beyond
the laneway behind the pub.

Her father did as she asked before adding, 'I'll say it didn't.
And as for that French gombeen you were on about, it could
have been worse. You could have married the eejit.'

'Don't say it, Dad.' Shannon gritted her teeth, knowing he'd
ignore her.

He couldn't help himself, and Shannon mouthed along
with him. ''Tis a lucky escape you've had there. You'd have had
to deal with a lifetime of bad River Shannon jokes.'

'It was Rivi*ere*, not River.'

'Riviere my arse, that's just a fancy French way of saying
River.'

Liam hadn't been smitten with Julien. Unlike Nora, who'd
fussed over him each time he and Shannon had called to see
them. Liam had accused his wife of being a closet Francophile
because she'd developed a habit of always greeting Julien with a
chirpy 'bonjour', and an even worse 'au revoir' when they left.
She was a wannabe Frenchwoman, he'd declared. A culture
vulture.

As for Shannon, well, she'd been smitten from the moment
she'd set eyes on him. He'd been brought into the medical
centre where she worked. She was a sucker for brooding brown
eyes and an accent and not the broad Irish farmer brogue from
around these parts either, thanks very much. As such, she could

have listened to the tall, dark and handsome tourist say, 'Oui, I'm in a lot of pain,' all day as she tended to his broken ankle due to a slip rock-climbing.

'Who does the eejit think he is? Spider-man?' her dad had said when she'd relayed how they'd met.

Liam pulled his oldest daughter to him and wrapped his burly arms around her. 'I know it's not how you saw things working out, Honey, but your mam and nan will feed you up over the holidays and get you back on your feet. Sure, you'll be grand. There's nothing good old home cooking can't fix.'

'Julien was a good cook,' Shannon mumbled.

'No one's as handy in the kitchen as your mam and nan, and a man who eats snails can't be trusted.'

'That's true, Daddy.'

Her cheek rested against the scratchy flannel of his shirt, and she breathed in the Old Spice she and her sisters still brought him for his birthday, knowing he deserved a medal for putting up with the dramas his five daughters had brought to his door over the years. You'd have thought there was a cut-off point when your children became adults, but somehow she'd missed the memo because here she was, back home again.

It was nice to hear him use her old childhood nickname too. Other fathers called their daughters things like 'pumpkin' or 'sweetheart', but not hers. Fancying himself an amateur botanist on the few hours he managed to snatch away from the pub now and again, Liam Kelly had chosen abbreviated versions of Connemara wildflowers for his girls.

Shannon was Honey, short for honeysuckle, and following off the rank was Imogen at thirty-two, otherwise known as Rose after the delicate white, guelder rose. There wasn't much that was delicate about Imogen. Hannah, thirty and the middle child, was nicknamed Pearl for heath pearlwort and was an eco-warrior. Then there were the twins. Grace and Ava were identical, apart from Ava, who had a small birthmark on her jawline

and whose chin had a gentler set to it than her sister's. To those
that knew them well, Ava appeared to be less robust than Grace
and had a fragility to her. They were the babies of the family at
a tender twenty-three years. They'd also answered to Penny and
Marigold when they were small.

It could have been worse, Liam would tell them when
they'd moan that their older sisters had pipped them at the post
for the best names. They could have been called Hog and
Weed.

'Bar, Liam.' Nora's voice drifted under the door as she
called up the stairs.

'It'll be grand to have all my girls home for Christmas.' He
gave Shannon one last squeeze before releasing her. 'Imogen
and the twins will be here tomorrow afternoon. I hope the traffic's not too bad.' Hailing as he did from a rural village where a
tractor on the main road constituted gridlock, Liam Kelly had
an obsession with the traffic in Dublin.

'I know how you work. It's the free labour you're after.'
Shannon smiled at him, aware it was all hands on deck this time
of the year at the Shamrock Inn. It wasn't just the pub that was
busy either. For as long as Shannon could remember, it had
been a tradition for the Kelly family to host Christmas dinner
for the residents of Emerald Bay who'd otherwise spend the day
on their own. It was a feast that was days in the making.

Liam winked. 'Speaking of which, get yer things unpacked
and settle in that gremlin creature spying on me you call a cat.
Then you can come down and have a brew.'

Napoleon meowed indignantly.

'And a Hobnob,' Shannon added.

'All right for some,' Liam muttered, opening the door and
thumping back downstairs.

She closed the door behind him and began to make kissy
noises to tempt Napoleon out of the wardrobe. He ventured out
warily, and she got down on her hands and knees, rubbing her

thumb over her fingers to bring him closer. He sidled toward her, and she scooped him up, cuddling him to her and resting her chin on his head.

'We'll be grand, you and me, Napoleon,' she said softly, unsure if she was trying to convince him or herself.

7

'How're you, Hannah Banana?' Shannon rhymed, thinking about dropping a kiss on her sister's head but seeing the matted snakes she'd coiled on top of it thought twice. Instead, she patted her shoulder and flopped down across from her seat. It was always a loaded question to ask Hannah how she was getting on because it could go one of two ways, depending on her mood. A lecture on globalisation, or a simple reply of 'grand'.

'Grand.'

Yes! Shannon gave a mental cheer. The beehives in the beer garden discussion must have worn her out. Nabbing herself a Hobnob, she jammed it in her mouth while she set about pouring a cup of tea. She was gasping.

'How's Napoleon?' Hannah asked, before adding with a grin, 'I can't believe he pooped in the wardrobe.'

'In the litter tray, Hannah. It's what he does. He's an indoor cat.'

'Either way, Imogen's going to be so fecked off with you for bringing a cat home. You know what she's like with her allergies.'

'Imogen's only home for five days. She can pop an antihistamine and lump it. And it's all a bit strange for him, being somewhere new, plus he had tuna for lunch and it's upset his system.' She'd left him sniffing the bedroom corners, having had a stern word about not marking his territory in her absence. 'Sure, he's all sorted now. I'll let him wander about down here tomorrow, and in a couple of days, he can check out the pub and garden under my supervision.' She was gratified to see her nan was over by the worktop pulling the steaming bread apart into scone-sized portions.

'Can I have the biggest piece, please, Nan, with lots of butter?' Shannon eyed the loaf hungrily.

'She won't eat her dinner, Kitty.' Nora, engaged in peeling potatoes, tsked.

'I'm not ten, Mam, and I will,' Shannon assured her. 'Pudding too, if some is going. I'm not fussy. Homemade vanilla custard or apple cake would be nice – anything. When did you become the Food Police anyway?'

'Since she and your daddy went to the doctor's and were told to lose some weight,' Kitty answered for her daughter-in-law in a disapproving tone. 'She's been a madwoman ever since. Sure, it's good to have a bit of padding on you in the wintertime, it helps fight the bugs off, but that doctor fella of yours would have us all emaciated and running marathons, Shannon.' Kitty Kelly was a firm believer in feeding up her family and anyone else who happened to need it. She couldn't be doing with cholesterol and the like.

'He's not my doctor fella. I'm employed at his medical practice is all, Nan, and if he says Mam and Dad need to drop a few pounds, then they do.'

'A lot of pounds,' Nora added. 'I'm determined to get my waist back.'

'You're not eating for two, are you?' Hannah's voice was

laced with suspicion, seeing her big sister reaching for another Hobnob.

Clearly Hannah hadn't lost her legendary ability to blurt whatever was on her mind without a thought as to the consequences. Shannon watched as her mam twirled around with lightning speed, wielding the peeler like a sword.

'Sweet Mother of Divine! Am I to be a grandmother? I'm only in my fifties.'

'I was in my forties, and it didn't stop you and Liam,' Kitty said, sagely slathering on the butter.

'That was different. We were married, for starters.'

Kitty raised an eyebrow. The maths on that had always been dubious.

'I'm not pregnant! I'm just hungry.' Shannon sighed. 'All the time.'

Nora wagged the peeler at Hannah. 'Stop giving your mammy heart attacks.'

Hannah was unrepentant as she rubbed her chin. 'Ah, I get it now. It's all right, Mammy. She's after trying to fill the gap Julien left, is all. Yes, we've seen it before. She uses food to fill the emotional void when a man leaves her.'

'Oh, feck off, Hannah.' Shannon scowled at her sister, who shrugged. However, Hannah's insight was surprisingly on the mark. Still and all, just because she'd done a year of psychology at uni before dropping out didn't make her Doctor fecking Phil.

Nora lowered the peeler. 'Come here to me now, Shannon. You've had a tough time, love, but Hannah's right. Your heart's been broken before, and you picked yourself up and carried on. Sure, I can remember you mooning about the place when that fella from Kilticaneel, the one with the nose on him, what was his name?'

'Brogan, Mam.' Shannon stayed where she was, knowing where this was headed.

'Brogan,' she said with satisfaction. 'Broke it off with you because he fancied—'

'Georgia,' Shannon supplied.

'Yes, her with the big bosoms. Your poor father never knew where to put himself when she called around. They were always after falling out of her top. Anyway, the end of the world it was. You lay around eating us out of house and home for a week or so, driving us mad with that Whitney Houston song, what was it called?'

'"I Will Always Love You".'

'You'd howl along to it, so you would, over and over, and the next thing we knew, you were all sunshine and light stepping out with—'

'Davey.' Hannah sniggered. 'I remember him. He always had his finger up his nose when he thought you weren't watching.'

'He had bad sinuses, and could we stop picking apart my ex-boyfriends' noses, please. They were a lifetime ago.'

'The point is, Shannon,' Nora said, 'you have been here before and survived, and you will again. And sure, you're home with your family now. So we'll look after you. Won't we?' She looked from Hannah to Kitty, who both nodded their agreement.

'No, Mam, I haven't been here before, because I'm thirty-four, not sixteen, and I thought Julien was the one, and this time around I was going to get my happy ending like you and Dad.' Shannon sniffed. Her family always brought out her dramatic side.

Nora left the sink and ruffled her daughter's hair. 'And you will, love. He wasn't meant for you, is all.'

Hannah stretched her hand across the table and, picking up her sister's, gave it a squeeze. 'And don't forget he had a mono-brow. Why don't you get the twins to sign you up on that dating app they rave about? It will be a distraction if nothing else,' she suggested. 'There's bound to be a lad over in Kilticaneel looking for action.'

Kitty cleared her throat noisily.

Nora shot Hannah a warning look. 'There'll be no talking about the action in front of your nan, madam.'

Shannon shook her head vehemently. 'That's not helpful. Besides, I don't have the energy, and even if I did, I'm not interested. I've officially taken myself off the market. You're single. Why don't you sign up?' She dislodged her hand beneath her sister's and swept both hands down her front. 'This here is a man-free zone.'

'Your man-free zone's got chocolate on it.' Hannah pointed to the brown patch on her cream polo neck.

'Jaysus wept, she'll be launching into "I Am Woman" next,' Nora said, returning to her potatoes.

'Or joining the convent.' Kitty slid a plate under Shannon's nose. She smoothed her granddaughter's hair. 'All good things come to those who wait.'

'Thanks, Nan.' Shannon watched the yellow blob of butter melt into the fluffy centre, unsure whether her nan was referring to the bread or men. Then, tucking in, she watched under her lashes as Nan, making sure Mam's back was to her, picked up the third plate and skulked toward the door.

'I know what you're up to, Kitty,' Nora said, stopping her in her tracks.

'Can't a mammy feed her son?'

'Not when he's starting with the middle-aged spread, no.'

'I'll have it, Nan,' Shannon offered, quick as a flash. Kitty banged the plate down in front of her.

'And when you've finished, Shannon, could you chop the veg for me. Hannah, you can take over the rest of these potatoes. You needn't think you'll be sitting around being waited on over the holidays,' Nora tutted, pulling her apron over her head. She hung it up. 'I'll go and see if your dad needs a hand.'

'Ah, Mam,' Hannah griped, dabbing at the crumbs on her plate with her finger. As soon as Nora had shut the door behind her, she looked across the table at her sister and held her hand out. 'Phone.'

Shannon frowned. 'Why? Use your own.'

'I can't. I want to check out Julien's new lady love, and he blocked me.'

'Hannah! What did you do?'

'PM'd him and told him he was an arse who didn't deserve you, that's all.' She grinned at her sister.

'You shouldn't have done that.' Shannon tried to keep a straight face

'But you love me all the more for it.' Hannah waggled her fingers. 'Now give.'

Shannon dug her phone out of her pocket and passed it over, squirming as Hannah swiped through his recent Instagram posts with an unreadable expression.

'Hmm, yes, I see. It's as I thought.'

'What?'

Hannah looked up at her. Her dark, elfin features were earnest. 'OK. Do you want my honest opinion?'

'I don't know.' Nobody did honesty like Hannah Kelly. 'Ah, g'won then.'

Kitty, too, was all ears.

'Julien has an Amélie fetish,' she replied, referring to their mam's all-time favourite film. 'I mean, yer woman's fringe is halfway up her forehead, and she has that gammon thing going on.'

'Gamine,' Shannon corrected.

'Same thing. I also think, given the size of her, this Audrey has a little biddy bite out of whatever she's supposedly feeding her face on for the camera and then bins the rest. It's a skinny girl thing. Yer woman there is responsible for contributing to greenhouse gas emissions.'

Shannon snorted and snatched her phone back, quickly scrolling through the posts with her nan leaning over her shoulder. She began to laugh. Hannah had a point.

Kitty straightened. 'You've got too much time on your hands these days, if you ask me.'

The sisters simultaneously rolled their eyes. They'd heard it all before.

'And I hit translate. Did you see yourself spending your life with a fella who captions his posts, and I quote, "Never a dull moment with this one" or "Office for the day"?'

Shannon was properly laughing now. The photographs of Julien and Angular Audrey cycling alongside the Seine and supposedly working with the Eiffel Tower backdrop were cringeworthy.

'My work here is done,' Hannah said, looking pleased as she got up and mooched over to the sink to pick up where her mam left off. Her sweater had a hole in the elbow, and she'd teamed it with baggy jeans held up with a wide brown belt.

Hannah might have the fashion sense of a flea but you had to give it to her, she stuck to her principles, Shannon thought fondly. And to refuse to buy new was top of her list.

She'd tried to convert her sisters to the joys of shopping in thrift stores but with little success. Unless you counted the fifties frock Ava had declared divine and forked out two quid for. Imogen, the family fashion plate, said it was all well and good wearing second-hand clothes to reduce greenhouse gases, save landfill space, help those in need, and conserve energy, but they smelled. Hannah, however, was fortunate because she'd look fantastic wearing a bin bag.

'Shannon, love, I was chatting to Isla Mullins the other day, and she was asking me if she could count on you joining in with the Emerald Bay Elves for the carolling this year?' Kitty said, tea towel in hand.

'Nan, I'm not sure I'm up to—'

Kitty overrode her. 'And I told her you'd be delighted to join in. Singing is good for your soul, Shannon, and the good Lord saw fit to give you a voice like an angel because he wanted you to share it.'

Hannah, who couldn't hold a tune to save herself, nodded her agreement, and Shannon scowled at her. She hadn't sung since the break-up, not even to Whitney.

'But I haven't sung in months, Nan. So I'll be terrible rusty.'

'Sure, it's like riding a bike. It's Friday night, Shannon. Dermot Molloy will be in with his pipes, and Ollie Quigley always comes armed with his fiddle. So your da won't need any persuasion when it comes to getting his tin whistle out.'

'It will be like the Corrs, only with the odds evened up.' Hannah grinned.

Kitty flapped the tea towel at her. 'That's enough out of you.'

Shannon sighed, knowing it was pointless to argue with her nan when her heart was set on something. Who knew, maybe a session in the pub would lift her spirits? It was only the Shamrock, not the Gaiety. She chomped down the rest of the bread and carried her plate to the sink.

'G'won, put your feet up for a bit, Nan. One of those game shows you like is bound to be on the telly. We'll sort things out in here.'

Kitty hung her pinny up over Nora's. 'No squabbling over your chores, you two. I can't be doing with listening to the pair of you blethering on.'

The sisters grinned, united on this front, as Shannon said, 'Ah, now, Nan, you know we can't promise anything.'

8

'Where are you off to?' Nora called out, straightening up from where she'd been leaning over the bar in conversation with Clare Sheedy as Shannon attempted to slink past unnoticed.

Shannon had been hoping to make it out the door in one smooth manoeuvre, having no wish to be included in her mam's conversation with Mrs Sheedy, a right Moaning Minnie.

Nora Kelly was a good listener, and she served as a sounding board for the women of Emerald Bay. Liam Kelly often joked she should have a Dear Nora column in the *Kiltica-neel Star*. Nora was also the founder of the Monday-night get-together group Menopausal and Hot and was fanning herself with a beer mat as she fixed Shannon in her line of sight.

Shannon smiled in Mrs Sheedy's direction before addressing her mam. 'I'm going to catch Freya before she closes the shop for the day and heads home.'

'And have you sorted that cat out? Your father's after telling me the smell was eye-watering in your room.'

'He's sorted, and it was the tuna, Mam. I told Dad he's not a smelly cat. How're you, Mrs Sheedy?' Politeness overruled her better judgement and eagerness to get on her way.

'Middlin', Shannon, if you want to know.'

She didn't.

'As middlin' as a mammy whose children are too busy to come home for Christmas can be. Sure, Nora, here's a lucky woman, having all her girls home in the bosom of her family for the big day.'

'Who's in whose bosom, Clare?' Liam asked, tongue in cheek, not looking up from his task of pouring a pint.

Nora shot him a look. 'Get your mind out of the gutter, Liam Kelly.' She put the beer mat down. 'C'mon, now be fair, Clare, you and Declan were invited to stay at your Kate's in Dublin over Christmas. It was your choice not to go.'

'Ah, Nora, you know how it is. At our age, we can't be doing with Dublin. Dirty, crowded place, so it is. Why they decided to buy that doll's house they call home is beyond me. They could have bought a mansion here for the money they paid.'

At our age?? Jaysus, Shannon thought, yer woman wasn't a day over sixty. She had a patient on her rounds who was learning Latin American dance in her eighties! She'd show Mrs Sheedy a thing or two.

'I'm only fifty-five, Clare, which is not over the hill.' Nora indignantly clarified their five-year age gap. 'And the only mansion in Emerald Bay is the Leslies' big house. The last I heard, it wasn't for sale. Sure, and you know it yourself, there's no work for young ones here either.' She was determined to jolly the woman along. 'Besides, they've lives of their own to be leading. Your children are only on loan.'

Shannon's eyebrows shot up. Lives of their own to be leading? Could she get that in writing?

Clare Sheedy sniffed. 'Well, I'd have thought our Jimmy might have come home to see us given we're getting on. Sure, in five years, I'll be drawing the pension.'

'Your sixties are the new fifties, Clare, and you know what airfares are like at Christmas. They go through the roof, so they do. And, wasn't it your Jimmy I saw in here last July? New York's hardly around the corner. You don't do too badly. Poor Maeve Doolin's son's barely been near the place since he crossed the water to England.'

'That's true enough.' Mrs Sheedy was sufficiently mollified to drain her tot of port, and Shannon used the moment to escape.

'I'll be back in time for dinner, Mam. Nice to see you, Mrs Sheedy,' she fibbed, before shooting out the door, making a note to call on Maeve tomorrow morning.

The damp afternoon was a shock after the pub's warmth, and she huddled into the puffa jacket she'd thrown on over her polo neck, shoving her hands in the pockets before setting off towards Freya's gallery and shop. Seeing Enda Dunne's ancient collie dog, Shep, a smile twitched. He'd taken up residence on the pavement outside Dermot Molloy's Quality Meats as was his habit when Enda settled in for a session at the Shamrock. He did well, too, according to Dermot, who said the canny collie could usually count on a sausage or two being tossed his way by a soft-hearted villager. He was very good at doing the moon eyes and was the best-fed dog in the entire Galway region. She paused to pet the docile old dog for a moment.

'Good boy, Shep.' She smiled as he flopped on the ground, insisting on a tummy rub. She obliged and then, telling him she had to get on her way, looked up to see Dermot scooping mince deftly into a bag. He waved out to her, and she waved back recalling her nan's comments about a singalong in the pub later. She loved listening to Dermot piping. She just wasn't sure about having to join in. Still and all, it would be nice to see his wife, Fidelma, and their brood of children, who all looked like miniature versions of their parents, this evening, she thought before carrying on her way. Across the road, Paddy McNamara was still deep in conversation with the supermodel in Heneghan's Pharmacy window.

'How're you, Paddy?' Shannon called across the street.

He swung around, bottle in hand, and raised it in greeting. 'Season's greetings to you, young Nora.'

'It's Shannon, Paddy.'

'This here's my lady friend, Bridget.' He waved the bottle toward the window and staggered about as though doing a jig.

The door to the pharmacy flew open, and Nuala McCarthy, in her white smock, appeared with her hands on her hips. 'Paddy, would you get on your way. You're putting customers off.'

'I'm not leaving without Bridget. I've told you, Nuala. We belong together.'

Shannon shook her head and tried not to laugh. Poor old Paddy.

The latest Cathy Kelly novel was on display in the window of the sunny yellow Quigley's Quill, and she eyed it. She could do with some escapism, and getting caught up in other women's complicated lives was an excellent way to forget her problems. The armchair was empty and, pressing her hands to the glass, she peered in the window. It was tempting to barrel in and make herself at home with the book. Rita, immersed in a novel behind the counter, would bring her a cup of coffee and a plate of biscuits while she read. Oh yes, it was tempting, all right. She took a step toward the door, but then retreated knowing that Freya would be annoyed if she wasn't her first port of call, and rightly so too. Besides, she'd only just finished her afternoon tea and shouldn't be thinking about biscuits.

Shannon summoned willpower and moved away from the window, jumping as a loud *parp-parp* startled her. The culprit was Mr Kenny on his motorised scooter sounding the car horn speaker his son had bought him last Christmas. He doffed his hat at her, and recovering herself, Shannon checked the road before stepping into it to greet him.

'You're still ignoring Sergeant Badger, then I see, Mr

Kenny.' She was fond of the elderly gent who was a law unto himself. He'd been a great pal of her grandad's.

'Pah, that eejit. I'll not have him telling me what I can and can't do. Besides, I've told young Keith Badger until I'm blue in the face. If it has an engine, it belongs on the road.'

'Fair play to you.'

'I remember when he was in short pants in cahoots with Cathal Gallagher. Village tearaways they were. Do you know they once smashed the window of the Shamrock back in the days when your grandad ran the place? They'd a slingshot they used to terrorise the village with. I don't mind telling yer, their mammies tore strips off them. It took those lads a year of scrubbing down the pavement with a bucket of soapy water outside the pub every Saturday morning to pay off the replacement pane. Sure, and look at them now. Him in the corner shop on every committee known to mankind. The other holding down the letter of the law.'

Shannon laughed. She'd see Sergeant Badger and Mr Gallagher through new eyes now. As for Mr Kenny, it was common to see him puttering down the Main Street in the high-vis jacket his son insisted he wore with a fleet of cars stuck behind him. If anyone dared sound their horn or shout out the car window at him to get off the road, he'd hold his walking stick up in the air. It was his version of a one-fingered salute.

'It's good to see you looking well again too. Although, you shouldn't be out and about on a day like this. You had me worried there for a while with that cough.'

'Ah, now, don't you be telling me what to do and all, Shannon.'

'I wouldn't dream of it, but it was a nasty chest infection you had.'

'Aye, it was. I thought I was on my way to answer to Him upstairs, but there's life in the old dog yet. 'Twas your nan's parsnip soup got me back on my trusty steed here.'

Shannon laughed. 'Nothing to do with the antibiotics then.'

'Kitty Kelly's soup's the best tonic there is. So you're home for Christmas?'

'A bit longer than that. I'm, um, regrouping.'

'Well, best of luck to yer. I'm off to see your father about a pint. It's good to have you home, lass.'

'Thanks, Mr Kenny. Ooh, there's a car coming – I'll let you get on your way.'

He revved his engine and sailed forth, and she grinned, stepping back on the pavement as the car sidled up behind him. It tooted impatiently, and he held his walking stick aloft by way of reply.

Carmel Brady was wiping the cabinets out inside the Silver Spoon, and she held up the cloth she had in her hand, waving it like a white flag upon seeing Shannon. She returned her greeting, spying the twirling sign for the Knitters Nook a short way ahead. If Shannon had a collar on her jacket, it would have been turned up to avoid being spotted by Eileen Carroll. Instead, she tried to shrink down inside her puffa and pick up her pace. As the village gossip, Eileen would be itching for the ins and outs as to her return to Emerald Bay. Eileen might be good friends with Kitty Kelly, but Shannon knew she could trust her nan only to share the bare minimum of her granddaughter's business with her nosy pal. So intent was she on getting past the woollens shop unseen, she didn't spot the icy patch on the pavement.

It all happened very quickly.

Shannon's legs slid out from under her. She was propelled forward, then backwards, frantically windmilling her arms as she tried to stay upright. It was a losing battle, and her mouth formed an 'O' in anticipation of hitting the footpath, but it didn't come because a sturdy pair of arms caught her.

'I gotcha,' an American accent twanged.

Shannon twisted to see whose arms she'd landed in and realised it was him: the Gore-Tex man she'd seen admiring the

Christmas tree earlier. He helped her upright, ensuring she was steady on her feet before dropping his arms to his side. 'There you go. That's my chivalrous deed done for the day.'

Flustered, with her heart still banging thanks to the adrenaline surge her near miss had sent through her, not to mention having been in close proximity to a strange man, she straightened her jacket, spotting the chocolate stain down her front with a grimace. She hastily zipped it up before looking up at him.

'Um, thanks a million. The last thing I need is broken bones.' She gave a small laugh even though what she'd said wasn't in the slightest bit funny.

'Glad to be of service.' He grinned, and the corners of his greyish-green eyes crinkled in response.

She'd put money on him being from Boston. They spoke fast, rounded their vowels and dropped their r's. Yes, definitely a Bostonian. He had a nice smile, too, Shannon decided. It wasn't perfect, as the clichés went about American teeth, but warm and genuine. She was mesmerised by how his mouth curved a little higher on the right-hand corner and oblivious to the fact she was staring.

He cleared his throat, and she blinked, coming out of her trance. What was the matter with her? Endorphins. That was it. They'd have been released in response to not having hit the ground and were making her crazy – endorphins, adrenaline, whatever. *Shannon, pull yourself together*, she instructed sternly.

'That was some pretty fancy footwork you had going on there.' That grin again. 'Miley Cyrus, eat your heart out.'

So much for pulling herself together because heat whooshed up her neck and spread to her cheeks. This time she avoided locking eyes with him. The only saving grace from her impromptu twerking on Main Street was that none of her sisters had witnessed it. They'd have had a field day.

'Sorry. I was teasing. I'm James.' He held out his hand, and Shannon stared at it. Julien had soft hands with long piano-player's fingers, but this hand was strong and there was a sharp white, half-moon scar under his knuckles. There was also no wedding ring, so her earlier assumption he was waiting on his wife was wrong.

Take his hand, you eejit. She gave it a quick shake, noting his firm grip, but didn't return the favour by telling him her name. 'Well, um, thanks again. Enjoy your time in Emerald Bay.' It was another inane comment, and it was time to put some distance between herself and the American fella responsible for making her behave like an eejit. She turned away and began to stride up the street, aware of his eyes on her back, but before she'd gone more than three paces, the door to the Knitters Nook was flung open.

Jaysus, no! Shannon thought as Eileen Carroll cornered her in a woolly cable-knit cardy buttoned to her chin and a pair of snug navy slacks.

'Shannon! I was hoping to catch you. I was very sorry to hear you and your young man are no longer courtin'.' Concern was plastered to her doughy features, and her tone of voice implied Julien had died, not run back to France. She caught the perplexed look on Gore-Tex man's face just before he turned and walked away.

'Ah, don't be sorry, Mrs Carroll. Sure, I'm grand,' she lied, adding flippantly: 'It wasn't meant to be, is all. C'est la vie.'

'You're home for good, your nan was telling me. And I hear you'll be leading the charge with the Emerald Bay Elves this year.'

Tell her nothing, Shannon. 'Just until I decide what's next. Sure, I'd have been home for Christmas anyway.' She didn't mention the carolling she'd been signed up for.

Eileen wasn't one to be fobbed off, and she leaned toward Shannon conspiratorially. 'Still, it can't be easy, not at your age, having to start over. I told your nan I thought it was wedding bells we'd be hearing this time for certain.' Her eyes widened behind the milk-bottle lenses of her glasses as another thought occurred to her. 'And then there's the clock to be thinking about.'

'And what clock would that be, Eileen?' Shannon stomped her feet against the cold and blew into her hands, hoping she'd take the hint that it was too cold to be standing about chatting.

She didn't. 'The ticking one, of course. I was only after reading the other day how a woman's chances of becoming a mammy go down with each year after thirty. And isn't it your thirty-fourth birthday you're not long after having?'

If Shannon hadn't been depressed before, she was now.

Eileen Carroll clucked like a plump hen. 'The thing is, Shannon, you young ones think you can have it all. A career first and then babbies when it suits you, but that's not what the good Lord intended when he created us. A woman's body is at its peak fertility from her late teens to twenties, and after that, well...' Her voice trailed off, and she shook her head, causing her sensible salt-and-pepper helmet to wobble.

I will scream, Shannon thought, gritting her teeth. 'Ah well, there's no need to worry about me and my ticking clock, Mrs Carroll.'

Her tone went over the top of Eileen Carroll, though. 'Yes, I suppose you're right. The fertility doctors can do all sorts nowadays to help things along their way if you have problems. Oh, and I heard Jean Grady's granddaughter's after freezing her eggs. Now, there's an idea. Have you thought about doing that? You know, to be of the safe side, like.'

'Um, no, I haven't.' Was she really having this conversation? In this day and age?

'Not to worry, because Mags Doon fell pregnant at forty-eight with her Leo. She thought she was through the change of life, but He had other plans.'

'Ah, I have a few years before the clock stops ticking then. That's good to know.' Shannon had had enough. 'You g'won inside, Mrs Carroll. You'll catch your death out here, and you don't want to be sick over Christmas.'

'You're not mistaken there. Enda Dunne's after taking bets on it being a white Christmas this year.' She sniffed. 'Not that I'd give that old fool a penny piece of my earnings. And where would you be heading this time of day yourself?'

'I'm off to see Freya,' Shannon said as the portly woman, at last deciding there was nothing more to be gleaned, took her leave.

'Thank feck for that,' Shannon muttered under her breath.

There was no such thing as an uneventful walk in Emerald Bay, she thought, putting her head down in the hope of making it to Mermaids without further mishap or references to her biological clock.

9

Shannon pushed open the pink door and stepped inside the brightly lit gallery. It was empty except for Freya, whose head was dipped while she fashioned a small lump of metal with a pair of pliers. Blue tendrils escaped from the messy bun she'd piled her hair into, and her dangly earrings swayed as she glanced up at the sudden gust of cold air, her face breaking into a wide smile as she saw her friend.

'Shannon!' Downing tools, she slid off her stool to come and greet her with a warm hug. 'Sorry, I'm whiffy. I've been using Liver of Sulphur on a Claddagh band. It gives a gorgeous antique finish, but it stinks! I'm burning scented soy candles to get rid of the smell, but I don't think I've won the battle yet.'

Freya was always one hundred miles an hour, Shannon thought, trying to keep up. There was a faint eggy smell trying to outdo a piney aroma, but it was nothing on Napoleon's earlier efforts, and she hugged her pal back like it had been years since they'd caught up instead of a month or so ago. The wool from the chunky cardigan Freya had on over her usual eclectic clobber tickled her nose, and she was released in time to blink back the threatened sneeze.

'Time for a cuppa or...' Freya pushed her sleeve up and checked the slender watch nestling amongst the stacked silver bracelets she always wore before grinning wickedly. 'It's officially wine o'clock. I don't close for half an hour, but it's been quiet this afternoon, and I doubt anyone will be calling in now. What do you say? I've got a bottle of red, if you fancy a tipple. Ooh, and a tube of Pringles.'

It was a no-brainer after her run-in with Eileen Carroll. 'A wine would be lovely, and I'm always up for crisps. Is that a new tattoo?' Shannon asked, catching sight of a dainty Celtic heart on the inside of Freya's wrist.

Her friend shoved the bracelets up her forearm and then thrust her arm out for Shannon to have a better look. 'Oisin and I got them done a couple of weeks ago in Kilticaneel. Like it?'

'It suits you,' Shannon said, remembering the tiny rose Freya had talked her into getting tattooed on her ankle to mark her twenty-first birthday. After that, she'd left the studio, vowing never again to pay to be in pain.

'Thanks.' Freya dimpled. 'It makes me feel close to him when he's not here.'

'Things are getting serious between you then?' Freya had been seeing the couch-surfing-artist-cum-dosser for nearly a year. She thought the sun rose and set over him, and now they were even getting tattoos together. *Rather her than me*, Shannon thought. She'd only met Oisin twice and had found him full of himself. He was a chancer who liked to be centre stage. Not that she'd mentioned this to Freya. So long as she was happy, that was what mattered. The thing was, she wasn't entirely sure her friend was.

Oisin had told Freya he was a free spirit who couldn't be tied to any one place because his art would suffer, and her friend had put a bright and breezy spin on this when she'd repeated it to Shannon. To her mind, though, this meant he wanted to have his cake and eat it too. And if he didn't have to pay rent while he was at it, so much the better. Still, she was in no position to be offering her opinion.

'Well, we're not talking wedding bells, if that's what you're getting at, but I think he's the one.'

'Where is he?' Shannon asked, half expecting him to materialise, paintbrush in hand, expression of artistic angst firmly in place.

'At an artist friend's retreat near Westport.' Freya's hazel eyes danced. 'I'm heading there once I shut the shop on Christmas Eve so I can spend Christmas morning with him, then I'll make my way to Mam and Dad's for lunch. Every Devlin from here to County Kerry and every island in-between is coming for their Christmas dinner this year.' She rolled her eyes at the prospect.

'And will Oisin be joining you?'

A shadow crossed Freya's face, suggesting Shannon had touched on a sore point.

'No. It's not his bag, the whole family Christmas Day thing. And sure, even if it were, I wouldn't inflict the gathering of the Devlin clan on him.'

Shannon's heart sank, and she wondered if her and Julien's doomed partnership had been as obvious to onlookers as Freya's relationship with Oisin was to her. Nevertheless, she summoned a smile. Freya was blind to her boyfriend's faults just as she had been Julien's, and she wouldn't take kindly to Shannon being a Negative Nelly.

Freya didn't pick up on her vibe, and she clapped her hands. 'Right, let's get this party started. I'll be back in a tick.' She swept off in all her Aran-knit, tie-dyed glory to the tiny room that served as a kitchen and storage space out the back, and Shannon decided to check out the paintings on display, heading toward a violent splash of blues which stood out starkly against the white walls.

She wasn't a fan of abstract art, mostly because she didn't get it. She pondered the canvas in front of her with her head tilted to one side. It was titled *Storm*, and to her, it looked like an angry child had been let loose with a tin of blue paint. Maybe she was a heathen, she mused. Then seeing it was by Oisin Duffy, she rearranged her features from sceptical to impressed in case Freya reappeared and quickly moved on.

The next offering was much more to her liking, and she stood in front of it mesmerised by the watercolour of Kilticaneel Castle with a moody sea in the background. The rainbow splash of colours against the slate sky caught and held her attention, though. If she weren't stony-broke and moving back under her parents' roof, she'd splurge on it.

'You'd have loved this one, Grandad,' she said wistfully. Freya had explained art to her once. It spoke to you, she said. And this painting was telling Shannon to throw caution to the wind and max out her card because she felt a connection to it.

'I sold that not long before you arrived. Thank goodness. Otherwise, it wouldn't have been worthwhile even opening today. It's been so quiet,' Freya said as she emerged from the back room with two wine glasses and the Pringles tucked under her arm.

'Oh. That's a shame. It made me think of Grandad straight-away.' Disappointment flared at it no longer being available, even though she knew she shouldn't be contemplating frivolous purchases. The whole point of coming home was to get her finances in order.

'An American bought it. I haven't had a chance to take it down yet. But, I tell you, Shan, if I weren't madly in love with Oisin, I'd have given yer man a gift with purchase.' She waggled her eyebrows suggestively, then held a glass out.

Shannon burst out laughing as she took the drink but then remembered her near-miss fall and narrowed her eyes. 'He wasn't a walking advertisement for active outdoor wear, was he?'

'With light brown hair, sea-glass-coloured eyes and a cute smile?'

Sea glass. That described his grey-green eyes perfectly. Not that she'd been paying attention or anything. 'Oh, I don't know about that.' Shannon pretended nonchalance. 'But I did just twerk for him outside the Silver Spoon. His name's James.' She turned around, careful not to slosh her wine as she gave a bottom-waggling demo.

This time, Freya laughed as she asked, 'James, is it? What happened?'

'It's Eileen Carroll's fault. I tried to keep my head down so she wouldn't spot me, and I slipped on an icy patch. It was all very undignified, and I would have gone over on my arse if he hadn't caught me.' Shannon took a sip of the ruby-red liquid.

'Your knight in shining armour.'

'My knight in Gore-Tex, you mean. The man looked like he was off for a weekend in the wilds with Bear Grylls.'

Freya sniggered over the top of her wine glass, her nose stud glinting under the bright overhead lights. 'I've missed you. It's good to have you home. I know Galway's not far away, but we're both so busy these days. We'll be able to catch up regularly now you're only down the road.'

'I've missed you too.' Texting just wasn't the same. They'd been inseparable when they were younger, but life happened, and they weren't teenagers anymore. Freya had her business to run, and Oisin – when he deigned to appear, that was – while Shannon had her work and... well, Napoleon.

They exchanged a smile, and Shannon raised her glass. 'I needed this, thank you. Will you be coming down to the pub later?'

'No, not tonight. Oisin said he'd FaceTime me. C'mon, let's sit down.' Freya led the way over to the workbench. 'You can have the stool.' She gestured to it, putting her drink and the crisps down before sweeping a clear patch amid the pieces of metal and tools, and hopping up on the bench, legs swinging back and forth as she asked when Shannon had arrived.

'An hour or so ago, and I've already dealt with a cat with an upset tummy, been roped into Christmas carolling with the Emerald Bay Elves and, despite my best efforts, getting cornered by Eileen Carroll on my way here.' Shannon filled her in on the conversation that had played out.

Freya snorted as she wrested the lid off the tube of crisps and held it out to Shannon. 'Honestly, that woman! You should have told her you were thinking of asking around the village for a sperm donor now you're back. That would have got her knitting needles a-clacking.'

Shannon took a handful of crisps. 'I wouldn't be asking for donations around these parts, thanks very much.'

'But, Shan, Lorcan McGrath's still single.'

'I thought he went to Lisdoonvarna to find a bride?' Shannon grimaced as she referenced the annual Matchmaking Festival held in the small spa town in County Clare.

'He did, but he had no luck. So he's on the prowl.' She held her hand up, fingers in a claw, and made a noise that was a cross between a growl and meow.

'Ugh, don't! And he's single because he doesn't believe in bathing more than once a month, and he's a face like a bulldog chewing a wasp to boot.'

Freya tried and failed to keep a straight face as she did her best impersonation of Eileen Carroll. 'Cop on to yourself, Shannon, because beggars can't be choosy, and the clock's ticking. You could have a little Lorcan babby running about the place in nine months if you played your cards right.'

'Freya!' Shannon was in bits. 'Stop it! You're making my tummy hurt.'

Freya was unapologetic as she tipped the tube, sending a

pile of potato crisps into her palm. 'These are so good,' she mumbled, shovelling them in. 'Once I start, I can't stop. I think I've got addictive personality tendencies.'

'I know I have. So give them here,' Shannon demanded, wanting more of the salty fix.

'I wonder how long he's in Emerald Bay for?' Freya passed the tube over.

'Who?'

'Yer American man. James, you said his name was.'

Shannon shrugged. She was more concerned with the crisps.

'You'd have told me if you'd been with anyone since Julien, wouldn't you?'

'Like a one-night stand, you mean?' Shannan paused, crisps halfway to her mouth.

Freya nodded.

'Yes, I would tell you – unless it was Lorcan McGrath. And no, I haven't, because for one thing I can't be arsed having to tidy me bits and bobs up, and for another, I'm officially celibate.'

'Ah now, Shan, life's too short to be living like a nun. Call in at Heneghan's on your way home and pick up a razor. They don't close until six. You'll be grand. And sure, look it, the best way to get over someone is to get back on the horse and go for an uncommitted, carefree ride round the block.'

'But I've no stallion to be riding even if I wanted to, which I don't. And I've never been any good at uncommitted and care-free. You know that.'

'Well, now's your chance. Have a fling. It will do you a world of good, and James is staying in town over Christmas. There's only the Shamrock Inn and Mrs Phelan's B&B to choose from, so I'd say the odds are good he'll be down the hall from you, especially since I told him how you couldn't get more cosy or authentic accommodation in all of County Galway than the Shamrock Inn.' She winked.

'You did not.'

'I did, too, with your best interests at heart.'

'Freya, read my lips. I AM NOT INTERESTED. And you wasted your time because we're fully booked.'

10

Shannon barrelled back into the pub rosy-cheeked thanks to the red wine and chilly early evening air. It was humming as usual, given it was Friday evening, and the tables and booths were filled with those who weren't in a hurry to get home or wherever they were headed next.

Nora looked up from where she was wiping down a table and tucked her hair behind her ears with her free hand. 'Chloe's after ringing in sick again.' She looked fed up. 'That's four days on the trot now. Your dad and I have been run ragged, so we have.'

'Ah, Mam, it's hardly her fault she's down with the flu. Poor girl.' It was a busy time of the year, and Shannon knew her mam and dad would have barely had a moment to themselves since the local girl who helped out over the dinner hour had been poorly. But she and Hannah were home now, and Imogen, Ava and Grace were arriving tomorrow. So they'd all be on board pulling their weight, and she might as well start now.

'Sure, look it, I've been eating crisps. I can wait an hour or so for my dinner.' She'd much prefer to hoe into the pot pie as soon as Mam took it out of the Aga, but they deserved a decent break, she thought, seeing the faint shadows under her mam's eyes. Besides, she was hardly going to fade away in the interim. 'You and Dad go and have yours, put your feet up while you're at it. Hannah and I can hold the fort for a couple of hours.'

'What were you doing eating crisps when you knew I was after cooking your favourite? On top of all that bread earlier too.' Nora's eyes narrowed.

Shannon thought it best not to add Maeve Doolin's shortbread to the list. 'Mam, do you want me to help out or not?'

'She does,' Liam called over from where he was pouring a beer for a lad in a high-vis vest and work boots who Shannon didn't recognise. 'And so do I.'

Enda had vacated his perch at the bar and finally moseyed off to take himself and Shep home, Shannon saw as she rubbed her hands together. So too had Clare Sheedy, which was a blessing.

'Right, that's sorted then. I'll give Hannah the word and check on Napoleon. I'll be back in two ticks.' She held up two fingers, receiving a startled look from Dermot Molloy at the bar before pushing through the door connecting the pub to their living quarters.

The kitchen smelled of delicious things to come, but it was deserted, and a lonely round of soda bread was on the breadboard. Shannon helped herself. She'd stuffed half of it in her mouth by the time she reached the stairs, and she froze hearing Nan's irritated tones drifting out of the living room. She and her sisters had long since suspected Nan had hidden eyes and ears everywhere, and she hastily chewed and swallowed, expecting a telling-off for helping herself so close to dinner time.

'No, you eejit! It's Istanbul that used to be called Constantinople, not Connemara!'

It was a contestant on the games show she was watching getting the ear-bashing, she thought, stuffing in the rest before haring up the stairs. Then, not wanting to frighten Napoleon, she opened her bedroom door slowly. 'Mammy's home, my dote.'

'Mammy? Jaysus, Shan, you're turning into a mad old cat lady, so you are. Although now you mention it, there's a strong resemblance between mammy and son. It's in the nose and whiskers.'

'Feck, Hannah! You gave me a heart attack.' Shannon's hand flew to her chest.

'Sorry.' Hannah grinned. 'I'm just after getting to know my nephew here.'

'Oh, shut up, but I'll have you know he's been there for me these last months.'

'He's had no choice. I closed the window, by the way. It was like an igloo in here.'

Shannon sniffed. Mercifully the eau de cat poo smell was gone.

Hannah sat cross-legged on her bed with Napoleon next to her with his legs splayed out as he lay flat on his back.

'Have you no dignity?' Shannon directed at him. He purred as Hannah tickled his tummy, then arched his neck and eyeballed his mistress disinterestedly from his upside-down vantage point.

'That would be a no to the dignity question.' Hannah laughed.

'Disloyal bugger,' Shannon muttered, forgetting what she'd come upstairs for in the first place. 'How's the new job going?' she asked, remembering her resolve to show interest in Hannah's new role.

Her sister's face was instantly alive as she waxed lyrical about the world's need for bees. Hannah was very good, Shannon thought. If she were still in her old apartment, she'd be looking into setting up a communal garden on the rooftop to attract the bees. She'd have got Aidan and Paulo on board at the very least. There was something else in Hannah's monologue, though. She kept mentioning a particular Feed the World with Bees co-worker called Dylan. But when Shannon asked her about this, her usually forthcoming little sister turned pink and clammed up. It was most unlike her, but Shannon let it slide, remembering why she'd come upstairs.

'I'm after helping out behind the bar so Mammy and Daddy can have their dinner in peace and rest for an hour or two. You can earn your keep too.' Then, spying the bag Aidan had pressed upon her earlier that day, she fetched the toy mouse.

'Thanks a million.' Hannah pulled a face. 'I saw Handsy Houlihan and the Nolan brothers down there earlier. That Colm's an octopus with the lady punters, so he is.'

Handsy Houlihan, otherwise known as Harry, was a middle-aged Kilticaneel estate agent who brayed instead of laughed and was partial to bad suits and an even worse comb-over. He lived in Emerald Bay with his long-suffering wife, Ciara.

'He'd never dare try the old "whoops my hand slipped" trick when Mam and Dad are about but, sure, he thinks it's open season if they happen to be out the back when one of us is clearing the tables. I don't know how poor Chloe sticks him or Colm. It's not in her barmaid job description,' Hannah continued. 'And both being old enough to be her grandfather. It was bad enough just Handsy drinking here, but I blame Mammy for encouraging the Nolans with that family discount she's after giving them.'

Colm Nolan was one of four brothers who trudged over from the neighbouring village of Ballyclegg, where they lived and where Nora Kelly too had grown up. As cousins of hers, Nora lopped ten pence a pint off for them, which made the half-hour walk to the Shamrock Inn worth it when you consumed the quantities the brothers did. They'd a sister, too, Maureen, who'd headed for Dublin as soon as she was able and had married a fella whose family ran a guesthouse. Nora said she was the best of the bunch, and she missed her, but of the sisters, only Imogen had met her and her daughters.

'Chloe's perfectly able for their sort. She told them all about her protective big brother having just passed his black belt in karate. It worked a treat.' Shannon dangled the mouse by the tail in front of a nonplussed Napoleon.

'But we don't have a big brother.' Hannah frowned.

'Neither does Chloe.'

'Ah, I see. I suppose I could drop in that I have a new fella on the scene who's into the bodybuilding.'

'Now you're getting the idea. Or you could tell Handsy you've caught the ringworm off me.'

'What?' Hannah recoiled. 'Ugh, Shannon, you should have told us earlier.' She began scratching her arms.

'Cop yourself on. I don't have it, but the last time he went in for the kill, I told him I'd a dose of the fungal infection and how the doctor told me it's terrible contagious and causes the "jock itch" in fellas. His arm was like a rubber band snapping back into place, so it was.' Shannon grinned at the memory

Hannah sniggered. 'Ringworm, got it. And give up. He's not interested in the mouse.' She untucked her legs and clambered off the bed, giving Napoleon one last tummy rub.

'I'm busting. I'll follow you down,' Shannon said, planting a kiss on Napoleon's furry head. 'But first, I'd better feed you, and I'm going to leave Mr Mouse here to keep you company.' She dropped the mouse down on the bed, then tipped some cat biscuits into Napoleon's bowl and checked his water before closing the bedroom door behind her and honing in on the bathroom.

Hannah had shooed their parents away and was fetching a glass to pour the pint of Guinness Rory Egan always partook of at the end of the day. It was his daily glass of vitamins, he'd state, quick to add that the black stuff was packed full of all the B's as well as iron and calcium. His sons, Shane, Michael and Conor, were holed up in a booth sipping their pints. So, while they might not be on waving terms with the Kelly sisters, they'd still drink in the family pub. Shannon shook her head, catching a faint fishy smell off Rory after his day out on his boat. He greeted her with a nod, being a man of few words apart from when it came to the Guinness.

She saw they'd a few blow-ins this evening, as they called punters who weren't locals. Old Evan Kennedy was holding court with a group of young Canadians proudly wearing either white scarves or beanies or both with a red maple leaf motif. The tourists were hanging off his every word, and Shannon didn't have to join them to know Evan would be spouting on about his connections with the American Kennedys.

Evan was adamant he was a second cousin thrice removed to the famous family. His party piece for the village's overseas visitors was how he'd been reunited with his long-lost relative, the late, great John F. Kennedy himself. Of course, he was Jack to him, and they'd met when he'd passed through Emerald Bay on his 1963 tour of Ireland. It was a tall tale that Evan could always count on to earn him an evening's worth of free ale.

Then there were the Nolan brothers. They were red-nosed heathens, the lot of them. Colm gave one of the young Canadians a suggestive look that made him look like the village idiot. Frankie and Brendan were engaged in a heated discussion about something, which was par for the course on a Friday night and usually ended with Liam manhandling them out onto the street to sort it out outside. As for Tom, he was examining the finger he'd not long had up his nose. Half-drunk pints littered the table around which they sat.

The back door opened, and Father Seamus blustered in, making a show of how cold it was outside by blowing on his hands and stamping his feet on the mat before making his way over to the bar.

'The usual is it, Father?' The moon-faced priest had presided over the village's stone church for as long as Shannon could remember. He lived in the presbytery farmhouse with his widowed housekeeper, Mrs Rae, who also doubled as the church organist. She kept him well fed. The priest was also partial to Bushmills finest and called in most evenings for a nip or two after his evening meal under the pretence of keeping an eye on his flock.

'Grand, thanks, Shannon,' Father Seamus said, making his way toward the bar. 'Just a tot, mind, to warm me up, like. 'Tis good to see you and your sister home. I understand from Kitty that we're to be graced with all the Kelly girls' presence at Mass on Sunday. Sure, that's a miracle worth notifying the Vatican of.'

'Of course, we'll be there, Father.' Shannon smiled beatifically before turning away to fetch the bottle of whiskey down, muttering a silent *Thanks a million, Nan.* Now she was back in Emerald Bay, there'd be no chance of any Sunday lie-ins.

Father Seamus seemed to be having a problem clearing his throat, Shannon thought as he eh-hemmed himself silly. She poured a hefty finger into the Waterford Crystal glass reserved especially for him.

'Here we are, Father. This will sort that frog in your throat out and have you warmed up in no time.' She slid the drink towards Father Seamus, who was still making a song and dance of clearing his throat. His face was glowing red, giving him the look of a tomato with eyes, a nose and a mouth. He took the whiskey and sloshed the golden liquid around before having a gulp.

'Your skirt, Shannon, eh-hem.'

'Oh, this?' She glanced down. 'Plaid's all the go this season. Although I suppose you could call it tartan too.' Why on earth was he in a tizz about her skirt? It was perfectly respectable.

He shook his head, looking as confused as she was, and Shannon was sure she heard him say, 'Well, I tried,' as he waddled off toward the blazing fire.

The door blew open again, and Shannon bit the inside of her lip, seeing who it was.

Gore-Tex man. She'd forgotten about Freya sending him their way. He had a backpack hooked over one shoulder as he made his way toward her. Shannon side-eyed Hannah. Her sister was following their father's instructions to the letter as she poured Rory Egan's Guinness infuriatingly slowly. Feck it. She'd have to see to him herself.

'We meet again!' James gave her that crooked smile.

It was a smile that would warm the cockles of any woman's heart. Not hers, though, Shannon determined as she forgot about Father Seamus's odd behaviour and mustered up a smile of her own, knowing it didn't quite reach her eyes.

'What can I get for yer?' She bit the inside of her lip again, reasonably sure of what was coming but playing innocent.

'I was hoping you might have a room available. I'm staying in Emerald Bay until after Christmas.' He gave an apologetic shrug. 'It's short notice so close to Christmas, I know, but I wasn't sure if I'd be staying on or not until today.'

It was as she'd thought. Fecking Freya and her meddling, Shannon mentally cursed. Like she'd told her friend, they were fully booked, which was a relief because the last thing she needed was to be confronted by his lopsided grin each time she left her bedroom.

She rearranged her face into an expression of sorrow, hoping she wasn't overdoing it as she said, 'No, I'm so sorry. Unfortunately, we've nothing available, but there's a grand B&B not far from here you could try your luck at. Or, Kilticaneel's not far away. There's bound to be rooms available there.'

'Shan, we do have a room as it happens,' Hannah interrupted as she let go of the Guinness tap and placed Rory's pint down in front of him. 'Mam told me the couple booked in this evening telephoned earlier to cancel. So Room Five's free.'

'That's great.' James beamed. 'I'll take it.'

'But you haven't even seen it,' Shannon blurted. 'And you don't know what it costs.'

Hannah eyed her sister suspiciously. 'Sure, it's a grand double room with an en suite overlooking Main Street. A bargain to be had at sixty-five euros a night. Is that get-up Gore-Tex?'

'Hannah!'

'Uh, yeah.'

Hannah nodded approvingly.

'You got the sustainability seal of approval,' Shannon explained.

'Glad to hear it. I'm sure the room will be fine, but if it makes you feel better, you could take me upstairs for a look before I commit.'

'I'll be fine here, Shan, while you take—?'

'James. I'm James Cabot, from Boston.'

A-ha, she'd been right in her earlier assumption about his accent, Shannon thought.

'It's nice to make your acquaintance, James Cabot from Boston. I'm Hannah Kelly.'

Hannah and James looked at Shannon expectantly.

'We already met,' Shannon mumbled.

Hannah's eyebrows shot up. 'Really? You've only been home five minutes. How?'

The flecks of green in James's eyes twinkled, waiting to hear what Shannon would say.

'I, um, I slipped on an icy patch on my way to see Freya, and James here happened to catch me before I went over.'

Hannah's eyebrows were in danger of merging with her hairline.

'I did, and yet I still don't know your name.'

'It's Shannon. Shannon Marie Kelly,' Hannah supplied for her sister before turning to serve the young Canadian woman who'd appeared at the bar.

There was nothing for it, Shannon thought. She'd have to show him the room.

11

Shannon stepped into the kitchen, aware of James behind her as he closed the door on the noise drifting through from the pub. Kitty, Nora and Liam were seated at the table, about to tuck into their dinner. The trio looked up to investigate the stranger standing a full head over Shannon, who'd just appeared in their kitchen.

'This is James,' Shannon said, stepping to one side as she introduced him. 'He's from Boston and looking to stay over Christmas. So I'm taking him upstairs to have a look at Room Five. James, this is Kitty Kelly, my nan, Nora and Liam Kelly, my mam and dad.'

'How are you?' James greeted.

To Shannon's ears, it sounded like 'how-ah-ya'.

'I'm sure the room will be great, and I'm sorry for interrupting your meal.'

He looked embarrassed, Shannon thought, which rather sweet but unnecessary. There was no such thing as interrupting the Kellys at dinnertime. It was the nature of the business they were in.

'Not at all,' Liam said, pushing his chair back.

'No, please don't get up on my account.'

Liam ignored him, getting up and extending his hand. 'Welcome. That's some deadly activewear you've on there, by the way,'

Nora and Kitty echoed his sentiment, and it was smiles all around for the handsome American.

James shook Liam's hand, receiving a hearty shake in return.

'Uh, thanks. I hike a lot on weekends at home.' He looked about the homey kitchen. 'It's a real family business you run here.'

'Sure, and there's three more of us arriving home tomorrow. Imogen, Ava and Grace.'

'Five girls. Whoa. That's a handful.' James laughed.

'They turned me grey, so they did.' Liam eyeballed Shannon before asking, 'What brings you to Emerald Bay for Christmas then, son?'

'I'm connecting with my Irish roots.'

It wasn't the first time they'd heard this from an American guest, and it was a satisfactory answer.

'Have you eaten?' Nora asked, always ready to lay an extra place at the table.

'I planned on settling in upstairs then driving over to Kilticaneel for dinner.'

'Oh no, you won't. Not when we've good food here going begging,' Kitty bossed.

'It does smell wonderful.' James inhaled appreciatively.

Mam and Nan better not give him my portion, Shannon thought mutinously.

'Grand. That's settled then. Shannon will show you your room, and then you're to come and join us.' Nora smiled, already up from the table to sort him out with a plate.

'Thank you. It's very hospitable of you,' James said.

'Not at all. Now, g'won with yer, the sooner you've had the

grand tour, the sooner you can join us.' Nora turned her back to pop the plate on the Aga to warm.

Shannon stalked from the room. It was a foregone conclusion that he'd be staying by the sounds of it. The door to the family living room was now closed, and when couples or small groups stayed, Mam hung a private sign on the door. However, a solo traveller was different altogether because she couldn't stand the thought of a guest holed up in their bedroom alone.

'There's telly in your room, but sure, feel free to join us in the living room,' Shannon added on autopilot as she made for the stairs. She was halfway up them when she heard James cough, and she realised he was still at the bottom of the staircase. Pausing, she looked back over her shoulder.

'Everything OK?'

'Uh.' He shifted awkwardly, his eyes fixed on the carpet.

Shannon thought he looked like he wanted to say something, watching his mouth move from side to side as she waited for him to elaborate.

'James?'

'I think I, uh, might have left my car lights on. I'll go outside and check before I join your folks.'

Satisfied, Shannon nodded and carried on her merry way, hearing Napoleon's annoyed mews as she reached the landing. She had a quick sniff, hoping the evidence of his motion earlier wasn't lingering. Instead, the whiff of peach air freshener made her cough. Either Mam had given the hall a good spray, or Dad had used half a can after sitting on the throne. He was forever getting told off for being heavy-handed with it.

'Is there a cat locked in somewhere?' James asked, brow creasing in concern as he caught her up, then sniffing, 'I can smell peaches.'

'Can you?' Shannon played dumb and pointed to the right. 'And there is. Napoleon, my Persian.' She didn't want to explain why he was shut in her bedroom, but she didn't want him to think she was a woman who locked her cat in her bedroom for no good reason either. 'I moved home from Galway today with him, so I've to keep him in my room until he gets used to being somewhere new. Don't worry,' she added. 'You won't hear him down your end of the hall. I'll check on him before I go back downstairs.'

'I wasn't worried about that. I love animals. You're doing the right thing keeping him in a smaller space, and if you take your time introducing him to his new surroundings, he should settle in without any problems.'

'You seem to know a lot about it,' Shannon said, a little snippier than she'd intended. She couldn't be doing with a know-all, not given she had four sisters who thought they knew it all. 'You're down this end.' She marched toward the last room on the street side of the pub. She didn't understand why she was being prickly, and she'd probably just destroyed every cliché he'd been holding onto about the charming Irish colleen.

'Sorry, I didn't mean to sound like an eejit, as you Irish say.'

Shannon stopped, hand on the doorknob of Room 5 as she risked a glance at him. He'd fixed her with that crooked smile again.

'Now you do sound like an eejit,' Shannon said with a half-smile to soften her words. 'You should have added "to be sure, to be sure".'

James ran his fingers through his hair and laughed.

'I'm a vet. That's how come I know about cats.'

'A vet?' Shannon queried.

He nodded confirmation.

'With your own practice?' Not that it was any of her business.

'No. An animal hospital employs me. I didn't want the stress or ties running a practice brings, and it means I get to focus on what I love: the animals.'

Either way, he was a vet. 'You don't know if tinned tuna upsets cats' tummies, do you?'

James looked a little taken aback by the question but gathered himself.

'If it's in spring water, it should be fine. Salt water's toxic, and oil's too rich.'

Shannon had a moment of panic hearing the word toxic, and she tried to think. She was fairly sure it had been in oil. Yes, definitely oil, she decided.

'That explains it. Thank you.'

James bit back a smile but didn't ask her to elaborate as she pushed the door to the guestroom open.

'This is you.' She flicked on the light and added, 'The key's in the door, and the pub's open until eleven most nights, but if you plan on being out later, just let Dad know. Have you any idea how long you'll be staying with us?' Then she registered the onslaught of floral patterns in the newly decorated room. *Jaysus, Mam had channelled her inner Laura Ashley in here,* Shannon thought, wincing. She'd clearly not asked for Imogen's input on the decorating front. But then again, Mam always thought Imogen got her creative flair from her. That was debatable.

'It's very nice,' James said politely. 'And, no, I'm not sure how long I'll be needing the room for, sorry.'

He had good manners. Shannon thought she'd give him that, trying not to laugh at how at odds he looked among all the meadow flowers in his survival gear. His lips twitched as if reading her mind, and she found herself smiling back before averting her eyes to point out the obvious.

'The en suite is through there.'

James slung his pack down on the bed and then ducked his head in the bathroom.

'It's great.'

'Mam will fill you in on breakfast and the like.'

James nodded, and there was a moment of awkward silence before Shannon turned on her heel. 'Grand. I'll leave you to it then.' She closed the door on her way out and took the stairs two at a time, eager to distance herself and their new guest. 'He'll be down in a minute,' she informed her family, moving toward the connecting door to the pub.

'Janey Mack Shannon!' Nora exclaimed.

'What?' Shannon swung back to see what had her mam riled.

'How long have you been prancing about with your skirt tucked up in your tights? And are you that hard up you can't afford to get yourself a decent pair without a hole the size of a saucer in their arse?'

Shannon stared at her mam and patted around the back of her skirt. Her face flamed as she yanked it free from tights that had indeed seen better days. It dawned on her what Father Seamus had been trying to tell her with all his throat-clearing earlier. Was it a sin to have flashed her backside at a man of the cloth, even if it was accidental? She'd have to google it. What was worse, however, was the realisation as to why James had hesitated to follow her up the stairs. Oh how she wished she could skulk off to bed and put today behind her.

12

'What's with you? You look like Mammy and her cronies from the Menopausal and Hot Monday group when their internal furnaces are roaring, so you do.' Hannah eyed her sister before slapping down Shane Egan's change and giving him an equally surly look back. He scraped the coins off the bar and picked up his pint, not bothering to acknowledge Shannon. Hannah tracked the fisherman with narrowed eyes as he meandered back to the booth where his dad and brothers were seated. 'I don't know what Ava saw in that stinky fishy gobshite.'

'Shush, Hannah.' Not only was her sister a blurter, she lacked volume control too. No matter if she was right. He was a stinky fishy gobshite, albeit a ruggedly good-looking one with his piercing blue eyes and six o'clock shadow, which had attracted Ava initially. That and the inevitability of them getting together, given they all got around in the same group.

The Egans were a fine-looking bunch of fellas and a catch for any woman partial to fish, but Shane had had a controlling streak about him where their youngest sister was concerned.

Maybe they were all too protective of Ava, her twin, Grace, especially, but she was the baby of the family. Even if it was only by forty-five minutes. It didn't help that her arrival into the world was fraught, and it had been touch and go there, thanks to a lack of oxygen. Ava was a fighter from the get-go, though. Either way, they'd all been relieved when she'd announced she was breaking things off with the fisherman and spreading her wings by moving to London, where Grace was based.

Nobody was waiting to be served, which was a small mercy, Shannon thought, helping herself to a glass of wine. She needed a minute or two to compose herself and try to piece together the tattered remains of her dignity. Why oh why hadn't she binned the tights?

The answer was simple. Because she couldn't be bothered hunting down a spare pair and going through the whole jumping and jiggling routine to ensure the crotch wasn't around her knees again.

Jaysus wept. What a day! Twerking on Main Street and prancing, as her mam had so eloquently put it, about with her arse all but hanging out in front of their American guest. At least she was a woman who preferred the full brief. That was something she supposed as she scrabbled for any tiny morsel to lessen the mortification she was currently experiencing.

Shannon rested the wine down on the bar top and placed her hands on her burning cheeks.

Dermot Molloy was a welcome distraction. Setting down the case he carted his uillean pipes around in, he waved over and called out, 'Will you be joining us tonight, Shannon?' Next to him, Ollie Quigley raised his head to hear her answer.

She remembered her conversation with her nan earlier and knew there'd be no getting out of it. So, not only was she dying of embarrassment, but now she would have to sing for her supper too. Sure, the evening was getting better and better.

'Only for a song or two, Dermot.' She tried to sound cheerful at the prospect. 'And I'm rusty, mind.'

'Ah, sure, now you've the voice of an angel, Shannon,' he said with a wink, opening the case. Ollie nodded his agreement.

Dermot's wife, Fidelma, called out a hello from where she was sitting with Carmel Brady from the Silver Spoon. The five Mullins children were all on their best behaviour with their hair combed neatly or tied in bunches as they sipped their Friday night treat, a glass of lemonade, and tucked into a bag of crisps each. By law, they were supposed to go home at 9 p.m., but the music would just be getting underway then, so a blind eye was turned until Fidelma took them off home for tennish.

Around now, Evan would up the ante with his Canadian audience, not wanting to lose them to Dermot and his pipes, Shannon mused, watching the wily old man sizing his competition up. She knew he'd bring up the curse of the Kennedys and how it had a long reach. All the way to Emerald Bay, in fact, because sure, he'd not been spared either. Hadn't his prize ram jumped the fence, never to be seen again? She took a slug of her drink, thinking she could recite his tale by rote. Then, seeing Hannah's hands were planted on her hips as she studied her face intently, Shannon asked, 'What're you staring at?'

'You. You look shifty. Tell me what happened,' her sister demanded.

'I don't know what you're on about,' Shannon squeaked, trying not to look like she had anything to hide.

'Yes, you do. You scratched your nose then. A sure sign you're fibbing. Is it to do with yer American man, James?'

'No.'

'Because I was picking up on the sexual chemistry between you earlier.'

'Hannah, you're mad. There was no chemistry, sexual or otherwise. I showed the man up to his room, is all.' *And showed him my bum while I was at it.*

'No.' Her dreadlocks wobbled on her head as she gave it a firm shake. 'I know you, Shan, and you're not telling me the whole story. I also know the sexual chemistry when I see it. Sure, it was like watching the baboons all over again, so it was.'

Shannon had another slug of the wine, and even though she knew her sister's reasoning would make no sense whatsoever, she still asked, 'Why are you comparing myself and American James to baboons?'

Hannah sighed as though she were dealing with a simpleton. 'Because of the sexual chemistry. I saw the baboons in a documentary about their mating habits. All posturing about, flashing their scarlet bottoms, they were pretending not to fancy the big male one. Though the big baboon did get aggressive with the lady ones, and American James struck me as an easy-going fella.'

'I was not behaving like a baboon!' Shannon was indignant, although thinking about it, she was scarlet, and she had shown him her bum.

Hannah gave her a look that read, *If you say so.* 'You have to agree he is ridey,' she said slyly.

'No, I don't because I'm not interested in men, like I already told you. *Any men.* And, if you think he's such a ride, why don't you get in there?'

'Not my sort. I couldn't date a man in chinos.'

'He wasn't wearing chinos. He was in Gore-Tex, and you said that's sustainable. Are the chinos not then?'

'It depends on whether or not the organic cotton's used, and he's in the chinos now.' Hannah gestured to where James had suddenly materialised, along with Nora, Liam and Kitty, who were dragging him about the pub introducing him to all and sundry.

'What's wrong with the chinos, because if he's into the Gore-Tex, he's probably into the organic cotton too?' He looked very well in the khaki trousers with his white sneakers. He'd teamed them with a white shirt, the collar peeking out the top of a grey sweater. Not that Shannon was checking him out in *that* way. She was defending the chino trousers, was all. Julien had owned a blue pair.

'Dad wears chinos whenever he and Mammy venture beyond Emerald Bay. They're his go-to good trousers. You know how he always says they're his casual but smart look, and Mam goes on about him scrubbing up well. It's cringe, so it is.'

'But those there are stylish chinos, not Dad chinos with all the pleats.'

'Still chinos.' Hannah snapped her focus back on Shannon. 'It won't work either, you trying to change the subject. What's got you behaving like a virgin on her wedding night? And if you won't tell me, I'll go and ask Mam what's going on.'

'Hannah!' Shannon was wasting her breath, and she knew there was nothing for it but to come clean. At least if she was the one who did the telling, she could downplay the horror of it all. The hole in her tights would likely take on the proportions of a Florida sinkhole if Mam told the tale.

'All right. I got my skirt caught up in the back of my tights earlier on. No big deal.'

Hannah's eyes rounded, and her hand flew to her mouth. 'What, flashing your arse about the place like?'

'I wouldn't put it like that.' Precisely like that, she thought.

Hannah began to smile. It spread across her face and morphed into a giggle which swiftly escalated into doubled-over laughter.

Shannon saw James glance over at the sudden burst of laughter and avoided his stare. She wished she could click her fingers and disappear.

'Sweet Jaysus, I'm crying laughing, and it hurts,' Hannah choked out thirty seconds later.

'It's not that funny.' Shannon said tersely, knowing if the shoe were on the other foot and it was one of her sisters who'd flashed Father Seamus and their American guest, she'd be in bits too. Then, catching a flash of khaki chino striding across the pub toward the bar from under her lashes, she realised he was headed their way.

'It is,' Hannah spluttered.

'He's coming over. Don't you dare say a word, or there'll be murder.'

Hannah was in no fit state to pour anyone a drink, and as she glanced up and saw James, her body shook even harder. If Shannon could have kicked her sister and got away with it, she would have, but she refrained, given it would only create more of a scene.

'What's so funny?' James asked, smiling as he reached the bar, Hannah's laughter infectious.

'Nothing,' Shannon muttered, barely making eye contact as she asked him what he'd like to drink.

'A pint of Heineken, please.'

She set about pouring his pint as Hannah straightened and gasped, 'I hear Shannon gave you a warm welcome.' A snort followed it.

Shannon pulled the pump and, angling the glass beneath the tap, risked a glance up at James, her eyes landing on his trembling lip as he did his best not to laugh.

'Your mom's Guinness and beef pot pie was the best meal I've eaten since arriving in Ireland,' he said, with only the slightest wobble.

Go away, Shannon muttered silently as the lager trickled into the glass, masking the sound of her stomach grumbling. *I don't want to make small talk with you.* However, good manners prevailed, and she raised her head to smile at him, hoping it didn't come across as a grimace.

It was all the encouragement needed.

'Napoleon had quietened down by the time I'd showered and changed.'

'Grand.' She shouldn't have smiled because James wasn't picking up on her body language vibe, and he took the smile as an invitation to carry on chatting. Next to her, Hannah was finally getting herself under control, but as she went to serve Rita Quigley, Shannon could sense her keeping a watchful eye on hers and James's exchange.

'Uh, I think that might be done.' He nodded at the pint glass she was holding.

Ah feck. Shannon blinked and realised the lager she was pouring was more head than beer and was also spilling over the edge of the glass into the tray.

'What do you call that?' Nora elbowed in alongside her eldest daughter, proclaiming her disgust as she took the beer from Shannon and tipped it out. 'She's not herself today,' she said, apologising to James. 'She's after doing all sorts.' Her brown eyes fixed meaningfully on her daughter.

Shannon felt prickly red heat creep up the neckline of the black polo neck she'd switched her chocolate-stained one for. Mam was right, she thought, she wasn't herself, and the last thing she needed was to be worrying about what this American tourist thought of her. What did it matter?

'You go and have your dinner. Then you can join your dad and the lads, love. A sing-song will do you good,' Nora directed, and Shannon was glad to leave, even if it did mean testing out her vocal cords. Anything to put distance between herself and Captain America. However, Hannah's stage whisper wafted down the length of the bar.

'See, told you. Sexual chemistry.'

'What're you on about?' Nora demanded, her brown eyes peering suspiciously at her middle child.

'The baboons, Mammy. The baboons.'

13

Dermot was seated near the flickering flames of the fire, playing a solo of 'Sliabh Geal gCua'. The haunting sound of the pipes he'd learned at his father's knees swept the crowded pub away to a mystical land of mist, stormy seas and stories. It was a mournful, lonely tune and Shannon knew there weren't many listening who wouldn't be rubbing at the goosebumps on their arms.

She saw her nan dabbing at her eyes and blinked back her own tears because the lament had been a favourite of her grandad's. It conjured up the smell of his pipe tobacco and the twinkling in his eyes as he told a story or two. The pipes always made her feel close to him. She gave her nan a smile, hoping to convey she understood her tears. Kitty's nostalgic smile back told her she did.

Shannon decided she'd stand to sing because she was full from her dinner, and the air could get down into her diaphragm when she was standing. Or so the singing teacher she'd gone to as a child had told her.

Hannah hadn't dared mention anything to do with primates while they scoffed down their meal, which was just as well. The pot pie had been comforting and delicious and had acted as a salve for her dented pride. Now Hannah was back helping Mam behind the bar, and Shannon found herself scanning the pub and smiling at the familiar faces who enjoyed the craic at the Shamrock Inn on Friday nights. James was seated next to Evan, talking to an attractive Canadian girl with the sort of hair that would never kink on a damp evening. Unlike her own, which was very kinked; she raised a self-conscious hand to it and tried to smooth a little of the frizz.

The pipes drifted off and were met by foot stamping, cheers, whistles and a cry for 'The Fields of Athenry'. Shannon caught her father's questioning look and gave him a nod. She got to her feet, standing to the side of the table, which would soon be cluttered with the pints the punters would buy by way of thanking them for the music. Her dad put the tin whistle to his mouth, and the crisp, pure notes sounded. Inhaling deeply, feeling her tummy swell, she opened her mouth and let the words fly free. Her eyes fluttered shut as her voice rang out sweet and strong. The people surrounding her faded, and all she was aware of was the music and the heartfelt lyrics about the potato famine. A blueprint of her country's memory. She was a storyteller, too, only instead of using spoken words like her grandad, she sang them.

Seeing there wasn't a dry eye in their vicinity, Ollie decided to up the ante, launching into a lively version of 'The Galway Piper' with his fiddle. Liam joined in, and Shannon felt the melancholy lift. They followed it up with 'The Raggle Taggle Gypsy', which had everybody clapping along, and the warm, festive atmosphere washed over her. Shannon forgot all her woes and began enjoying herself in a way she hadn't done since Julien left. She'd forgotten how euphoric singing made her feel. Or maybe she'd chosen to forget because she'd not been ready to feel the joy it brought her until now.

· · ·

It was getting late when Dermot called time, and Shannon felt light and giddy. She realised the emotion she was experiencing was one she hadn't felt in a good while. Happiness. And she beamed as her dad gave her a proud wink.

'Voice of an angel, all right,' Dermot reiterated his earlier sentiment before raising his pint to his lips. Ollie stopped fiddling with his fiddle long enough to agree.

The pub would quieten now as people made their way home or wherever they were going, Shannon thought, waving goodnight to the Gallaghers from the corner shop. Her mam had tasked Hannah with clearing the emptying tables, and she was wiping the bar top down.

Isla Mullins, owner-operator of Emerald Bay's Irish souvenir shop, stepped into her line of sight. She was only five or so years older than her mam, but her spectacles, along with the haircut, a Nessie pudding-bowl special, put a good ten years on her. In her pea-green hoodie with its black map of Ireland emblazoned across her chest, Isla was hard to miss. She was a firm believer in wearing what she stocked in the shop and was quick to tell you she'd often closed a sale in the pub after a customer had admired her attire.

Shannon doubted she'd shaken on any deals tonight, unable to picture the Canadian group in pea-green hoodies.

'You know yourself you could have been a professional singer, Shannon. Sure, you're up there with the great woman, Mary Black herself.'

Shannon had never been good at accepting a compliment. Her mam had told her repeatedly that all she had to do was say a simple thank you, and there was no need to be self-deprecating. It didn't come naturally, though, and she replied with a dismissive flap of her hand, 'Ah sure, I can hold a tune is all, Isla.'

Isla ignored her. 'Well, I know I speak for all the Emerald Bay Elves when I say how delighted we were when Kitty told us you'd be joining us for this year's carolling as an honorary elf.' She leaned forward conspiratorially. 'Between you and me, a couple of our more senior elves are tone-deaf. So I'm counting on you to carry them along.'

Shannon nodded, trying to rally an enthusiasm she didn't feel.

'We've a rehearsal tomorrow in the church hall at two o'clock sharp, and I mean sharp because I'm after organising young Gina Brady to man the fort at the shop, and Eileen Carroll's knitting group has booked the hall for three thirty. She closes the Knitters Nook early on Saturdays, and we don't want to be annoying her when she's a pair of needles in her hands. Now then, what size would you be?' Isla pushed her glasses back over the bridge of her nose and scanned Shannon top to toe. 'About a ten, if I'm right?'

She'd run with that, Shannon decided.

'I was last time I checked, Mrs Mullins. Um, why?'

'For the tunic, like. And don't worry, it's fleece-lined, so pop a vest on underneath, and you'll be grand. Geraldine's a wonder on that machine of hers. She'll whip you one up in no time. It was her made all the tunics and hats for the small sum of twenty euros. You'll need to sort yourself out with a pair of green tights.'

Shannon stared blankly at Isla Mullins. Surely she wasn't expecting them to dress up as elves? And, worse, pay twenty euros she could ill afford for the privilege. What was wrong with a bobble hat, scarf and coat? No, there was no way she'd be singing her heart out to 'Jingle Bells' while wearing an elf costume. It wasn't happening.

'I'm a firm believer in looking the part. It adds to the overall festive feel,' Isla added.

Shannon would be having words with her nan, so she would. She'd not mentioned anything about looking the part.

'So, we'll be seeing you tomorrow afternoon.' Isla looked at her expectantly from behind her thick lenses. 'And don't forget to bring your subs.'

Shannon assumed she meant the twenty euros. Isla could be intimidating when she wanted to. She was a hard woman to say no to, which was why so many tourists went home with leprechaun snow globes, shamrock tea towels and curly red wigs. 'Two sharp at the hall,' Shannon confirmed as Isla bustled off. She wished she'd had enough bottle to have said a polite no, that Nan had been mistaken because it wasn't her thing. She hadn't lived in Emerald Bay for the best part of her life, though, without learning to rub along in a small village. Sometimes you had to make compromises. It was just that dressing as an elf was a very, very big one. And twenty euros! Twenty fecking euros!

A yawn escaped, and it hit her how tired she was. It had been a big day, and the emotional upheaval tinged with relief at leaving the apartment in Galway was catching up on her. She felt guilty as her thoughts turned to Napoleon. She should have gone up earlier, but the night had gotten away from her. Another big yawn escaped. She'd earned her bed, she thought, deciding to skulk off and leave Hannah to the clearing up. It would serve her right for being such a smart arse earlier. Checking the coast was clear, she began slinking toward the door to the family quarters. She was almost there, the door handle in reach and her hand about to grasp it, when she felt a tap on her shoulder.

She spun around, hoping it wasn't Isla again, having forgotten to tell her she'd also need special elf boots, and was surprised to see James behind her instead. She'd thought he was getting cosy with the fabulous hair girl, but here he was standing in her personal space, so close she could smell the citrusy spice of his aftershave. It was all very unsettling, and she wanted to take a step back but knew she'd collide with the door if she did.

'That was wonderful.' James's eyes were alight, and his

cheeks ruddy thanks to the lager he'd had and the warmth of the fire. He held up his phone. 'I recorded it for my mom. She'll love it. Do you sing professionally?'

'What? No!' Shannon laughed at the notion and pointed to his phone. 'And please, don't be putting any videos on YouTube or whatever. In cyberspace, there's one out there of Dad dressed as an Irish dancer, red wig and all, doing the fancy footwork for St Paddy's a few years back. We threatened to disown him.'

James laughed. 'Well, what do you do if you're not the next Enya?'

A dreadlocked head bobbed between them. 'When she was ten, she wanted to be in that nineties band, B*witched. Remember "C'est la Vie"?' Hannah hummed the chorus, and James shook his head, bemused.

'No, I can't say I do. Were they like the Spice Girls?' He flashed his crooked grin.

Hannah nodded. 'Only better, because they were Irish obviously, and Shan here was mad on them.'

Shannon shot her sister warning daggers, knowing it was as futile as sticking her finger in a hole in a dam trying to stop her when she was in mid-flow. And away she went.

'She made all of us sisters practise the "C'est la Vie" dance moves with her before kicking Imogen or me out of the group before the live performance for Mam and Dad. It depended on which of us she was annoyed with, because there were only four members in the group. Shannon was a stickler for detail. The twins were made permanent because two of yer B*witched wans were twins. She was a tough manager,' Hannah finished with a butter-wouldn't-melt smile.

James had his head tilted to one side, and amusement flickered across his face as he tried to keep up with Hannah's monologue.

'I wanted to be in NSYNC myself.'

'Snap!' Hannah cried jubilantly. 'Shan had a big crush on

Justin Timberlake. She'd a huge poster of him on the bedroom wall.' She demonstrated how big using her hands. 'It would make Imogen cry. They shared a room, and we don't know why it upset her, other than she wasn't a JT fan herself.'

'Go away, Hannah,' Shannon said through gritted teeth,

Hannah, catching her mam flapping the cloth she'd been wiping down the bar with at her, moseyed off to clear the tables.

'I've got three brothers,' James said once she'd gone.

Clocking his sympathetic tone, Shannon forgot all about her sweaty palms and how her eyes kept being drawn to his mouth as she said, 'You'll have an idea what I have to put up with then. And you've not met Imogen, Grace or Ava yet.'

She decided he had a nice laugh as he nodded, 'Oh yeah. I get it, all right.'

Her hand trembled with the urge to fan herself because all of a sudden she felt hot, but she kept it by her side, aware she'd look like her mam if she began flapping her hand in front of her face. 'Well, I'm heading up now. I have a neglected cat to be fussing over.'

'I'm not far away myself. I've got an earlyish start in the morning.'

'Are you off to see the sights and delights of this part of the world then?'

'I plan to, but tomorrow, I've someone to call on.'

'In Emerald Bay?'

'Uh-huh.'

Shannon waited for him to say who exactly. Emerald Bay was a small village. Everybody knew everybody, but he didn't say any more, and the silence stretched awkwardly.

It was none of her business anyway, she thought, opening the door.

'You didn't tell me what you do,' James said.

'I'm a practice nurse for this region.' Shannon flicked the

light on in the kitchen and, having no wish to explain her role, said, 'Goodnight then.'

'Yeah, goodnight.'

She closed the door firmly behind her and leaned against it for a moment, surprised to find her heart was banging against her chest. James had put her on a spin cycle. Did he not know the meaning of giving a person breathing space? She decided she'd be keeping her distance while he was under the same roof. This American with the sea-glass-coloured eyes would not put a crack in her man-deflecting shield, even if he did have a lopsided smile that made her legs turn to jelly. She was not interested. 'I'm a strong, independent, single woman,' she whispered to herself. 'Who does not, repeat, *not* want a fella.'

14

It was silent on the landing, which was a good sign. Napoleon must have settled down, Shannon thought, padding down to her bedroom, and the peachy pong wasn't nearly as whiffy now either. She was eager to see her furry friend and hoped he'd not attended to any more business in the litter tray. Then, pushing the bedroom door open, she flipped on the switch. As light flooded the room, she saw all was as it should be and, standing in the doorway, a smile teased her lips as she spied Napoleon.

He'd made himself at home by curling up to sleep on her pillow and was giving off snuffling snores. Shutting the door, Shannon pulled the curtains, spying Mr Mouse peeking out from under Imogen's bed which meant, despite his earlier disinterest, he'd been amusing himself in her absence. *Good*, she thought, moving toward the head of the bed.

'Hello, fella. Sorry I've been gone so long. I promise I didn't forget you. So who's a clever boy for catching the mouse then?' She was glad Hannah wasn't about to hear this exchange.

Napoleon opened one eye and stretched as she patted him, unbothered by the fur floating down to settle on her pillow.

'It's been such an odd day. For you too, I suppose. We'll sleep well tonight.'

Her cases were still at the foot of the bed, and she wished she'd taken the time to unpack them earlier because she really couldn't be bothered now. Ah well, they'd have to wait until the morning. Besides, Dad had sprayed the peachy yoke in the closet, too, and unless she wanted to get about smelling like James and the Giant Peach, it would be better to leave it airing out overnight. She'd still have time to stake her claim in the wardrobe tomorrow morning before Imogen, a wardrobe hog of old, arrived. A shudder rippled through her at the thought of Imo's reaction to a litter tray being in there. 'One thing at a time, Shannon,' she said aloud. 'I'll deal with it when I have to.'

Was it the blue case or the red she'd packed her toilet bag and pyjamas in? Unable to remember, she tried her luck with the red one first. She laid it down flat and, opening it, saw her journal resting on top of the clothes she'd shoved in. They badly needed to be hung up but, ignoring them, she picked up the hardback notebook she wrote in each day and flicked through it, sitting back on her haunches.

Her neighbour Aidan had given it to her on one of her Friday-night visits across the hallway of the apartment building. When she'd opened it and looked at him, puzzled by the blank pages inside the whimsical cover, he'd explained that it was a gratitude journal, to help her through her break-up journey. Shannon had had to interrupt to ask him to please never use the word 'journey' again. He'd apologised, saying he'd been watching too much reality TV, and told her the idea was for her to take ten or fifteen minutes to record the things that had happened during her day which she was grateful for.

'What, like my family, you lads, Freya, Netflix and Tayto crisps? That sorta thing?' she'd asked.

'Kind of. But make it a rule not to be repetitive and think about why it is you're grateful.'

'Because you all love me, and I love Netflix and Tayto crisps,' she'd stated the obvious.

'No. Don't just write "Aidan gave me a Lion bar, and I enjoyed it".'

Shannon's ears had perked up. 'Have you a Lion bar for me too? Because I'd be very grateful if you did, and it would help me through my break-up.' Nope, she couldn't bring herself to say the 'j' word, not even for a Lion bar.

'No. I'm using it as an example.'

'Oh.'

'What I mean is, instead of Aidan gave me a Lion bar—'

'Which you didn't, by the way,' she griped.

He carried blithely on. 'Write, "Today, Aidan gave me a satisfyingly chewy caramel and wafer bar smothered in milk chocolate".'

'I fecking well wish you had.'

'Do you get what I'm saying, Shannon?'

'I think so.' She'd promised she would try her hardest to find three positive things to write in it each day.

It was a promise she'd kept too – well, to a point. But there'd been days where she'd not found much to inspire her, and on those days, she broke the repetitive rule and wrote she was grateful for her cosy sloth-patterned flannelette pyjamas, Napoleon and cups of tea with sugar in them. All three were constants she could count on post-break-up with Julien.

Now, she put the journal to one side as she rifled through the clothes locating her ancient quilted toilet bag first and her pyjamas second.

The flannelette PJs had been tucked away for the duration of her and Julien's relationship. He'd never said so, but she'd known he wasn't the sort of man who would appreciate the joy a woman could feel when slipping into a pair of well-worn, cosy pyjamas, all set for a night in front of the television. He'd bought her silky garments which rode up her backside and which she'd felt obliged to wear. She'd been so intent on arranging the skimpy excuse for knickers so they didn't disappear permanently one night that she'd missed the ending of the Ryan Reynolds romp they'd been watching. The day Julien had walked out, all the underwear he'd ever bought her had gone in the bin, every last wispy pair of them.

Shannon undressed, kicking the holey tights to one side with a scowl as she vowed to buy a new pair from the Bus Stop corner shop tomorrow. She was grateful for being able to wear comfortable underwear, this was referenced in her journal, but she wished she hadn't opted for a white pair of knickers under her black tights. Then, clambering into her pyjamas and fetching the crisps Aidan had given her as a parting gift, Shannon ripped the bag open, stuffing in a handful. She set them down on the bed before searching through her handbag for a pen.

'No, not for you. You've had plenty to eat today.'

Napoleon had roused himself to check out the cheese and onion aroma, and he gave Shannon a look that said, *I don't want them anyway*, before stalking back to his pillow and snuggling back down.

'Good boy.'

She sat cross-legged on the bed and turned to a fresh page in the journal, frowning at the blank lines as she clicked the ballpoint pen she'd located on and off. It was a habit that had got her into trouble in her school days, but it helped her think. She glanced at the crisp bag and decided to start at the beginning of her day by writing in her loping style:

Aidan gave me a survival kit to take with me, which I was touched by, and I enjoyed the Lion bar on the drive home. He also forgave Napoleon and gave him a mouse.

I had a lovely cup of tea, a shortbread and a cosy chat with Maeve Doolin.

Shannon paused, frantically clicking the pen. She should be grateful she hadn't broken a leg skating over on the ice today but was reluctant to mention James in her journal. Besides, the skirt-tucked-up-in-tights debacle overrode that, so she decided to skip over that part of the day.

> *I called in on Freya, and she made me laugh until my stomach hurt.*
>
> *Nan made brown bread, and I got to eat it hot and fresh from the Aga. Mam made my favourite meal, and she even made a pastry 'S' to go on top of my pot pie.*
>
> *Napoleon bonded with Hannah.*

There was something else, Shannon realised.

> *I sang again, and it felt wonderful.*

Snapping the book shut and stashing it in the top drawer by her bed, she changed into the PJs and, picking up her toilet bag, said, 'I'll be back in a tick, Napoleon,' before venturing down the hall to the bathroom.

The sounds downstairs were muted as she shut the bathroom door and pulled her hair back from her face with an Alice band. While she was brushing her teeth, a tube left on the vanity caught her eye and picking it up, she saw it was a face masque. It was also French and looked expensive. Therefore, Imogen must have left it behind the last time she'd come home. Shannon read the instructions, noting you left it on overnight. There'd be no chance of trying it once Imogen arrived home, so tonight was the night.

She finished her teeth and, with her face washed, shiny clean, slathered on the thick, goopy mask, leaving a ghostly white film on her face. She'd have to put a towel over her pillow tonight because Mam would go mad otherwise.

As she opened the bathroom door, a towel draped over her arm, she nearly collided with James.

'Uh, goodnight again.' He gave her that funny lopsided grin as he caught sight of her greasy face and pyjamas.

'Goodnight,' Shannon squeaked, scurrying off to her bedroom. Why hadn't she put her dressing gown on? And why oh why did he have to catch her looking like a ghost in sloth pyjamas? Imogen would have said it was karmic payback for using her things without asking.

Tomorrow is a new day, Shannon, she told herself, scooping up Napoleon and lifting the covers so he could investigate. She draped the towel over her pillow, thinking this mask she'd coated on better fecking well have miracle properties before flicking the light out and climbing into bed.

'Napoleon!' she groaned a moment later as a smell wafted up toward her.

THREE DAYS UNTIL CHRISTMAS

The warmth of a home and hearth to you
The cheer and good will of friends to you
The hope of a childlike heart to you
The joy of a thousand angels to you
The love of the Son and
God's peace to you.

— IRISH CHRISTMAS
BLESSING

15

'Mam, I'm popping out. Do you want me to pick anything up from Heneghan's or the Bus Stop?' Shannon asked, breezing past her mother and coming to a halt as she reached the door. 'Oh, I almost forgot. We're expecting two more on Christmas Day. I called in to see Maeve Doolin on my way home yesterday, and she confirmed she's coming to us and asked if she could bring someone with her for Christmas dinner. Of course, I said it wouldn't be a bother.'

'The more the merrier, so long as we have a rough idea how many we're catering for. So who is it Maeve's after bringing?' Nora asked, curiosity stamped on her face as she looked up from the shopping list she was adding to. She eyed her daughter closely. 'You're looking very well this morning, Shannon, and I hope it's tights you're after getting from the Bus Stop.'

'Thanks.' Not that she'd be telling her mam she'd Imogen's face mask to thank for her glowing skin. 'I am, and Maeve wouldn't say,' Shannon answered the remaining questions. 'She was quite secretive. I'm a little worried about who this visitor of hers is, to be honest. Her arthritis was paining her too, so I'll pick up a hot-water bottle from Heneghan's while I'm out and drop it in later this morning.' She glanced at the wall clock and saw it was after ten. She was a free woman between now and this afternoon's carolling practice in the church hall, which she hoped would not be a dress rehearsal. The less time gadding about dressed as an elf, the better.

She'd slept soundly in her old bed, not waking until nearly eight when Napoleon had jumped on her chest and meowed it was past his breakfast time. She'd sorted him, then clambered back into bed, lying on her back as she picked free the strands of hair stuck in the remnants of the sticky mask. Listening to the various creaks on the landing, trying to guess whose was whose until it grew silent. That was when she'd peeked out of her bedroom door to ensure no one – no American, more to the point – caught her in her morning glory, before padding to the bathroom.

It had been a pleasant surprise to see her skin look better once she'd washed it, and she'd decided it was almost worth having got caught out last night as she'd admired her minimised pores in the mirror. More's the pity, she'd only get to use the mask the once with Imogen arriving home today. Heading back to her bedroom, she'd hung her clothes up and opted for jeans after yesterday's debacle, almost regretting her choice as she sucked her tummy in and wiggled and jiggled the zipper up. Then, pulling a warm cinnamon-coloured sweater over the top, Shannon headed to the kitchen, where she was relieved to find nobody had snaffled her leftover soda bread. Saturday morning was off to a good start, and feeling positive, she munched on jam-slathered toast.

'I hope it's not that big red-nosed son of hers after a free dinner who'll be joining us.' Nora interrupted her thoughts.

'No, it's not him. He's a selfish eejit who can't be arsed bringing his family over from London to spend Christmas with his poor mammy. Maeve downplays it, but I know it saddens her. She'd love to see more of her grandchildren.'

'Just remember you said that when your dad and I are old and grey and moaning about our creaking bones.'

'Mam, I'll still be living here in another thirty years at the rate I'm going,' Shannon stated glumly.

Nora laughed. 'You'll sort yourself out, Shannon. Sure, our guest, James, was singing your praises this morning as he tucked into his full Irish, so he was. He's quite taken with you. It's a pity he's only over on holiday.'

Shannon wished she had her mam's faith in her ability to get her life back on track. Having seen the sly look she'd given her when she'd dropped James's name into the conversation, she dug her nails into her palms to stop herself asking what exactly it was he'd been saying. She didn't want to add fuel to the fire her mam was trying to stoke.

'I've told you, Mam, I'm off men – Irish, American or whatever. I'm not interested. Where is everyone, anyway?' Shannon asked in an abrupt change of subject.

'Hmm, if you say so. Your dad's out the front. The man from the brewery's calling in this morning. Kitty's at the church hall with her card-making group, although they're after making origami Christmas decorations today, and Hannah's off saving the world in Kilticaneel with her friend Meghan. You know the one who stomps around in those Doc Marten boots looking like she put a hole in a bin bag and stuck it over her head?'

Shannon laughed at the spot-on description of Hannah's pal. She was glad her sister was out, because she'd not be answerable for her actions if she started on about the baboons again this morning. Mam was bad enough.

'Don't you want to know what he was after saying then?' Nora asked.

Of course, she did, even if she had deliberately waited until she heard an engine start in the car park before venturing down-stairs. He'd been true to his word, having got away earlyish.

She might not have seen him this morning, but she had been in his bedroom.

Mam had set her the task of making his room up. Shannon thought you could tell a lot about a person by the state of their bedroom as she straightened the bed covers, and James was tidy. Unlike herself, he'd put his clothes away. He'd also hung his wet towel up instead of leaving it in a heap on the bathroom floor, as many guests were apt to do. She'd replaced it with a fresh fluffy towel and set about wiping out the basin. The citrus and spice aftershave she'd caught on him last night had been strong in the small space, and she'd seen he used a herbal-scented shampoo as she wiped the shower out. It had seemed too intimate to know the brands of toiletries he favoured, and feeling suddenly claus-trophobic, she'd been glad to make her escape.

Now she answered her mammy. 'G'won, I can see you're dying to tell me.'

'Well.' Nora put the pen she was holding down. 'He said you'd a beautiful singing voice and a natural stage presence. His mammy over there in America thought so too. James sent her a video, so he did. Isn't that nice? And he also said my breakfast was the best he'd had since arriving in Ireland.' She puffed up a little at this.

Shannon didn't mention he'd said the same about her Guin-ness pot pie last night. Any more puffing up, and she'd float off like one of those helium balloons.

'I was hardly on a stage, Mam.' Shannon batted the praise away, secretly pleased. 'Do you want me to pick anything up while I'm out?'

'No, you're grand. And you do have the voice of an angel, Shannon. It's a blessing, so it is, and it made my heart full, hearing you sing last night.'

'Ah, thanks, Mam.' Shannon kissed her on top of her head.

'I tell you, Shannon.' Nora moved on with lightning speed, as was her way. You had to get in quick when there were eight of you under one roof, or you'd never say what it was you wanted to say. 'It's some racket Cathal and Brenda have got going at that shop of theirs. You want to see the price they're charging for a tin of beans these days. I could be dining on a fillet steak for what they're asking. Sure, we'd all be in the poor house if the greedy Gallaghers had their way. I'm all for the shopping locally but not at triple the price. Anyway, it's the big shop at the Tesco in Kilticaneel tomorrow. They're open Sunday, and if we go early, it shouldn't be too chaotic. You can help me with that. Oh, and don't forget, your sisters are arriving this afternoon.'

This time, Nora glanced up at the clock with a frown.

'Imogen promised she'd ring me when they're leaving, and I've not heard a word. I hope they're not all after lying in their beds until midday feeling sorry for themselves. I don't want them driving down in the dark.'

Shannon hadn't forgotten they were coming today, and she thought it quite likely Ava and Grace had dragged Imogen out to make the most of their night in Dublin, but she didn't say this. 'Ah, they'll be on their way soon enough, don't worry, Mam. Did I tell you Nan's roped me into singing the carols with the Emerald Bay Elves? And Isla Mullin has summoned me to a rehearsal at the church hall for two this afternoon. So, I'll be seeing you.' She left her mam to her list.

'Morning, Dad, Enda.' Shannon sailed through the pub.

'Would you put in a good word for me when you see your nan, young Hannah? She's a fine woman so she is.' Enda looked up from his pint.

'That cat of yours isn't after doing his business again, is he?' Liam demanded.

'It's Shannon, Enda.' She didn't know why she bothered. 'And, no, Dad.' Napoleon had, of course, because what did her dad expect – for him to hold it in? Mercifully, it didn't warrant a peach air freshener frenzy like yesterday. This morning, Napoleon had been in good form, seeming to accept he was to spend another day in the bedroom. Tomorrow, she'd let him out and about when she'd nowhere she needed to be. It had been heart-warming to see him having a grand old time mauling Mr Mouse when she'd closed the door on him earlier.

'Bye, Dad.'

Shannon escaped into the frosty morning and shoved her hands in the pocket of her puffa, stepping out of the way of a group of bored-looking teens. They shuffled past full of angsty anguish, enveloped in aerosol clouds as they vaped themselves silly. Although vaping hadn't been a thing when she was that age, sneaky cigarettes had, and she smiled at the memory. She'd not have sidled down the Main Street bold as brass like this lot, though. Mam and Dad would have eaten the head off her if they'd caught her. Back then, she'd thought Emerald Bay was a proper backwater, and she and Freya used to spend hours imagining a glamorous life across the water when they were grown up. Yet here they both were, still in Emerald Bay.

On closer inspection, she realised she knew all the gang's faces. Their mams had been bringing them to the surgery since they were babies. The last time she'd seen them, she'd been handing out jellybeans after their booster tetanus shots. It made her acutely aware of the passing of time because that had to have been a good four years ago.

'How're you, Nurse Kelly?' Ella Finlan asked politely, her arm firmly entwined through that of Kyle Hogan, who was looking conspicuous in his gangsta rapper get-up. He had a weighty backpack slung over his shoulder, and Shannon wondered if they'd been stealing booze from their mams' and dads' alcohol cabinet to sample down at the bay. Been there done that – only the once, mind.

'Sound as a pound, Ella, thanks. Those things are bad for yer, you know.'

'Have you any jellybeans on you, Nurse Kelly?' Ella's pal Ruby McGinn in all her bronzed highlighter glory asked with a cheeky flick of iron-straight blonde hair.

'No, but I have got a big vaccination needle I'd be happy to use if you're suffering from smartarsitis there, Ruby.'

They giggled on their way.

Shannon watched them for a moment, guessing they were headed for the park by the church. The trees down the back had always been a popular spot for getting up to no good. Was the holly bush still there? she wondered. It had been a thing to hold a sprig over the head of a boy you liked, to steal a kiss. Her breath was white on the clear, sharp air and, forgetting about the teens, Shannon made her way toward the Bus Stop, the village's corner shop. She passed the time of day with Brenda Gallagher first before picking up two packets of black tights and, recalling her conversation with Isla, scanned the shelf for a green pair. To her amazement, they were in stock. Then, seeing the price, she felt resentment at using her hard-earned money to buy elf tights.

'Isla asked me to order those in for the carollers, like. Will you be joining them then, Shannon?' Brenda asked, scanning them through.

'I will, Mrs Gallagher. Oh, and would I be able to get twenty cash out, please?'

'Thanks be to God for that!' Cathal Gallagher poked his head around the storeroom door. 'At least one of you will be able to hold a tune.'

'Ah, ignore him,' Brenda said, tracking Shannon's gaze. 'And the chocolate, too, is it?'

Her hand hovered over the Lion bar, but she snatched it back, remembering her tussle with the zip on her jeans earlier. Maeve was sure to offer her another piece of shortbread this morning when she swung by and, given the amount the tights were about to cost, let alone the twenty euro, she knew her finances wouldn't withstand having to stump up for a new wardrobe in the next size up, on top.

'No, just the tights and money, thanks, Mrs Gallagher.' Mam was right, she thought, wincing as she swiped her card while Brenda put her purchases in a brown paper bag. It was daylight robbery in here.

She left the shop with money in her purse and her parcel, seeing patches of emerging blue overhead. A sure sign that once the morning mist had melted away, they'd be in for a clear winter's day. So much for the snow, she thought, meeting and greeting familiar faces on her short walk to Heneghan's Pharmacy.

Paddy McNamara was staring morosely in the window at his cardboard supermodel lady friend.

'How're you, Paddy?'

'Not so good today, Nora lass. Bridget here's had a terrible upset. Her perfume's disappeared.'

He was right, Shannon thought, seeing the space where yesterday there'd been an oversized bottle of Seduce Me. 'Ah, there are some muppets out there all right, Paddy. And I'm Shannon. Nora's daughter.'

'Aye.'

It was too cold to stand about like so, and Shannon dug around in her pocket, producing a handful of coins. 'Why don't you get yourself a cup of tea and a scone at the Silver Spoon. Warm yourself up, like.'

'That's very kind of you, Nora. I always said that Liam Kelly was a lucky man.'

'I'm Shannon. Liam and Nora's daughter, Paddy,' Shannon repeated.

He ignored her. 'But what about Bridget, here? Sure it's her who's suffering.' His wily eyes locked on Shannon's pocket. 'What's she to do without her perfume?'

Against her better judgement, she dug even deeper and gave him all change she had left in her pocket, knowing that it would be the Shamrock Inn and not the Silver Spoon he made a beeline for as soon as her back was turned. She'd have been better off buying him a takeaway hot drink and scone instead of giving him money. Still and all, it was Christmas, and a leopard wouldn't change its spots. Paddy was Paddy, and at least he had a roof over his head thanks to his old da leaving him his cottage.

'God bless you, Nora Kelly. Sure, tea and a scone are just the ticket to cheer my Bridget up.' Paddy gestured to the leggy cardboard cut-out. 'Bridget, are you after forgetting your manners?'

'She's grand, Paddy.' Shannon nipped her bottom lip to keep from laughing at the consternation on Paddy's face, not bothering to correct him this time. It was a lost cause.

She left him as he turned right toward the Shamrock Inn and, wiping her feet on the mat, pushed open the door to the pharmacy. A bell announced her presence.

Feck, she thought, seeing Mrs Tattersall sitting near the dispensary with her customary disgruntled expression firmly in place, trolley by her side. It was one of the anomalies of life in a village. You could go weeks sometimes without bumping into someone, and at other times they were there every time you rounded a corner. Then, telling herself off for being uncharitable toward the woman, especially given the time of year, she headed the old bite off with a wide smile. 'I haven't forgotten that candle, Mrs Tattersall. Morning, Niall, Nuala,' she called out brightly.

The shop was warm, its shelves overflowing with Christmas gift sets, and it smelled like fancy soaps. She'd always liked calling into Heneghan's at this time of year when she was a child, not just because Nuala kept a basket of barley sugars under the counter, which was passed out to the children while they waited for their mam or dad, but because she'd enjoyed seeing all the new Christmas stock.

'Well, be sure you don't go forgetting now, Shannon. You young ones have brains like sieves. I blame those phone yokes you're all glued to. They've put holes in yer brains, so they have, and Mr Tattersall's after having a terrible night with his knees.'

'I promise the candle's top of my list,' Shannon appeased the woman, who made an indecipherable sound before picking up a women's magazine. She made a show of flapping it open and murmuring in disgust over the scanty fashions the young ones were gadding about in. 'They'll cost the health service millions, so they will, with the chest infections they'll be after getting, and there's Mr Tattersall having to wait weeks to see a specialist, so.'

Niall Heneghan looked up from the pills he was counting in the dispensary to greet Shannon with an amused smile, while Nuala bobbed up from behind a Vitamin C stand where she was unpacking a delivery.

Shannon thought she was probably keeping out of Mrs Tattersall's line of sight, not that she blamed her one little bit.

'Morning, Shannon, I heard you were back. How're you?' In her white smock and blue cardigan, Nuala was about her mam's age and was one of those women who never looked any different from the last time you saw her. She'd worn her auburn hair in the same short pixie cut forever and was always immaculately groomed, showcasing the latest colours for the pharmacy's only cosmetic brand, Nu U Woman, with her make-up and nails. Today, her rich tea-coloured eyes were popping with moss green and warm browns. The shades looked gorgeous on her, Shannon thought.

'I love how you've made up your eyes there, Nuala.'

''Tis Nu Woman's latest ombre shades. I've applied a smoky eye, Shannon, and the trick is in the blending. The colours would look very well on you too. Have you a minute or two to spare? Because I could demonstrate them on you.'

'I'd like that.' Shannon dimpled as Nuala hurried off to fetch a stool for her to sit on. A makeover could only lift her spirits.

'Your skin's looking dewy. What's your secret?' Nuala asked as she daubed the eyeshadow brush in the palette.

'I'm after pinching Imogen's fancy face pack.'

Nuala smiled, and Shannon filled her on in Imogen, Grace and Ava's impending arrival while she flicked the brush on the back of her hand to tap off the excess shadow. Her strokes were featherlike on Shannon's eyelids.

'I hear Paddy's made a new friend in Bridget,' Shannon said, her eyes closed.

'You start with the neutral base, Shannon. I'm putting it all over your lids.'

Nuala smelled of a perfume Shannon didn't recognise, though she guessed from its musky base notes it must be Seduce Me. It was rather lovely, and she hoped it worked where Niall Heneghan was concerned, for Nuala's sake.

'He's putting the customers off, is what he's doing, Shannon. The tourists keep a wide berth and cross the road when they see him loitering there. They all think he's a flasher in his dirty mac about to show them his tackle.'

Shannon coughed back a giggle.

'I'm applying the darkest colour next to your lash line. Did Paddy tell you we were after being robbed?'

'The perfume in the window?'

'Yes. Seduce Me. I'll spray you, if you like?'

'Grand, not that I plan on being seduced.'

'Chance would be a fine thing, I'd say.' Nuala's sigh was weighty. 'Blending the moss green in the middle of the lid now. Whoever the eejit was who stole it has only gone and pinched themselves a gorgeous bottle of coloured water. It was for display purposes only.'

This time, Shannon did laugh.

'It'll be the hooligans over from Kilticaneel. Mark my words,' Mrs Tattersall informed them both.

16

Shannon tapped the steering wheel along to the beat, waiting until the last notes of Ronan's classic hit 'Life Is a Rollercoaster' before turning the engine off. That song always put her in a good mood. She examined Nuala's handiwork in BB's rear-view mirror, deciding the woman was a magician. Somehow, with those brushstrokes, Nuala had made her eyes double in size and brought out the gold flecks in her boring old brown irises. Of course, she'd bought the eyeshadow kit, it would have been rude not to. Adding the hot-water bottle had turned down the volume on her whispering conscience as she'd zapped her card for the second time that morning. At least she'd refrained from buying the bottle of Seduce Me after Nuala had sprayed her wrists. Mrs Tattersall, not wanting to miss out, had held her arm out. Her face had been a picture when Nuala told her the scent's name. Shannon didn't fancy Mrs Tattersall's chances with Mr Tattersall, given his bad knees, but she'd kept this to herself.

She couldn't sit here on the side of the road admiring her enormous eyes all day, though, and so she opened the car door. Getting out, she saw a car parked on the opposite side of the road. She'd been so engrossed in her new look she hadn't noticed the bog-standard hire car until now, and she wondered if it was Maeve's mystery visitor come calling. Maybe she should do a U-turn and drop in tomorrow. She didn't want to pry, but the hot-water bottle would be a comfort to her friend, and she didn't need to stay long. Besides, she was burning with curiosity after Maeve's caginess yesterday. Her mind made up, she strode up the front path thinking how the little cottage looked like an illustration from a children's fairy tale under today's blue sky.

She tapped on the door and took a step back to wait, but unlike yesterday the door swung open only moments after her knock. Slack-jawed, she registered who was standing in the hallway looking for all the world as though he owned the place.

It was James.

'Shannon! Hi. Maeve didn't say you were calling in.' He stared hard at her. 'There's something different about you?' Then, hastily added, 'In a good way, I mean.'

Given the last time he'd seen her, she'd had illicit white goop smothered over her face, this wasn't surprising. Shannon didn't move or reply because she was too taken aback at seeing him there, but she noticed that his lopsided smile didn't seem to come so easily to him today. He even had shortbread crumbs down the front of his sweater, which meant he was well and truly getting his feet under the table.

He opened the door wider to usher her in, but she didn't move. 'She's not expecting me. I swung by to drop something off for her. What are you doing here?'

'I'm, uh, I'm visiting—'

'Whoever that is, come in and close the door. You're letting all the cold air in,' Maeve called out bossily.

She was right, Shannon thought. Doing as she was told and marching past James, she headed straight for the kitchen, determined to get to the bottom of why he was here.

'Ah, it's you, Shannon.' Maeve beamed from where she was ensconced in her chair, the blanket draped over her knees and a cup of tea in hand. 'What's different about yer?' She studied her keenly. 'You're putting me in mind of Bess.'

'Your old Labrador?' Shannon managed a laugh. 'Thanks a million.'

Maeve hadn't finished, though. 'It's your eyes. Bess had that look, too; God rest her soul. She even won over Declan Donnelly, the postman, and that's some feat.'

Emerald Bay's now-retired postman was well known for his aversion to dogs because he had had his fingers nipped at one time too many. So, if you looked at it like that, it was a compliment Maeve was paying her, Shannon supposed.

'Nuala's after trying some new eyeshadows on me.' The fire enticed her to warm her backside in front of it, but instead, she held up the bag she was carrying. 'I bought you a hottie.'

'She's done a lovely job bringing out your best feature, so she has. The eyes are the window to the soul.' Her mouth puckered. 'Poor Nuala, pining away like so. He's a fool, that Niall Heneghan, for not seeing what's right under his nose. And you're a wee dote for thinking of me, Shannon.'

'Ah, sure, it's nothing. I was passing anyway,' Shannon fibbed.

Maeve's cheeks were pink, matching the blouse she was wearing, pinned at the neck by a pretty rose cameo brooch. She'd taken trouble with her appearance, and there was the same air of fidgety excitement about her again today. Peripherally, Shannon saw James loitering uncomfortably in the doorway. So he was her mystery visitor, but who on earth was he to Maeve, and why was he here?

Her mind churned over Maeve's cryptic comments about a relative having called to see her. How were they related if James was who she'd been talking about? Via some distant cousin who crossed the water to America years ago, perhaps?

He'd mentioned last night that his reason for being in Emerald Bay was to connect with his Irish roots. She'd never in a million years thought Maeve would have featured in that equation.

The wily little woman's chortle distracted her.

'I can almost hear the cogs whirring, Shannon. James told me he was staying at the Shamrock Inn, so I know I don't need to introduce the pair of you. He's come all the way from Boston to meet me. Can you imagine? He also told me how much he enjoyed tapping his toes to the session in the Shamrock last night and what a treat it was to hear you sing. I've not heard your lovely voice since you performed in the church hall in your school play. What was it called, now?'

Shannon was glad of the excuse not to have to respond to the indirect compliment. '*Grease*. I played Sandy, and Kellen Duffy took the role of Danny. He'd terrible breath on him. I think he used to eat a clove of garlic before each performance to pay me back for the time I told Father Seamus he was after sneaking the communion wine. I had to call on all my acting talents when we did the grand finale: "You're the One That I Want".'

Laughter sounded over by the door, and Maeve, too, was amused. Shannon was pleased.

'Why don't you make yourself a cup of tea, Shannon? The kettle's not long boiled, and I think there's a piece of shortbread left in the tin – unless you ate the last of it?' Maeve's eyes sparkled in James's direction.

'I held back, but only just. I'm determined to get Maeve's recipe to take home with me.'

'Good luck with that,' Shannon muttered, feeling very much on the back foot watching the exchange, unable to recall seeing Maeve this animated in a long time. It was all very unsettling, and a cup of tea was in order because she wasn't leaving until she got to the bottom of things. 'I'll fill this while I'm at it.'

She indicated the hottie and, turning away, overheard Maeve tell James to sit down.

'You're making me nervous hovering like so, boyo.'

Shannon glanced back over her shoulder. She thought he was acting shifty, watching him through narrowed eyes as he settled on the sofa where she'd sat yesterday. Another thought wrestled for attention. If he was indeed related to Maeve, why come crawling out of the woodwork now? The routine motion of making the tea and filling the hot-water bottle gave her time to mull the situation over. Just because he'd appeared seemingly out of the blue didn't mean he had an ulterior motive. It wasn't like her not to give someone the benefit of the doubt either, but she was protective of Maeve and would hate to see her hurt or taken advantage of. With this in mind, she kept one ear cocked, trying and, to her frustration, failing to hear their conversation over the whistling kettle.

There was one piece of shortbread left, and telling herself it was for her rattled nerves, Shannon helped herself. Then, carrying the fat hot-water bottle wrapped in a tea towel, she asked Maeve where she'd like it.

'It's me hip that's giving me bother today. I tell the pair of yer, old age isn't for the faint-hearted.' Maeve gestured to her left side.

Shannon arranged the bottle there so the heat would penetrate through and hopefully soothe the stiff joint. It was pleasing to see her friend visibly relax.

'Oh, that's grand, that is.'

James was watching Shannon with an expression she couldn't read, and it made her hand tremble when she carried her cup and saucer through, placing them down on the side table alongside Maeve's. There was no way she'd be joining him for a cosy chat on the sofa, and instead, she fetched a chair from the table, placing it next to her friend. Shannon wanted to convey that, while Maeve might be widowed with a son living far away in London, she was not alone.

Amusement plucked at the corners of Maeve's mouth, and she reached out and patted Shannon's hand. 'It's all right. I promise you it's not my millions James is after.'

Shannon turned the colour of Maeve's blouse at her thoughts having been read so accurately.

'No! I'm not. I'm not after anything except getting to know Maeve here,' James declared, hand on heart, to Shannon, who couldn't meet his eye.

'There's a rumour going around Emerald Bay, you see, James, that I'm sitting on a tidy nest egg.'

Shannon opened her mouth, unsure of what she was going to say because she couldn't dispute this. It was true, but Maeve held up her hand, silencing her, and she shut it again.

'Oh, I've heard the stories, Shannon.'

Of course, she had. It was Emerald Bay they were talking about. There were no secrets here.

'The version that tickled me most was that rebels back in the day stashed money for the cause here on the property. You know Ivo's grandfather was a volunteer?'

Shannon nodded. She'd heard that version and the one about Ivo winning big at the Galway Races and tucking the prize money away because he was frightened of alerting the locals to his newfound fortune by spending it.

'Of course, whether or not I am a wealthy widow is nobody's business but my own.'

Shannon mused, *That's me told*, dipping her head to drink her tea.

'But I appreciate you looking out for me, my dear. I know you have my best interests at heart.'

Maeve's body was frail, but her mind was strong, Shannon thought.

'I can assure you, Shannon, I don't intend to hurt Maeve in any way,' James said.

She risked a glance over the top of her teacup. James might be good-looking with an endearing, quirky grin, but that didn't mean he was trustworthy. His expression was guileless and the insistence in his voice genuine, but weren't they all the marks of a good conman? She was yet to be convinced.

'I told you I'd had a visitor yesterday, Shannon.'

'James.'

'Yes. And, like you, I was cautious after our initial telephone conversation.' Maeve smiled apologetically in his direction. 'I know the elderly and vulnerable are fair game to these scam artists who are after wheedling your bank account number out of yer by saying you've won the lottery. I do listen to the radio and read the paper.'

'I know you're well informed about what's going on in the world, Maeve,' Shannon appeased. It was true. Maeve was able to hold her own when it came to current affairs and was more informed about the state of the world than Shannon, who preferred to bury her head in the sand and play her easy-listening music when it came to politics.

'I didn't ask for any bank account details when I telephoned either,' James interrupted. 'In case you were wondering.'

Shannon was puce as her teacup clattered down in its saucer.

'I can assure you, Shannon, James's intentions are honourable.'

'They are,' James affirmed.

Their conversation sounded like a Victorian melodrama, and Shannon waited, but nothing more was forthcoming. 'How are you related then?'

James turned to Maeve for guidance, and she gave a slight shake of her head.

'If you don't mind, Shannon, I'm not ready to talk about that. Not yet.'

Shannon's mouth worked as she processed that Maeve had shut the conversation down much as she'd done yesterday. She couldn't very well press her on it. She'd have to respect her wishes, and as for James, well, she hadn't made her mind up despite Maeve's assurances. She could sense the underlying current. They had things to be talking about, and three was a crowd. 'I'll leave it to you then.' She deposited her empty teacup and Maeve's on the worktop.

James also got to his feet. 'I'll see you out.'

Shannon baulked at his over-familiarity in the Doolin house and received the sort of loaded frown her nan was good at from Maeve. She'd decided that the ability to convey what you meant in one look was a skill you only learned after a certain number of decades under your belt. And she'd just been told to behave herself. So she gritted her teeth and refrained from snapping, *I don't need seeing out.*

Maeve gave a satisfied nod. 'Shannon, dear, I nearly forgot my manners. Thanks a million for the hot-water bottle. I'd been missing it.'

Shannon took hold of her older friend's hand, pressing it gently between her own. 'You're welcome, and if you need me, all you have to do is pick up the phone. My number's on the pad by the telephone.'

'You're a wee dote, Shannon,' Maeve said once more. 'Don't think I don't appreciate what you do for me.'

Shannon searched her face for clues as to who James was to her, but she was a closed book. Giving her one last smile, she followed James down the hall.

'I figured out what's different,' he said as they reached the door.

'What?' Shannon looked up at him warily.

'Your eyes.'

What was she supposed to say to that? He must have heard her telling Maeve she'd had her eye make-up done at Heneghan's earlier. But before she could formulate a response, he spoke again.

'And your manner.'

This time the question rolled forth unbidden. 'What do you mean?'

'You're so confident and assured when you're caring for someone.'

'It's my job to be. I'm a nurse.' She knew she sounded spiky but couldn't help it.

'No, it's more than that.'

He was right. It was. 'Maeve's my friend, not just my patient.'

'She's a lucky woman.'

'She's a special woman.' Shannon opened the door and was hit by a blast of arctic wind. She needed to get away. He was standing too close once more, and the scent of the aftershave she now knew to be Dior was doing peculiar things to her senses.

'I'm beginning to realise that, Shannon. And I'm sorry I can't tell you more, but I've got to respect Maeve's wishes. It's her story to tell, not mine. Besides, I don't know all of it yet either. I promise you can trust me, though.'

Shannon nodded. If he was a scammer, he was up there with the best.

'Can I ask you something?'

Jaysus, what now? She moved away to stand on the front path, trying not to gasp at the frigid air before turning, eyebrow raised, waiting.

'What perfume are you wearing?'

Whoosh! She felt the heat flood her face like her mam having one of her hot and hormonal moments. There was no way she'd say the words 'Seduce Me' aloud to him. Groping around for a reply, she flapped her hand vaguely. 'Oh um, I don't know. It's something Nuala from the pharmacy sprayed on me.' If she was a racehorse, it could be said she galloped to the sanctuary of her car. As she started the engine, it occurred to her. Maybe he'd wanted to know what the perfume was for a specific reason. Perhaps he wanted to buy it for his girlfriend back home. She knew nothing about James Cabot other than he was a vet from Boston who was somehow connected to Maeve Doolin, who also happened to have sea-green eyes and a lopsided grin.

'What do you think's going on between James and Maeve, Grandad?' Shannon asked as she drove past Emerald Bay seeing seagulls circling above the fishing boats.

But today, there was no rainbow reply.

17

The Shamrock Inn was busy, given the number of cars parked outside, Shannon saw as BB skidded into the reserved spot alongside the sleekly tapered red sports car that was Imogen's pride and joy. Her sisters were home then, and she wondered which of the twins had drawn the short straw by having to contort themselves into the tiny back seat for the journey down from Dublin. Her money was on Ava, with Grace being the more dominant of the two. It wasn't that she was bossy per se; it was just how the dynamic worked between them.

It would be good to see them all, although she dreaded the inevitable litter-tray altercation with Imogen. Still, she wouldn't think about that now. Pulling BB's handbrake up, she checked her phone for the time. It was a good two hours before she was due at the church hall for carolling practice, plenty of time to catch up. She picked up the package containing her new eyeshadow kit and tights, knowing she could count on some ribbing from all four of her sisters where her elf outfit was concerned. Hmm, what about wearing an oversized coat over the top? It was doubtful Isla would let her away with it, but for the sake of her dignity, she'd have to try at least.

She opened the door, bracing herself for the cold temperature outside her cosy wee car. Climbing out, she glanced up at hers and Imogen's bedroom window. Had she met Napoleon yet? If so, she hoped they'd bonded enough for Imo to understand the necessity for a litter tray in their bedroom. The thought of her sister falling for his sweet little Persian face buoyed her, because how could she not? Shannon went so far as to picture Imogen combing his coat through and announcing it was indeed a relaxing pastime as she ventured inside the Shamrock and stood stock-still.

It was as if she'd walked into one of those American Star Trek conventions, only instead of Mr Spocks, the tables were filled with men of middling years whose faces were shaded by tweedy caps. Upon checking out the bar where her mam and dad were busy serving, she saw that the tweedy cap men were clad in variations of a similar theme. Diamond-patterned sweater vests with long socks pulled up to the knees so their trousers looked like knickerbockers. Was this some modernised version of Morris dancers?

Nora glanced up from pulling a pint and smiled at her baffled expression while Liam, passing one of the men a bag of pork scratchings, waved her over.

Shannon made her way toward him. 'Who's all this lot?' she whispered, leaning over the bar.

'The Glenariff Golfers from Galway. They've been playing in a tournament on the range near Ballyclegg.'

Ah, that made sense. She hadn't walked into a parallel universe where the world had been taken over by men in tweed caps after all.

'Your sisters are here. The traffic was terrible. 'Twas a gridlock out of the city, so it was.'

Shannon smirked. She wouldn't have expected anything less. 'So there was more than one tractor on the motorway?'

'Sarcasm is the lowest form of wit. Make yerself useful and

toss a log on the fire before you disappear. It's getting colder by the minute today.'

Shannon did so, stepping back as it hissed and spat, then took a moment to rub her hands together in front of it. Her dad was right. It was freezing. She wondered if Nan had been baking in anticipation of her sisters' arrival and made her way through to the kitchen, not wanting to miss out.

A happy sigh escaped as she breathed in the homely aroma of the fresh batch of Christmas mince pies cooling on the work-top. Kitty was in the middle of dusting them with icing sugar while Hannah, Grace and Ava were seated at the table. There was a pot of tea in their midst and no sign of Imogen. Hopefully, this was a good thing.

'Good trip, girls?' Shannon asked, soaking in the sight of her youngest two siblings with their heart-shaped faces, clear blue eyes and red hair.

'Look who's here.' Kitty put the sieve down with a cheery smile speaking before either of the twins could reply. 'I should have known you'd have smelt the baking and come running. You've never been any different.'

Nan had a point, Shannon thought, grinning over at her sisters as she reached out for a pie even though she knew she'd get her hand slapped. Nan didn't disappoint.

'Wait until I've finished, madam.'

Shannon winked. 'God loves a trier, Nan. Where's Imo?'

Grace grinned at the exchange. 'She's gone up to your room to make some calls. You know what she's like. She's always working, even when she's supposed to be on holiday.'

It was true. Imogen's clients were wealthy for the most part and used to having people at their beck and call. If she was making calls, she wasn't unpacking, which meant Shannon had a reprieve from explaining why there was a litter tray in their wardrobe. She breathed easier.

'Honestly, she told us to pack lightly, but you want to see

the size of her case. I thought Ava and I would have to sit on the roof. She did let me take a turn behind the wheel, though. That car of hers purrs. I felt like Bella Hadid or the like with the wind in my hair. It was nothing like riding in that old rust bucket you bomb about in.' Grace batted this at Hannah across the table.

Hannah pulled a face. 'You've got no hair for the wind to blow back, and at least I have a car.'

Shannon realised that Grace's hair was much shorter than when she'd last seen her. She'd had it lopped off into a beguiling bob that hugged her jawline and made her neck look long and elegant. It suited her.

'And as soon as I can afford to, I'm going all-out electric,' Hannah elaborated.

'There's no need to run a car in London, and you'd best get feeding those bees then. She's been driving us potty going on and on about them, so she has,' Grace bantered back.

Shannon smiled, repeating her sister's catchphrase. 'No bees. No food.'

Hannah straightened indignantly. 'It's true! And I'm not giving up where the hives out the back here are concerned either. We've all got to do our bit. Imo's got a roof garden. She should be planting wildflowers and bee-friendly plants, not those arty yucca things she's got going on. It's Dublin, not the Med she's after living in. And what about you two?'

Grace and Ava shook their heads. 'We're in a tiny terrace, no garden, sorry.'

'Good for you, Hannie,' Shannon said. She meant it too. If there were more Hannahs, the world would be a better place. 'How was Kilticaneel?'

'The same as always. Meghan gave me a hand with the fliers I wanted to distribute for my more hives campaign.'

Ava, getting up from the table, wasn't quite as enthused about the journey west of the capital as her older twin. 'The drive down was grand if you don't mind freezing your arse off in the back seat because someone insisted on having the window down, so all the motorists coming the other way had a clear view of her.' She pulled a face at Grace, who batted her lashes and smiled innocently. 'Honestly, Shan, my knees were up around my ears for two and a half hours.' She hugged her sister hello. 'You're looking well, by the way. I love the eyes.'

Shannon laughed, squeezing Ava back. She'd been right then. Poor old Ava had lucked out. She was the quietly observant one of them, she thought fondly. Not much slipped past Ava.

Grace, too, got up, and as she crossed the lino toward her, Shannon thought how she and Ava were two peas in a pod apart from their hairstyles and outfits. However, she knew that if you scratched beneath the surface, you'd find two very different personalities.

Grace followed the latest trends and was currently clad in thick-soled white trainers, faded denim, wide-legged jeans last seen some time in the nineties and a fluffy cardigan that ended just above where her jeans began. On the other hand, Ava would have fitted right in with the hippie set in Marrakesh in the seventies or dancing at Coachella in her yellow minidress, tights and knee-high boots. She even had a paisley headband knotted around her head with a cascade of fiery hair protruding beneath it.

'I love the hair, Grace. Very Lady Mary, *Downton Abbey*, only with red hair,' Shannon said, moving in for a second hug. Then, 'Stop sniffing at me like you're a fecking dog.'

'I can't help it. You smell gorgeous. New perfume?'

'No, although I wouldn't mind a bottle if you're looking for Christmas present inspiration. Nuala gave me a squirt of it when I called into Heneghan's earlier. It's called, um, Seduce Me, but keep that quiet.'

Hannah snorted.

'Don't you dare say it!' Shannon pointed a threatening finger at her.

'I wasn't going to say a word about the sexual chemistry.'

Grace and Ava's heads turned left and right like they were watching a tennis match.

'Who's got the sexual chemistry?' Ava asked.

Kitty put the sieve down, all ears too.

'The baboons,' Hannah replied mysteriously.

'I'm warning you. I won't be responsible for my actions.'

Hannah ignored her, bringing the twins and Kitty up to speed. 'The baboons *and* Shannon and our American guest James have got the sexual chemistry. James is fit, if you bypass the chinos, and he fancies her. She's after flashing her arse at him last night too, and she fancies him back, only she won't admit it because she's determined to carry on comfort eating and mooning after Julien.'

'Hannah!'

Kitty hastily handed Shannon a mince pie. It was a diversion tactic. The sort you'd use on toddlers, and it worked a treat.

Shannon informed the room staunchly that she was not looking for a new love interest in between crumbly bites. Not now, not ever, going on to elaborate on the skirt tucked in tights episode in case they thought she had been going around flashing her knickers at James. She drew the line at defending his chinos, though. Or that it was looking likely he was related to Maeve Doolin. It was time for a change of topic. 'Did you see the cardboard supermodel in the window of Heneghan's on your way through the village?' she asked the twins once she'd hammered her point home.

'We did,' they chimed.

'What happened to the usual talcum powder gift sets and tinsel?' Grace asked.

Shannon shrugged. 'I don't know, but I do know the supermodel is Paddy's new lady friend, and she goes by the name of

Bridget – according to Paddy, at any rate.' She relayed the scandal currently rocking Emerald Bay: the brazen theft of the display bottle of perfume from the pharmacy window.

Ava laughed and rested her hand on her chest. 'Sure, Emerald Bay's like gangland London with all the goings-on.'

Shannon smiled. It didn't take much to beat the village drums, and theft was right up there.

'You two don't look too bad, all things considered.'

'What do you mean, "all things considered"?' Ava frowned.

'I mean, given your party-hard lifestyle in London, I figured you'd be painting the town red with Imogen last night.' She'd seen her sisters' photos on Instagram and Facebook at various pubs and clubs, their arms wrapped around different girls and guys Shannon didn't know. Whenever she FaceTimed with either of them, they were always hungover or about to head out for the night. They must live week to week because maintaining a full-on social life like theirs and paying rent etc. in London wouldn't come cheap. Still, she'd not been shy and retiring at their age either and, given her current financial predicament, wouldn't be giving them a talk about the virtues of saving their hard-earned pennies.

'We gave it a nudge, but a fry-up sorted us out,' Ava replied.

'Really? I can't imagine Imogen has bacon and eggs in the fridge on standby. Chia seeds and granola, maybe.'

'She didn't. We left her to her almond milk green smoothie and went to a cafe down the road,' Grace supplied.

'Here we are,' Kitty said, placing a plate of mince pies on the table. 'We'll not be having any talk of the chia seeds and green smoothies at my table, thanks very much. I can't be doing with all that bird-food fodder. Grace, call your sister down.'

'Do I have to?'

'Yes, or there'll be no mince pie for you.'

Shannon helped herself to a second pie. 'So, how's life in the world of freelance copywriting?' she asked Ava as Grace scraped her chair back once more and ventured out to the hallway to holler Imogen's name from the bottom of the stairs.

Shannon listened to her sister chat about how she'd work coming out of her ears, and when Grace, whose job title was social media coordinator, sat back down, she asked her the same question. But, unfortunately, she'd forgotten how Grace could talk on Instagram Reels vs Facebook Stories for hours. Her eyes were about to glaze over when an unholy shriek startled them into wide-eyed silence.

It was Hannah who spoke up. 'I'm guessing Imogen just met Napoleon.'

Or found the litter tray, Shannon added silently.

18

Shannon was the first out of her seat, charging up the stairs like she'd a rabid dog nipping at her heels to fling open the bedroom door. Imogen, clad from head to toe in designer Sweaty Betty activewear, was standing on the bed as though about to embark on a pillow fight. Given that her sister had an aversion to getting sweaty, her clothing brand amused Shannon for a nanosecond, but then the horror masking her immaculately made-up face as she pointed toward the carpet drew her back to the situation. She gauged the scene registering one hairy paw protruding from under the valance and a sorry-looking Mr Mouse who'd been batted into the space between hers and Imogen's beds.

'It's a rat, Shan! Get Dad,' Imogen ordered with a note of hysteria as she wrung her hands.

'Nice to see you too,' Shannon said. Then, unable to help herself, she began to laugh, and Hannah, who'd been peering over her shoulder trying to see what was going on, joined in.

'It's not funny, you two. Rats carry diseases. We could all catch the fecking bubonic plague. It was the rats that spread that, you know.'

'It's not real, Imo. It's too small to be a rat,' Shannon explained.

'It could be a babby rat.'

'It's a toy mouse,' Shannon said, as though explaining something to a small child. She ignored Imogen's squeals of disgust as she bent down and picked it up by its soggy tail.

'See.' She dangled its mauled body in front of her sister.

'Urgh, get it away from me! Dirty, dirty thing!'

Shannon saw the paw had shot back under the bed at all the carry-on.

Hannah backed Shannon up. 'It's a toy, Imo. You can get off the bed, but as you're dressed like you're out to win the Longford Royal Canal Run, you should probably jump down and spring into a burpee or something. What brand is all that get-up anyway? Tell me, and I'll give you an eco-rating out of ten.'

Imogen looked from her younger sister to the first off the rank but didn't move from the bed.

'Shut up about your eco-ratings, Hannah,' she said. 'And, if this was your idea of a joke, Shannon, I'm not laughing. I nearly had a heart attack when that thing shot out from under the bed.' Her glossy lips pouted, and doubt laced her voice as she asked, 'So, c'mon then, tell me how it moved from under there to out there? Have I missed something? Is one of you secretly dating Dynamo, and he's after sharing his magic secrets with yer?'

'That would be down to Napoleon,' Shannon replied, dropping the mouse and wiping her hand on her jeans.

'Who's Napoleon? Ah, Jaysus, Shan, you're not after picking up another French fella, are yer? What's wrong with an Irishman? And why's there a carpeted miniature jungle gym by the window, and what's that and that?' She was pointing at the food bowls and litter tray warily.

'No, I'm not, and I didn't set out to meet a Frenchman in the first place. It just happened!' Shannon avoided the litter box and food and water bowl enquiry.

'No, she's not. But it's an American she needs to be picking up.'

'Shut up, Hannah.' Shannon gave her sister the elbow, and then, thinking of her poor cat hiding under the bed, undoubtedly traumatised by Imogen's shrieking, she dropped to her knees and crawled across the floor to lift the valance cover.

'What else is under there?' Imogen demanded, still standing on the bed.

'Shush, Imo, you're scaring him. C'mon, Napoleon, it's all right. It's only your Aunty Imo being her usual eejitty self.' Shannon followed this up with kissy noises.

Imogen, who could be slow on the uptake, suddenly saw the light. 'Didn't you and that French fella get a cat? I'm allergic to cats, Shannon. You know that.' She gave a psychosomatic sneeze.

'A few sneezes and itchy eyes never killed anyone.' Shannon was unsympathetic as she tried to entice Napoleon out. Imogen was dramatic, and she knew they'd adopted a kitten because she'd telephoned her full of excitement the day they'd brought Napoleon home.

Something else occurred to Imogen, and adopting a sage older sister tone, she addressed Hannah: 'You'd do well to remember this, so listen up. Pets are always a forerunner to children. Every one of my friends who had a fabulous life is now shackled to motherhood. And it all started with a trip to the pet shop with their fella. Sure, they all came home like Shan here did with a dog, cat, rabbit or, in the case of Siân, who always likes to be different, a chinchilla. But then, a year later, whammo! They're pregnant, and it's goodbye to life as they knew it. I don't have any pets, not even a friendly squirrel in the tree in the courtyard – nada. And it's why you should think on before you go down that rabbit hole too.'

Hannah spoke up. 'I do my bit volunteering for the ISPCA on Saturday mornings, Imogen, but I'm not ready to commit and bring an animal into my fold, apart from the bees, although they're insects and not very friendly. So at the very least, you should be looking at planting wildflowers in that roof garden of yours.'

'You don't have any pets because you live in a squat,' Shannon retorted, still peering under the valance, trying to coax Napoleon out.

'I do not. I pay rent. There's just a lot of us living there, is all. The prices in Cork city are obscene. It's renter capitalism, so it is.'

'Shut up, Hannah,' Shannon and Imogen dueted like TikTokkers on a video clip.

Hannah, never one to do as she was told, carried on: 'Although it's a good thing Shannon didn't get pregnant because Julien would have left her with a baby and a cat. Although between you and me, Imo, I reckon she thinks Napoleon's her babby. She calls herself mammy and everything.'

'Stop talking about me as if I'm not in the room. C'mon, Napoleon,' Shannon coaxed. He refused to budge, twin yellow eyes boring into her. She glared up at her sister. 'It's your fault. You've scared him, and he's had enough upset with Julien leaving and now the move home.' She hauled herself upright and trooped over to the wardrobe to retrieve the cat biscuits.

'Shannon, that better not be what I think it is.'

'It is what you think it is,' Hannah informed Imogen then, in case they weren't on the same page: 'It's a litter tray, and he's after doing the smelliest poo ever in it.'

'Mam!' Imogen hollered.

'What are you shouting about?' Ava asked.

Grace, hustling in behind her to see what all the commotion was about, added, 'Mam's behind the bar. She won't hear you, and Nan won't come running either. She's putting her feet up with a cuppa.'

Shannon had had enough, and abandoning the idea of

tempting the cat out with food, she got down on all fours before lying down on her tummy and wriggling half under the bed, stretching her arms long until she got hold of Napoleon. Then, sliding his protesting furry form out from under the bed, she stood up, holding him close to her chest to make him feel safe. 'This is what she's shouting about.'

'Ava, Grace, meet your nephew, Napoleon Kelly, Shannon's love child. He takes after her baby daddy with a face like an arse, but he's part of the family; therefore, we must all love and accept him,' Hannah informed her sisters.

'Feck off, Hannah,' Shannon flung back.

The twins had a moment where they were both wedged in the doorway as they vied to get to Napoleon first.

'He's so cute.'

'He's so sweet.'

Napoleon preened regally before hissing in Imogen's direction.

Imogen scowled, jumping down from the bed with a thud that would have had Kitty looking at the ceiling and muttering something about there being a herd of elephants roaming about upstairs.

'Imo, you knew I had a cat and that I was moving home.' Shannon aimed for a truce.

'Yes, but I didn't think you'd bring him home with you.'

'Well, what did you think I'd do? Give him to the ISPCA? What kind of person would that make me?'

'No. Of course not, but maybe a friend or something.' She sneezed again. 'It's a serious allergy, Shan.'

'Sneezing isn't anaphylactic shock, and I'm a nurse. I'd save you if you did suddenly have an attack.' How did Imogen look like she was wearing no make-up when she had a full face slapped on? Her hair, a warm extravaganza of caramel and blonde balayage, always looked effortlessly tousled, too; when Shannon and her sisters knew from the amount of time she spent hogging the bathroom, it wasn't. She softened her tone. 'Look, how's about I pick you up a box of antihistamines from Heneghan's on my way to church? That should see you right.'

'And what about the litter tray?'

'It's only for another day or two. I was planning on letting him have a sniff about the place later and, once he's used to it, I'll let him explore outside. He won't need it then. He's fully house-trained, I promise.'

'Why are you going to church?' Ava asked.

'Um...'

'Nan roped her into doing the carols with the Emerald Bay Elves. She told me they've elf costumes to wear and all.' Hannah again.

Ava, Grace and Imogen began to giggle.

'Yes, yes, very funny,' Shannon said. However, the thought of her gadding about dressed as an elf did defuse the Imogen– Napoleon tensions, and Imogen sat down on her bed.

'So who's this American Hannah thinks you should be copping off with?'

Hannah piped up with the story she'd not long told Ava and Grace, and predictably Imogen was in fits over the thought of Shannon parading about with her skirt caught up in her tights. She was also all ears where James was concerned.

If it meant her sister would accept Napoleon, Shannon was happy to be the source of her amusement, but she wouldn't stand for her getting matchmaking notions. She was beginning to feel like a parrot as she repeated herself: 'I'm single. Napoleon and Dad are the only men I want in my life. So don't be getting any ideas. Got it?' She looked to each of her sisters, fixing them with her steeliest gaze until they nodded their understanding.

'I've been seeing someone, as it happens.'

All eyes swung to Imogen. She was very picky when it came to the opposite sex, so this was breaking news.

'How did you meet?' Grace fired off.

'He's a client who booked me to reconfigure the floor plan of his penthouse suite.'

'And you added your personal touch. Isn't there some interior decorator's moral code about dating clients?' Hannah queried.

'I prefer interior designer,' Imogen said snootily. 'I did the necessary training, therefore designer, not a decorator. And there's no code. Or if there is, then I've broken it.'

'Name, age, physique, height and shoe size?' Ava demanded in one big breath.

'He goes by Nev, short for Nevin, he's pushing six foot and fit in both senses, with big feet and you know what they say about big feet.'

If they didn't, the lurid wink would put them right, Shannon thought, not noticing she hadn't answered the age question.

'What's he like then apart from being rich, I mean? Because he must be if he lives in a penthouse and can afford to get a new layout.' Grace sighed. 'I'm so in the wrong line of business because all I ever get to meet are nerdy start-up business types who think they're going to be the next Mark Zuckerberg once I get their social media campaigns sorted. And all the fellas I meet on Let's Get it On or Tinder are only after one thing.'

'Surprise, surprise.' Shannon shuddered at the thought of dating apps.

'Try working in copywriting,' Ava offered up glumly.

'I meet quite a few interesting fellas in the Feed the World with Bees business, as it happens,' Hannah joined in. 'But I've yet to come across a keeper. Get it? Bee, keeper.'

There was a mass rolling of eyes.

Shannon decided not to ask after Dylan, Hannah's co-worker at Feed the World with Bees whom she'd been name-dropping yesterday. Instead, she stayed silent because they all knew how she'd met Julien when he was brought, hobbling and in agony, into the surgery. They'd all lectured her on having a 'fixer' mentality. It had been Imogen, in a rare show of insightfulness, who'd hit closest to home by saying Shannon needed to feel she could fix her romantic partners and that it stemmed from having not been able to save Grandad. She'd added that it had not been her fault, so she needed to move on from it and meet someone where the relationship started on an even keel, i.e. no broken bones. Insightful it may have been. It hadn't stopped Shannon from falling hard for Julien, though.

'Have you got a photo? I haven't seen anything on Insta?' Grace asked. 'And why's he not joining us for Christmas?'

'He's not into all that superficial social media stuff.' Imogen sniffed.

This caused raised eyebrows in light of her own carefully staged Instagram page. Grace, in particular, was put out, given her line of work.

Imogen saw their scepticism. 'Mine's for my business. And we're not at the meeting each other's family stage yet. Besides, I don't want to scare him off.'

'Thanks a million,' Ava said.

'You know what I mean. The Kelly family en masse is intimidating.' Imogen reached over for her phone. It had dropped out of her hand when she'd clambered onto the bed in terror. Her fingers worked a hundred miles a minute, and then she held the phone out for them all to see.

Shannon inspected the bright, shiny photo of Imogen looking glam with her oversized sunglasses, probably Gucci or something, as she snuggled into George Clooney. On second glance, she realised it wasn't George, but Imogen's new fella had that same silver fox Georginess about him. 'Suave,' she offered, trying to hide how shocked she was by their age gap.

'Worldly,' from Grace, who was also blinking rapidly.

'Sophisticated,' was Ava's squeaked verdict.

'Old,' Hannah stated.

'He's not old. He's mature.'

'He's got to be Dad's age at least. Ancient. And that's why you don't want to bring him home,' Hannah butted back. 'He's a sugar daddy.'

She had a valid point there, Shannon thought. Not the sugar daddy part, because Imogen was self-sufficient and independent, but he was at least the same age as their dad.

'I'm not going to rise to the sugar-daddy bait, Hannah. As for age, it's just a number,' Imogen replied enigmatically. 'And don't mention Nev to Mam and Dad yet. Or else.'

Hannah was about to launch into an 'I knew it' rhetoric when her nose curled. Ava's followed suit, as did Imogen's, while Shannon, guessing who the culprit was, began to shrink inwardly.

Grace's brow puckered as she exclaimed, 'Jaysus, is there a blocked drain or something? Or have Mam and Dad been hiding bodies about the place? What's that smell?'

All eyes turned to Napoleon, who innocently lifted his paw and began to lick it.

———

19

Shannon, her hands thrust in the pockets of her puffa as she walked toward the church, was lost in thought. She was mulling over what their mam and dad, Dad in particular, would have to say about the man in Imogen's life being the same age thereabouts as him. Quite a lot, she imagined, recalling how he'd behaved like a Neanderthal, all but thumping his chest when Grace had brought home a fella she'd met while she was away at college. The poor lad had only been eight years older than her. Imogen's Nev was closer to thirty years older. Nope, she wouldn't want to be in Imo's shoes when Dad caught wind. She didn't blame her for not inviting Nev to spend Christmas with them in Emerald Bay.

Imogen had always played her cards close to her chest when it came to the men in her life. And the fact she'd confided in her sisters as to Nev spoke volumes. The glow radiating from her hadn't just been thanks to her BB cream either. Imogen was smitten. She'd been holding something back, though. You didn't share a room with someone for over half your life without being able to read the signs, and Imogen's had been a blinking neon that said there was more to her burgeoning relationship with Nev than she was letting on.

If Shannon were to take a stab at it, she'd say Nev had children, and it was this and knowing how Mam and Dad would react when they learned of their age difference that was taking the shine off things for her sister. It was quite likely Nev had been married and procreated at some point. If so, odds were his offspring were close in age to Imogen. Hmm, tricky. Maybe they thought she was a gold digger? Either way, she'd be wheedling all the details out of her sister while she was back in Emerald Bay.

She was aware of Carmel Brady of the blow-up Santa in the window giving her a wave from across the street, and she waved back. The poor woman was in danger of tipping over, thanks to the enormous Dermot Molloy's Quality Meats bag she was half dragging along beside her as she passed by the fishmongers.

'How're you, Mrs Brady? You want to watch you don't pinch a nerve lugging that about.'

'It's the turkey, Shannon.'

'Why don't you call in at the pub and get Enda to give you a hand? Sure, he's sat on his backside doing nothing but supping and mooning after my nan. I'd help you myself, only I'm running late for a two o'clock appointment.' She didn't want to risk the wrath of Isla Mullins by being late for the rehearsal. Especially given Isla had made a point of saying she'd organised cover for the shop for the hour and a half they had the use of the hall. Nor did she wish to annoy Eileen Carroll when she was armed with her backup crew and knitting needles.

'I might do that. Is it the carol singing you're off to?'

'It is.' There were no secrets in Emerald Bay.

'My Gina's after watching Isla's shop until four,' Carmel Brady clarified. She glanced at the watch on her left wrist. 'So you'd best get on your way because I make it one fifty-eight now, and Isla will have your guts for garters if you're late. You know what she's like.'

Shannon did, and she hurried on her way.

Her mind turned to Ava as the white stone church with its annexe that served as the community hall came into her line of sight. She'd been perky chatting about work and life in London, which seemed to involve a serious amount of partying, but the perkiness had a forced note to Shannon's ear. Her break-up with Shane Egan had been a nasty one. She was burning the candle at both ends, as their mam would say, and if you looked closely, you could see shadows under her eyes. Maybe she was anxious about seeing Shane again.

Shannon worried about her sisters. It came from being the oldest in the family.

A wailing like a one-sided catfight or Kate Bush doing her 'Wuthering Heights' number off-key startled her, and her hand froze momentarily on the church gate. What an earth was that? She'd have liked to have turned around and gone home, but it wasn't worth the retribution.

With trepidation, Shannon squelched around the back of the pretty church and opened the door of the not-so-pretty but practical hall that had been tacked on to the back of the church like an afterthought sometime in the sixties. The source of the wince-inducing sound was none other than one of Santa's little helpers. The elf also strongly resembled the retired Doctor Fairlie's wife, Helena. She was running through her scales, warming up and enjoying the draughty hall's acoustics as she opened her lungs.

Jaysus wept, Shannon thought, eyeing the half-dozen or so other elves milling about, all 'me, me, meeing' with their song sheets in hand. They were going to sing a few carols in the square on Christmas Eve, not audition for *Britain's Got Talent*. She recognised every face peeking out from under their green-and-red striped elf hats complete with pom-poms, the pointy ears stitched on the side a nice added touch. Shannon also knew what ailed each of them. Mrs Shea was beleaguered by recurring bouts of oedema, which left her poor ankles and feet so swollen she couldn't get her shoes on. Mrs Bradigan had started with Type 2 diabetes, and so on. Mrs Greene homed in on her, cutting in front of Isla Mullins, who was tapping her watch, asking Shannon if she had any suggestions for the terrible indigestion plaguing her. She had to lean in to hear her over the background din.

Shannon knew she'd have covered everything from insomnia to Mrs Lafferty's husband's haemorrhoids by the time the practice was over. You were never off duty when you were a nurse. At least not in Emerald Bay. She also knew the last time the gathered elves' thighs had this much exposure was in the sixties when the mini was the height of fashion. What had Nan got her into? She owed her a lifetime of soda bread on demand for this.

'Shannon.' Isla Mullins, the self-appointed senior elf had elbowed her way past Mrs Greene to hand her a shopping bag. 'You can get changed in the jacks. Quick as you can, mind, so we can get things underway. Chop, chop.'

Shannon did as she was told, stepping around the old boombox that belonged on the shoulder of an eighties relic, and as she reached the Ladies, she heard Isla telling Helena Fairlie that she was sufficiently warmed up now and she'd do well to rest her voice. 'Thank God for that,' Shannon muttered, pushing open the door to be greeted with the scent of pine disinfectant and the sound of a dripping tap.

If it was draughty in the hall, it was freezing in the loos, and she shivered as she pulled her sweater over her head. At least she had a thermal on underneath. That would stop her from turning blue. Folding her sweater, she placed it in the bag Isla had given her. Then, holding the short green tunic with its faux black belt up, she inspected it warily.

A rap on the door echoed.

'Shannon, it's ten minutes past two.' Isla made her irritation clear.

'I'm coming!' She slid the tunic on, deciding to leave her jeans on underneath. She'd deliberately left the green tights at home because there was no way she would risk laddering them, not given what they'd cost her. It would be her luck to put a fingernail through them as she rolled them up her legs. No, jeans would have to do. Isla could suck it up. Then, retrieving the hat, she jammed it on her head.

In her absence, Isla had assembled the group in three rows, leaving a space between Mrs Tattersall and Mrs Bradigan. *Great*, Shannon thought, clocking Mrs Tattersall, whose current facial expression suggested Mrs Bradigan on her right was culpable for the cabbage smell currently circulating.

'Centre, front,' Isla barked at Shannon, shoving a songbook at her as she ran over to take her place, the pom-pom on her elf hat batting her on the face with each step. 'I'm sure you'll know most of the words to the carols I've chosen for us to sing, but just in case, you've your songbook to take home and study.' Then she pushed play on the boombox and, picking up a baton, began to conduct them through the opening bars of 'Silent Night'.

By the third line of the song, Shannon wished with all her heart that Helena Fairlie, two rows behind her, would fecking well be silent and that Mrs Bradigan would refrain from eating the colcannon between now and Christmas Eve.

20

A disgruntled Shannon flung the door to the Shamrock Inn open, clutching her elf costume bag. The pub was quieter than it had been earlier, and she registered Hannah was behind the bar chatting to Enda. She didn't bother greeting her as she put her head down and, with the door to the kitchen firmly in her line of sight, made a dash for it.

She was in no mood for chit-chat, and she was also deaf in one ear, thanks to Mrs Fairlie's trumpeting. Her husband had been the village doctor but had long since retired, and these days the residents of Emerald Bay had to trek over to Kilticaneel for their medical appointments. The villagers held him in high regard, along with Mrs Fairlie, so no one could bring themselves to tell her she couldn't carry a tune to save herself. Not even Isla, who usually never held back.

Shannon had made one pit stop on the way home, and that was to buy the promised packet of antihistamines for Imogen. Nuala had rung up an exorbitant amount on the till, which she hadn't begrudged paying, unlike the tights. If it meant Napoleon could have free run of the family quarters without Imogen harping on, it would be money well spent. As she'd bagged the pills up, Nuala informed her no arrests had been made over the theft of the enormous bottle of coloured water masquerading as Seduce Me, despite Sergeant Badger's enquiries. She'd also speculated whether the robbery would make the *Kilticaneel Star*. Shannon doubted it would be front-page news, but you never knew, things might be quiet on the Kilticaneel crime front. Paddy had been holding vigil at the pharmacy window once more engaged in a heated one-sided conversation with Bridget staring silently and sultrily down at him as Shannon made her way home.

'Emerald Bay's Singing Elf returns,' Hannah announced, a crisp halfway to her mouth.

'Does Mam know you're into the crisps?' Shannon asked as she reached the door. They weren't allowed to help themselves to stock from behind the bar and, given her healthy appetite, she'd be the one the finger of blame was pointed at.

'No, but she can hardly complain when I'm manning the fort, can she?'

'Why are you out the front?'

'Because Dad's gone off to Kilticaneel for a last-minute appointment, which we all know means he's gone to get Mam's Christmas present, and Mam's out the back trying to calm Imogen down. The twins got a special exemption from helping out until they've unpacked.'

'What's happened?' Shannon had a bad feeling Napoleon would be in the mix there somewhere.

'It turns out Imo really is allergic to cats. Her eyes have puffed up, and she looks like Miss Piggy. She went ballistic because she was due to FaceTime the fella we're not supposed to mention in front of Mam and Dad. Grace gave me an update five minutes ago, and she'd locked herself in the bathroom. Mam was trying to talk her down.'

'Christ on a bike,' Shannon muttered.

'Did you get those tablets you said you would pick up for her?'

'They're in here.' Shannon tapped her jacket pocket.

'Well, hopefully they'll sort her out. You'd best give her one.'

'Give me a crisp first.'

Hannah obliged, complaining as Shannon took a handful. 'Oi, there's hardly any left!'

'It might be my last supper,' Shannon spoke through her mouthful as she ventured through to the kitchen.

She could smell fish, she thought, looking to her nan, who was stirring a pot on the Aga while Grace mashed a pan of potatoes. Fish pie, she deduced. Imogen's favourite. Nan was going all out. She was even adding shrimp to the mix, she saw, spying the shellfish defrosting in a bowl.

'Did you bring the tablets home with yer?' Kitty asked. The 'tablets' were said with reverence as though it were the holy grail itself Shannon was after bringing home.

'I did.'

Kitty stopped stirring and fetched a glass, catching sight of Grace as she did so. 'If you don't watch it, the wind will change and leave your face like that, young lady.'

'What's up with her?' Shannon stage-whispered as her nan filled the glass.

Grace stopped mashing. 'It was supposed to be my turn for the favourite dinner tonight, not Imo's. I was looking forward to Nan's lasagne, not fish pie.'

If anyone ever accused their nan of not being an adventurous cook, she was always quick to correct them and say, 'Sure, don't I make a grand lasagne, and that's Italian, you know.'

Shannon liked fish pie, although she wasn't so taken with the fishy smell in the kitchen at this moment in time. Still and all, she knew the result would be creamy and melt-in-the-mouth comfort food. Mind, she was equally partial to Nan's lasagne.

'Shannon, stop thinking about food and fetch a pill from that packet and be quick about it,' Kitty ordered, holding a glass of water out to her.

Shannon took it, putting it down before ripping open the brown Heneghan's Pharmacy bag. She popped a tiny white tablet from the blister pack and, grabbing the water, headed for the stairs. She half expected her nan to call after her, 'May the force be with yer.'

Ava and her mam watched her advance up the stairs from where they were camped outside the bathroom.

'Thank goodness you're back,' Nora said as Shannon reached the landing. 'Did you bring the tablets?' Again the reverent tone.

'I did.'

'Good. You want to see the state of her. She looks like Quasimodo's sister, so.'

Ava confirmed this with a nod.

'Mam, I heard that!' came bellowing through the bathroom door. 'And if that's Shannon, tell her it's the fecking cat or me. Oh, and tell her I know she's been using my La Nuit face masque, too.'

'Shannon,' Nora admonished. 'How many times? You're to leave your sister's things alone.'

Shannon ignored her mother. 'Do you want the antihistamine tablet or not? And don't make me choose between you and Napoleon, because Napoleon respects my privacy. He'd never dream of trying to read my diary.'

'I was twelve, Shannon, let it go,' Imogen called back through the timber door.

'I've told her she can't lock herself away in there. Not when we have a paying guest who doesn't want to be privy to her carry-on.' Nora sighed. 'There're only three days left until

Christmas. I've better things to be doing with my time than standing outside the bathroom door trying to calm this madam down.'

'Is he back then?' Shannon tried to act casual, feeling Ava's wily gaze on her.

'No. I haven't seen James since this morning,' Nora replied, and then she rapped sharply on the door. 'Imogen Kate Kelly, I won't tell you again. Open that door!' She threw an exasperated look at her daughters in the dim light of the hallway. 'Do you think you two can handle this from here on in?'

'Yeah, we've got this, Mam,' Ava assured her.

Nora threw her arms up in the air and then headed downstairs.

Shannon was suddenly struck by fear for her beloved Persian's welfare. 'Is Napoleon all right, Ava? She hasn't deliberately let him outside or anything?'

'He's grand. Don't be worrying your head about him. Let's get her sorted.'

'I'm not opening the door while Mam's there,' Imogen shouted. 'She thinks I look like Quasimodo.'

'No, she doesn't,' Ava soothed.

'She didn't say that. She said Quasimodo's sister,' Shannon corrected.

'Not helping, Shan,' Ava said. Then as they heard the lock slide back, she gave her sister a thumbs up.

The door opened a crack letting a sliver of light out.

'Pass it over.' A hand snaked through the crack.

Shannon pressed the tablet into Imogen's palm.

'Water,' Imogen demanded. 'I'm not drinking from the tap.'

'Well, either open the door properly or give me your other hand.'

'You'll laugh at me.'

'No, I won't. I'm a nurse. I deal with this sort of thing all the time, and my patients are quick to comment on how professional I am.' Shannon made the last bit up.

'Just you then.'

'I'll go and check on Napoleon,' Ava said, and Shannon nodded gratefully.

A moment later, the door slowly opened.

'Jaysus.' Shannon stared. Imogen's eyes were two pink, swollen slits.

'You said you were professional! You wouldn't say that to a patient.'

That was true. Shannon handed her the glass of water, putting her imaginary nurse's hat on.

'Get that antihistamine down you, for starters, then go and lie down on Ava's bed, and I'll wrap some frozen peas in a tea towel. You can rest them over your eyes. They'll help soothe it. You'll be good as gold by tomorrow, I promise.'

'I was supposed to FaceTime Nev.' Imogen sniffed, before popping the tablet in her mouth and swallowing it down with a gulp of water.

'I know, but you can still talk to him.'

'Yeah, but I was hoping to do more than just FaceTime.'

'Not in our room, you weren't.'

'You don't have to worry, I'm not feeling a femme fatale at this moment in time. And what about Napoleon? Can he go and stay with Freya or something? It's only for a few days.'

'No! It wouldn't be fair. The move's been traumatic enough. But, listen, I'm sure Ava will swap rooms with you, and if you take the antihistamines regularly, you'll be sex-timing Nev in no time. I'll even move your clothes across to the twins' wardrobe for you.' Ava was her pick to share with, being the most easygoing of her sisters.

'And keep me regularly supplied with cold compresses until the swelling goes down.'

'Deal.'

'And snacks and drinks, should I require them?'

'Feck off, Imo Don't forget I'm already doing you a big favour by keeping quiet about a certain fella's age.'

'Aagh!' The bathroom door slammed shut.

Shannon turned around and saw James on the stairs behind her, an eyebrow raised quizzically.

21

'Did I interrupt something?' James asked Shannon. Their guest paused midway up the stairs and looked up at her uncertainly. 'I can go away and come back later if I did.'

James was channelling his Bear Grylls look this afternoon, and Shannon wondered if he'd gone hiking because he'd been in jeans and a sweater earlier, not that she was taking notes about what he was wearing. 'No. It's nothing. It's just Imogen being Imogen. She's very dramatic.' This man had a knack for timing, Shannon thought. Why did he have to decide to come upstairs at the precise moment she was telling her sister to feck off? 'And besides, you're our guest, so please don't feel you can't come and go as you please just because Imogen's having a meltdown.' Her voice sounded oddly formal.

'I can hear you!'

Shannon couldn't help but grin, although she knew she'd not be grinning later when Imogen had her running up and down the stairs like a housemaid from the 1920s. Her sister had never been a good patient. If the rest of them had a cold, then so far as Imogen was concerned, she had the flu and would keep you posted with minute-by-minute updates on her symptoms.

As James took the last few stairs and joined her on the landing, he stepped a little too close to her again, and Shannon automatically went into fight or flight mode. Her heart amped up its beats per minute, and prickles of sweat popped on her forehead. She wished she could click her fingers and hide in the bathroom alongside Imogen. But as it was, with the bathroom door behind her, she couldn't even take a step backwards to create breathing space. He was close enough for her to see his eyes had crinkled in response to her smile, and in this light, his greenish-grey irises had turned a bottomless green. Aside from being ready to tackle Nature in all her fierce glory, he was also at ease and utterly oblivious to the body heat she felt sure was radiating off her in waves. Was it an American thing, this standing-too-close business? Whatever it was, it gave her the hot flashes, or power surges as Mam called them, and she had to dig her fingernails into her palms to stop herself from fanning her face.

'Imogen's your younger sister, right?'

'One of them. Imo's between Hannah and me. Although the way she's after carrying on you'd think she was the baby of the family. The three of us have the Nolan brown eyes and hair from Mam's side but that's where the similarity ends. Grace and Ava, the twins, are the babies of the family. They're redheads with blue eyes, which comes from the Kellys.' Shannon knew she was burbling. He'd asked a simple question and received a family tree for a reply.

'Feck off, Shannon. I've every right to be upset,' Imogen shouted through the door.

James laughed. 'Siblings, huh? It's the same in my family.'

Shannon nodded and tried to take a nonchalant sidestep in the direction of her bedroom. The smell of the fish Nan had bubbling in the milk downstairs was getting stronger. Dad would definitely be marching about with the peach air freshener later. Poor Napoleon's mouth would be watering at the fishy aroma, and it was his teatime to boot. She'd decided this was her excuse to make a quick getaway when James began speaking again.

'I just met Grace. She was telling me about life in London and promised to write me a list of the hidden gems most tourists miss for when I make it over there.'

Curiosity outweighed her need to run down the hall to her bedroom and close the door.

'Well, take her recommendations with a pinch of salt, because you're in for a list of London's top ten pubs and clubs from what she and Ava have told me. So are you headed for the UK after Ireland then?'

'Not this time. I've got to get back to the clinic, but I plan on coming back.' James was in no hurry to move off. 'I parked on the coast road and followed the cliff path to the bay this afternoon. The castle ruins are quite something, and the bay is beautiful. I couldn't believe how clear the water was.'

'Clear and freezing this time of year,' Shannon answered, noticing with amusement the nuances of his Bostonian accent.

'What?'

'Your accent. The way you say pahk instead of park.'

Mischievousness played at the corners of his mouth as he said, 'Pahk the cah in Hah-vahd yahd.'

Shannon burst out laughing, and James gave her his crooked grin. But then, the energy between them changed, and the sparkle left his eyes as he became serious and touched her arm briefly. His fingers fleetingly on her arm made her feel like she'd been branded.

'I want you to know I won't hurt Maeve, Shannon. I can promise you that.'

Shannon chewed her bottom lip as she met his open, honest gaze. She believed him. Something shifted in his eyes, and his face softened. Jaysus wept! Was he going to kiss her?

'Imogen's after having had an allergic reaction to Napoleon, her eyes are terrible swollen. Like Miss Piggy's so,' she blurted, gratified to see James blink as though coming out of a trance. The moment, or whatever it was, was gone.

'I noticed. It didn't look like much fun.'

A wail sounded from the bathroom.

'Sorry.' James winced and gave Shannon an apologetic shrug. 'I didn't mean to make things worse.'

Shannon gestured at the door and mouthed, 'She's a drama queen.'

James cleared his throat. 'I'll go to my room now so you can tell her it's safe to come out.'

Shannon watched him go, feeling confused. Had she imagined things when she'd thought he was about to kiss her? And why did her body begin behaving like a hormonal teenager at her first dance around him? She shook the questions away because they didn't matter. She might be attracted to their American guest. He might even find her attractive. That didn't mean anything would happen between them, though, because she wouldn't let it. 'You can come out now, Imo. He's gone.'

The door opened once more, and Imogen huffily pushed past her, making a beeline for Grace and Ava's room. She opened the door and stood with one foot inside the bedroom and one in the passage. 'I see what Hannah means now.'

Shannon's hands settled on her hips. 'What do you mean by that?'

'The baboons,' Imogen replied, banging the bedroom door shut. 'And don't forget my peas!'

Shannon stomped back down the stairs filling her nan and Grace in on the Imogen situation as she retrieved a clean tea towel and a bag of peas.

'He's very nice, your American,' Grace said slyly from where she was sitting flicking through a magazine now dinner was in the Aga. She received a swat with the tea towel from Kitty.

She'd have been very good with the lassoing in the rodeo, would their nan. She was very quick, Shannon thought.

'Don't be teasing your sister. There's been enough shouting and carry-on this afternoon.'

Grace was undeterred. 'And he looks very well in all that Gore-Tex. I think it's a "Me, Tarzan, you Jane" sort of a thing.'

Shannon knew she shouldn't ask for clarification, but she did anyway.

'I mean, he looks rugged in all that outdoor gear. The sorta fella you'd want to rescue you if you were lost out on the moors.'

'You'll be calling him Heathcliff next,' Shannon muttered.

'You could do worse, you know, Shannon. He's a fine fellow, so he is,' Kitty said, draping the tea towel over the hook.

'Thanks a million, Nan.'

Kitty was unperturbed as she moved on. 'Your mam's after getting the oldest Molloy girl who's home for Christmas to help behind the bar for an hour this evening so we can sit down for a proper family dinner.'

'Holly,' Shannon supplied her name. 'She worked here over summer a few years ago.'

'That's her, and a lovely young woman she's grown into. Do you know she's after getting a part in *Fair City*?' The long-running Irish soap opera was Kitty's not-so-secret vice.

'No. Good for her.' Shannon vaguely recalled Holly had headed for Dublin in search of fame and fortune.

'Tell her what her lines were, Nan?' Grace grinned over at Shannon.

'Well, she played a girl admitted to the hospital with the stomach pains, and you want to have heard the way she said, "It's my stomach that's after hurting." Very believable she was. It was like watching your Meryl Streep wan with appendicitis, so it was.'

Shannon and Grace snickered and then, receiving an unamused stare from Kitty because *Fair City* was no laughing matter, Shannon hastily said, 'It will be nice to have a family dinner, Nan. It's been strange taking shifts to eat. Still, Chloe being sick couldn't be helped.'

A banging overhead sounded, and the threesome raised their eyes toward the ceiling.

'What on earth was that?' Kitty asked, her blue eyes wide.

'It sounded like someone banging on the floor with a shoe,' Grace deduced as the thumping sounded again.

'Imogen!' Shannon said, stomping back upstairs and tapping on the bedroom door. She didn't wait for a reply as she stormed into the room. Imogen had drawn the curtains as though paparazzi might be lurking in the laneway running down the side of the pub. The telltale shoe was on the floor next to the bed. As for Imogen, she was lying prone on the bed, the back of her hand resting on her forehead like a Southern belle swooning.

'Here.' Shannon thrust the peas and towel at her and made to leave.

'Do we have a bell I could use?' Imogen called weakly after her. 'It would be easier than the shoe. So as I can let you know when the peas need replacing.'

'No, we don't. And if you so much as touch that shoe again, I'll shut Napoleon in the bedroom with you.'

Shannon was pulling the door behind her when she heard Imogen add, 'Don't crush any of my clothes when you're carrying them through, Shannon; otherwise you'll have to iron them before hanging them up.'

Shannon took a deep breath and told herself these were the sacrifices motherhood wrought, closing the door to seek out Napoleon.

22

It was no surprise to anyone when Imogen refused to come downstairs for her dinner, which meant Shannon had to traipse back up the stairs with a plate for her. She'd found her sister still reclining on her bed, eyes covered with frozen peas wrapped in a tea towel which she'd briefly lifted as she ordered Shannon to set her fish pie down on top of the drawers by her bed. Imogen's clothes were now squeezed in alongside Grace's, and the clutter on the bedside table suggested she was making herself at home.

Poor Grace and Hannah weren't happy about the swap and would be even unhappier when they went up tonight to find the bedroom smelt like Egan's fish shop, Shannon had thought, closing the door on her. On the other hand, Ava had confided she hankered after getting a cat, but the shared terrace house in London had a strict no-pets policy. As such, she was happy with the new arrangement. So was Napoleon, who'd lapped up all the attention his Aunty Ava lavished on him.

Shannon sat down for dinner and tucked in. The fish pie would be next-level comfort food if she weren't hyper-aware of James seated directly opposite her. His hair had been damp, curling slightly around his ears when he'd come downstairs to join them at the table, and he'd changed into a sweater and his chinos. She watched him sneakily as he scraped up the last of the pie's creamy filling, somehow managing to finish his meal despite the Spanish Inquisition.

Nora and Liam had wanted to know if he ever frequented the pub featured in *Cheers*, a well-known sitcom set in Boston that had run through the eighties. Then Hannah had begun grilling him about the bee population of Boston. Finally, Grace and Ava were curious whether he lived in a brownstone – he didn't. Shannon had stayed quiet throughout the questioning, toying with her food, but she'd been all ears listening to his responses. It was Kitty who turned the topic of conversation to his family.

As forks had scooped up chunks of firm white hake and tender vegetables, James replied by telling them he was the youngest of four. All boys. Their dad, a firefighter, had been killed on duty when they were small, something that had elicited sympathy around the table. He'd been too young to remember him, he'd said, before telling them that Hazel, his mom as he called her, had done an incredible job of getting four boys unscathed through their teens and off to college.

Shannon had detected pride and something else she couldn't pinpoint in his voice when he spoke of his mother. The brothers had all taken different career paths, like her and her sisters. His oldest brother, Alex, was an architect who'd married his high school sweetheart. Next in the pecking order was Oliver, a self-proclaimed player who dabbled successfully in finance, and then came Brayden, a year older than James. He was a builder who was after a chequered dating history at long last with a woman his mom approved of. The Cabot clan had high hopes she'd be joining the family one of these days.

Shannon had wondered what sort of woman his mother would approve of. But as Hannah asked, 'And do you have a wife, husband, partner, special anyone back home in Boston,

James?' she'd forgotten about what sort of woman would fit into the Cabot family as she aimed a kick under the table at her. Unfortunately, her foot connected with Grace, who, startled, dropped her knife and fork onto her plate with a clatter, making them all jump.

Nora had glowered at Shannon, who was feigning innocence, while James looked on amused. They were all holding their breath, waiting for his reply to Hannah's question, though.

'There's Harry.'

There'd been a collective sigh around the table. Even Liam's sigh had sounded like he'd the weight of the world on his shoulders at the news James was gay. All three sisters shot a commiserating glance over at Shannon, who could have happily thumped them. Disappointment mingled with relief at having misread the signals, because even if she was interested, which she wasn't, he was off the menu so far as she was concerned.

'My beagle.'

Hannah, Grace and Ava were all smiling once more. 'Your dog, ha ha ha,' they laughed, a little too hard. Nora was just about hysterical, and Liam looked at his wife in alarm.

'My best friend,' James corrected, sea-green eyes fixed on Shannon. It was as though an invisible thread connected them. 'He's staying with my brother while I'm away.' James dug out his phone and pulled up a photo of man with his best friend to pass around the table. The affection on both the beagle and James's faces was apparent for all to see.

Kitty, informing James he was a fine-looking dog indeed, noticed Shannon's plate as she handed him his phone back. 'You've hardly touched your dinner, Shannon.'

'Sorry, Nan, I'm just not that hungry.'

'Are you sickening for something?' Kitty frowned and planted her hand on Shannon's forehead. 'You're not hot, but it's not like you not to finish what's put in front of you.'

It wasn't, but her stomach was tied tighter than the reef knot she'd perfected for her Ladybirds' badge.

'She's sickening for something, all right.' Hannah grinned.

Shannon didn't dare aim another kick because it would be James's shin her foot connected with this time, knowing her luck, so she'd let it slide.

Now, as Shannon excused herself from the table, getting up to stack the plates, Grace began filling the sink with hot water, and Ava fetched a clean tea towel. To Shannon's relief, Hannah made herself scarce before she could be roped into doing anything. James was telling Kitty how much he'd enjoyed the fish pie, and she was lapping up the praise.

'Did you let Napoleon check the place out?' James asked Shannon, watching her piling the plates on top of one another.

Liam spoke before Shannon could reply. 'She did. Gave me the willies, so it did, seeing his pushed-in face peering at me around the door like so. I thought it was a new breed of rat.'

'Dad, he's gorgeous,' Shannon protested.

'If you like pushed-in faces.'

James was laughing at the exchange.

'Ignore him. He's winding you up,' Nora said, passing her plate to Shannon.

Shannon turned her focus on James. 'Napoleon had a good wander about the place, thanks. He didn't seem fazed at all, and I've left the bedroom door open so he can come and go. Nan giving him a piece of fish won him over. I think he's going to like his new home. And remember you're not to let him out.' She directed this final remark at her family members.

'She carried him through to the pub. Tell James what Enda said, Shannon,' Liam chuckled. 'You've probably seen Enda propping up the bar as you come and go, James. He's a soft spot for Kitty here.'

'And not so much as a scrap of encouragement do I give the

old fool either. I'm not that sort of woman. So that you know,' Kitty directed to James.

James nodded. 'I wouldn't have thought you were, Kitty.'

Shannon gave him points for keeping a straight face. As for Enda, she'd been affronted at the time but could see the humour now as she told James how Enda had asked her what she was doing carting a guinea pig about the place. 'Yesterday, he called Napoleon a ferret. So my poor cat is going to wind up with a complex.'

James laughed again. 'Poor Napoleon. Will you let him outside at all?'

'Only if I'm there to keep an eye on him.'

'That's probably wise.'

'Cats are supposed to roam about catching mice and things.' Liam snorted.

'Not Persians, Dad. Ask James if you don't believe me. He's a vet.'

'They're docile, Liam, which makes them vulnerable in the wild, and their long coats get tangled and matted easily if they're left to roam. Also, they're prone to respiratory issues if they spend too long outdoors.'

'On account of their pushed-in faces like?'

'Uh, I'd say it's down to the unique shape of their heads,' James replied tactfully.

'Thank you,' Shannon said, carting the plates over to the worktop and hearing her dad asking James whether he'd had a chance to explore the area.

She loitered alongside Grace, waiting to hear what he'd say. There'd been no mention of his connection with Maeve over dinner, but then her family had been more interested in knowing about his life in Boston than what had brought him here.

'Not yet, although I had a good walk along the coast road to Emerald Bay. I think I'll go for a drive tomorrow. I thought I'd get away early and explore. I've got a Lonely Planet book in my room, but I'm open to suggestions.'

If Shannon had turned around, she'd have seen a crafty look cross her father's face. But, as it happened, she was glad she was pretending to be busy passing plates to Grace to wash when he spoke up, because abject horror would have shown on her face at what he said.

'I've got an idea. Thanks to her nursing rounds, Shannon knows this place like the back of her hand. Sure, she'd make a grand tour guide for you tomorrow. Nobody can say the Kellys don't go the extra mile for their guests.'

Had her father just volunteered her services as a tour guide for James? Shannon froze, plate in hand. Then, as Grace elbowed her, she rearranged her expression to one of regret and turned around.

'Ah, Daddy, that would have been grand, but I can't. Sorry, James, but I'm after promising Mam I'd help her with the shop over in Kilticaneel tomorrow morning for the Christmas dinner. It's a big job.'

Nora was having none of it. 'Not at all, Shannon. Grace or Ava can come with me.'

'I'll go with you, Mam,' Grace volunteered, and Shannon resisted the temptation to stomp on her foot. Anyone would think she was suffering from restless leg syndrome with all these urges she was after having to kick or stomp.

'That's settled then.' Liam sat back in his chair with his hands resting on his middle. 'Shannon will show you around the place.'

'I'll pack you a picnic and flask to take with you.' Nora smiled smugly, pleased with the way things were panning out.

James picked up on Shannon's vibes and gave her an apologetic shrug, mouthing 'Sorry' over the table.

She'd been raised not to be rude, and she shook her head to signal it was fine, and it would be, she told herself. A tour of the local area was not code for getting it on in the car. Even if it was, BB was far too small for that sort of carry-on. 'I'll enjoy seeing the countryside through fresh eyes,' she said, trying to make up for coming across as a reluctant tour guide. 'Um, I think I'll head up now and check on Napoleon.' Shannon took to the stairs.

'Is there any chance of pudding, Nora, my love?'

'Not for you, Liam!' drifted up the stairs after her as she made her way toward her bedroom.

There was no sign of Napoleon there, and she found him inspecting the bathroom. 'Hello, fella,' she said, picking him up and cuddling him. 'I'll be heading back downstairs soon because I'll go and pull my weight in the pub, but I thought I'd come and see how you're getting on.'

His purring made her smile, and she enjoyed the warmth of him as she nuzzled his head. 'And don't you be listening to Daddy when he says you've got a pushed-in face. You're a fine-looking fellow.'

Shannon set him down and headed for her bedroom. She'd write in her gratitude journal now because later, Ava would be in the room too, and the journal was private. It was her thing.

She could hear muted sounds below as she settled herself cross-legged on her bed and opened the notebook, unsure of what she would write. She'd enjoyed having her eye make-up done by Nuala and had received compliments, so she started by writing that down. It was good too that Napoleon was making himself at home, she thought, penning that next. Then, she tapped the biro to her mouth. There was something else, but it was hovering just out of reach. She closed her eyes, trying to grasp it, and then it came to her.

I haven't thought about Julien all day.

TWO DAYS UNTIL CHRISTMAS

This Christmas may you have
Walls for the wind
And a roof for the rain,
And drinks bedside the fire,
Laughter to cheer you,
And those you love near you,
And all that your heart may desire.

— *IRISH CHRISTMAS*
BLESSING

23

To her amazement, Shannon had slept soundly, but even so, the alarm on her phone going off at seven was a rude awakening. Ava mumbled in the bed opposite her, 'Turn it off, Shan. I'm on my holidays.' And bleary-eyed, she did so, aware that if she didn't push the covers off and get out of bed, she'd likely nod off again. Napoleon mewled his annoyance at being woken when she unwittingly flung the covers over him but was mollified by breakfast. She'd move his food and water bowl downstairs before she left this morning; it was time to let him have his first taste of the big outdoors, she decided, watching him hoe into his biscuits like he'd been on a two-day fast.

The shower sorted her out, but it was far too early to try and emulate Nuala's smoky eye, so she settled on a lick of mascara and lip gloss. It would be the normal-sized eyes for her today, she thought. Then, rubbing at the steamed-up mirror, Shannon inspected her hair. It could do with straightening, but what was the point? She'd be pulling her woolly hat down over it. No, better to spend the time squeezing in an extra cup of coffee than faffing with her hair. A quick brush and she'd have to do.

Shannon could see a chink of light peeking out from under

James's door as she made her way down the passage, which still smelt faintly of last night's dinner. She could hear Mam, a morning person, moving about in her room but knew her dad wouldn't appear downstairs for at least another hour. She paused outside Grace, Hannah and Imogen's door listening out for a few seconds. There were no sounds of life aside from Imogen's snoring, which was a relief. Imo was adamant she didn't snore, but Shannon would know those snorty eruptions anywhere. It was a blessing her sister was still sleeping because she'd had enough of being at her beck and call last night. Hopefully, the swelling around her eyes would be gone this morning because Imogen had proven to be one of her more challenging patients.

Napoleon padded down the stairs after her and, switching on the kitchen light, Shannon made her mind up; now was as good a time as any to let him sniff the fresh air, especially if it meant he did his morning business outside. Stopping only to flick the kettle on, she opened the back door, glad she'd dressed for warmth, not glamour, as the frigid air blasted her. 'Come on, young man.' The Persian poked his head out but didn't venture forth. She had to nudge his backside with the door to close it behind them. Mam would go mad if she let all the warmth out. Napoleon sat on the step, and after giving her one of his haughty looks at having made an undignified exit, he turned his attention to the shadowy beer garden and surveyed his kingdom.

'C'mon, put your paws on the grass and see what it feels like,' she coaxed, wandering onto the lawn. She pointed to the mist-shrouded fields. 'But over there is out of bounds. D'ya hear me?'

Napoleon stretched a cautious paw out and set it down on the frost-tipped grass, then another paw, before sniffing his way toward Shannon. His tail slunk along on the ground as he investigated this new, mysterious world, and Shannon walked closely alongside him, coming to a halt by the shrubby bushes down the far side of the garden. 'Now g'won with you and do your business. I promise I won't watch.'

Napoleon obliged, disappearing into the shrubbery, and as he scrabbled about, Shannon blew into her hands to warm them. The sky grew lighter, and the last twinkling star was snuffed out. It looked like it was going to be another clear day. That was something, she thought, huffing out a cloud of white.

A smile twitched as she recalled how she and Imo used to get a twig and pretend they were smoking on mornings like this when they were small. One morning Mam, catching them at it, had given them a great big lecture on smoking being a dirty, filthy habit. It hadn't stopped them from returning to their game once her back was turned. A robin redbreast flitted about the garden, and Napoleon stalked from the bushes. His yellow eyes trained on his prey, but the bird was too quick for him, darting away to visit another garden. She hoped he wouldn't be too much longer, or there was a risk of her turning into an ice statue, she thought as he continued to explore.

She stifled a yawn because she'd been late to bed last night despite knowing she was in for an early start today. Mam and Dad had shooed them away from the bar, which meant when Freya had called into the pub, she'd pulled up a seat alongside her, Ava, Grace and James, whom her sisters had insisted join them by the fire for a drink. They'd rescued him from Evan Kennedy, cutting him off mid-stream as he launched into his favourite 'curse of the Kennedys' story. When James had got up to visit the little boys' room, Freya leaned in and whispered in Shannon's ear that she'd no idea it was possible to rock a pair of chinos, but James had pulled it off. Shannon had not commented.

Freya's phone had sounded then, and their conversation ceased as she snatched up her phone and scanned the text.

Shannon, seeing her friend's smile fade, had asked if everything was all right.

'Grand. It's just Mam reminding me what to bring on Christmas Day.'

She didn't have to say she'd hoped it was Oisin, and right then, Shannon would have dearly loved to give the fickle artist a piece of her mind. But, as this wasn't possible, she did the next best thing and filled Freya in on the tour of duty she had to undertake tomorrow with James. It had shifted her friend's focus off her useless boyfriend and restored her previous good mood.

Later, when she'd been lying in bed with Napoleon tucked in beside her, Ava, having finished thumping the pillow as she got comfortable in the strange bed, said, 'James is nice, Shan, and funny. Did you hear that story about the woman who brought her cat in thinking he had an abnormal growth, but it was his willy? I was in fits.'

'It was funny.' Shannon smiled in the dark. She'd been bent double as James had relayed how he'd had to keep a straight face as he explained what it was the woman had seen.

'He likes you. Hannah's right.'

'Listen, Ava, when you've had someone you think is your forever rip the carpet out from under your feet, you'll understand why I don't want to go there.'

'Sorry,' Ava had whispered back. 'I should know better.'

Shannon had reached over, and her sister had grasped her hand. 'It must have been tough seeing Shane tonight,' she'd said as Ava squeezed her hand back.

'It was. I hate that you can be so close to someone, and then when you break up, you become like strangers.'

'Mm.'

They'd changed the subject then and talked about Imogen, tossing their opinions on the age gap between their sister and her new beau back and forth before agreeing they were both done and needed to get to sleep.

Now Shannon watched as Napoleon completed one more circuit of the beer garden and then strolled toward her. 'Good boy.' She scratched him behind the ears before opening the door to sizzling bacon. He shot in after her.

Nora, ready for the day ahead, was at the stove pushing Dermot Molloy's finest streaky bacon around the pan along with two sunny-side-up eggs. 'This should set our guest up for the day,' she said, seeing Shannon. 'Did you sleep all right, love? It must be nice being back in your old bed.'

It was. There was something to be said for a single bed with flannelette sheets in winter. 'I did, thanks, Mam, and that smells amazing. Can I have a rasher sandwich?' Shannon asked, hopefully fixing herself and her mam a cup of coffee. She stood alongside her, nursing her mug. Napoleon, who was also partial to a rind now and again, mewled at her feet.

'Shannon, if I trip over him...' Nora warned.

'Come and say hello to me, boy.' James surprised them, neither woman having heard him come downstairs. Shannon noted that he was dressed to tackle the wilds of Connemara and survive whatever the weather had to throw at them once more.

'Good morning, James.' Nora greeted him with a warm smile. 'You're looking the part in your outdoor wear there. Breakfast won't be long now. The bacon's sizzling in the pan, so you settle yourself at the table, and Shannon will make you a drink. Tea, or is it coffee today?'

'Coffee, white, with one sugar would be great, thanks, and good morning, ladies.' James strode toward them and bent to pick up Napoleon, who wriggled, miffed at being carried away from the Aga.

Shannon watched as he sat down at the table with him and how as soon as he began stroking him, Napoleon settled down contentedly. He'd a crescent-shaped scar on his knuckles, she'd noticed when she'd shook his hand outside the Knitters Nook after their impromptu meeting, and even though it was none of her business, she couldn't help asking whether it was a veterinary war wound.

'This?' James held his hand out for inspection.

Shannon nodded. 'I hope you don't think I'm being nosy.'

'She's always been a Nosy Nellie,' Nora butted in.

'Mam!'

'It's fine. I could tell you it's the result of a tussle with a fierce animal, but I'm afraid it's courtesy of a hen.'

'A hen?' Shannon's eyebrows shot up.

'A chicken's foot, to be precise. Don't ask. Suffice to say they've sharp claws.'

Shannon smiled and set about making a third coffee. She put it down in front of him before opening the fridge. There was a shelf full of wrapped parcels and, frowning, Shannon fetched the tomato and brown sauces. As she set them down on the table, she wondered which James was, tomato or brown? Of course, it was tomato sauce for herself. But then she wondered why she was wondering about it in the first place. She shook the thoughts away, asking her mam, 'What's with all the mystery packages in the fridge? They look like lucky dips at the fair.'

'It's for the picnic. I've made ham and egg sandwiches. There's cheese and your nan's after wrapping half a loaf of brack for you. Oh, and there are some apples from Rita Quigley's tree you can help yourself to. I'll fetch the old picnic basket out from under the stairs.'

Shannon's eyes drifted to the flask that appeared on the worktop, waiting to be filled. Her mam intended to pack them off the best part of the day by the looks of things. Was James aware of what her family was trying to do? The Kelly clan were not subtle, and she'd have thought their matchmaking attempts glaringly obvious. It was highly embarrassing, but before drifting off to sleep, a plan to get through the day had formed last night. She would treat her tour guide role much as she would her nursing round, only she was carting her patient about with her. She'd behave like a professional and an adult instead of a tongue-tied teenager. The old saying of every cloud having a silver lining was prophetic in so much as today would also allow her to press him once more about his tie to Maeve.

James, listening to the exchange, thanked her. 'It's very kind of you to go to so much trouble, Nora.' He'd called her Mrs Kelly until she'd told him he was making her feel ancient.

'Not at all. Shannon, fetch us some plates would you, please, and put the toast on? You can butter your bread if it's a butty you're after.'

'What about you, Mam? What are you having?'

Nora's eyes looked to the ceiling. If Liam were up, they'd hear his footfall overhead. 'You can butter me a couple of slices too. Just don't be telling your father I'm after eating bacon. We're supposed to be watching our weight. It's the low-fat granola for him again.'

Shannon smiled and did as she was told.

James was a tomato sauce man, Shannon noted as their hands reached for the container at the same time. They both snatched them back as though they'd had an electric shock.

'Uh, sorry, You go first.'

'No, you're the guest.'

'Thanks.'

Shannon watched as he squeezed a dollop on his plate, missing the amused expression on her mam's face at their awkward exchange. She suspected she was in for a long day rubbing elbows with James in BB's close quarters.

24

'Meet BB,' Shannon said to James as he followed her outside, and she aimed her keys at the yellow Honda Jazz. The lights flickered, and the locks popped.

'Short for Big Bird?'

'Good guess. My dad, as you can see' – she gestured to Liam's Hilux – 'has a thing for yellow vehicles being visible on the roads, especially given the amount of driving I do on my nursing round.' She shrugged. 'And the colour's grown on me because I'm very fond of BB.'

James picked the Lion bar wrapper off the passenger seat and, ducking his head, folded himself into the car while Shannon clambered behind the wheel.

'I haven't tried one of these,' James said, inspecting the wrapper.

'You don't know what you're missing,' Shannon informed him. She took the wrapper, stuffing it in the driver's door pocket. Then, starting the car, acknowledged her mam waving them off. All that was missing was a handkerchief in her hand because she looked like she was waving them off on an epic

MICHELLE VERNAL

voyage, Shannon thought, rolling her eyes and waiting until James's seat belt clicked before reversing out of the car park.

As soon as she'd put the car in gear, Robbie began crooning about loving angels.

'Sorry.' She turned the volume down.

'Don't be. I don't mind a bit of Robbie Williams.'

'Really?'

He nodded. 'My brothers are all into nineties grunge. You know, Sound Garden, Nirvana. They think it gives them a rebellious edge, given they wear suits to work.'

Shannon nodded.

'Apart from Brayden, he's more into hip-hop. You want to see him on building sites with his cap on back to front, and his builder's crack on show.'

Shannon burst out laughing at the picture painted.

James grinned over at her. 'Me, I like music that's easy on the ears.'

A fellow easy-listening convert, Shannon thought, feeling a connection as she turned the music down but not off.

BB crawled through the fairy-light-lit and bunting-strewn village. The Christmas windows sparkled, and the shops' lights began to flicker on, providing a cosy invitation to step inside and escape the cold. The sky resembled a heavy grey eiderdown this morning, but at least it wasn't raining, Shannon thought.

'Uh, Shannon, a man on a motorised scooter is heading right for us.'

'Ah, don't be worrying, that's Mr Kenny. He's king of the road on that thing. It's an unwritten rule that he always has the right of way.' She swerved, waving, and then glimpsed Paddy up ahead. He was outside Heneghan's once more, chatting to his cardboard lady love. She shook her head, seeing the bottle-neck of whatever tipple he'd got his hands on protruding from the pocket of his greatcoat. Remembering the scandal currently rocking Emerald Bay, she relayed the story of the great perfume bottle heist to James. It was gratifying to hear him laugh.

Her grip relaxed on the steering wheel as she decided that perhaps this sightseeing trip they were embarking on wouldn't be so bad after all. But then James rearranged his long legs, making himself comfortable, and Shannon's body grew hot. She fiddled with the air conditioning, turning the temperature down even though she knew it wouldn't help. The nearness of him filling the space in the seat next to her was the problem.

She glanced to her right and was surprised to see Isla putting her blackboard out on the pavement, advertising her current bargain-priced wares. It was a welcome diversion. The village's souvenir shop owner was eager to offload all the leprechaun snow globes she possibly could if the 50 per cent discount she was offering was anything to go by. Shannon tooted the horn, and Isla looked up and waved over, eyebrows raised as she saw the passenger sitting alongside her star Emerald Bay Elf.

Eileen Carroll unlocked the door of the Knitters Nook, spun around at the horn sounding, and her mouth formed a comical 'O' as she saw who was sitting beside Shannon.

Rita Quigley, making her way to Quigley's Quill, waved, and Shannon waved back, while inside the Silver Spoon cafe, she could see Carmel Brady chatting to an early-bird customer.

The shops must be subscribing to extending Christmas opening hours, Shannon guessed because the street would be deathly quiet this time of the morning any other time of year.

'It must be nice living somewhere like this where everybody knows everybody,' James remarked, unaware that the news Shannon was chauffeuring the American tourist staying at the Shamrock about the place would have already begun to whip through the village like wildfire. It might even knock the perfume heist off the front page.

Shannon thought of Ava and Shane. It wasn't nice living in

a small village when your relationship broke up. At least she hadn't had to see Julien again once he'd left. That would have been unbearable. Ava had spent last night avoiding looking in the direction of the alcove where Shane Egan and his brothers were seated. She'd seen Shane staring over at her sister, though. It was as if he was willing her to acknowledge him. If she'd felt him boring holes into their backs, then Ava would have too, despite her carefree chatter. He hadn't dared come over while her sisters surrounded her. That was something. It would have been awkward for them all. Her mind turned to Christmas Eve. Then there was the carolling too. She'd never have been roped into the Galway equivalent if there even was one.

'Not when your nan puts your name forward to join in Christmas carolling with the Emerald Bay Elves, and you find out you have to wear an elf costume to look the part,' Shannon stated.

James creased up again. 'Seriously?'

'Seriously. I've even got a little elf hat with a bobble on it.'

'Now that I've got to see.'

Shannon didn't risk glancing over at him; she kept her eyes trained on the road ahead as they left the shops of Main Street behind. Then, thinking about what he'd said, she realised she hadn't answered him properly. 'I appreciate the community side of village life more now I've been away for a while. But when I was younger, I found it claustrophobic. You couldn't get away with anything without someone seeing you and reporting yer to yer mam and dad. I was desperate to move away. So were my sisters, which is why they've scattered to Dublin and London. Ava, in particular, had a nasty break-up with a local fella, and Emerald Bay is suffocatingly small in those circumstances.'

'I'd imagine it would be. Although on the other side of the coin, living in a big city like Boston can be lonely. It's strange how you can be surrounded by people but the anonymity of city life means you still feel alone.'

Shannon nodded. She could see what he was saying. 'Not you, though. You've got your family around you.' It wasn't a question, more a point of fact.

'I'm lucky, yeah, but there have been times when I've felt alone despite them all being close by. Does that sound weird?'

'No. I understand, but I think when that happens, it's not about who's around you but rather how you're feeling inside.'

'Yeah, that's it. This is a deep conversation before nine a.m.' James grinned to lighten his words. 'So you're home for good?'

'For now, at least. And it's not so bad.' Shannon surprised herself by saying this because she might have been dreading coming back to Emerald Bay, but it would always be home.

'You lived in Galway, right?'

'I did. There was good craic to be had there.' Heartbreak too. Not that she'd mention this, but around every cobbled corner, there'd been memories of Julien. Coming home had given her space to breathe again.

'It's a great town for sure, from what I've seen. Although I think I experienced one of the worst hangovers of my life after a pub crawl with a fellow American staying at the same hotel as me.'

This time Shannon laughed.

'What brought you back to Emerald Bay then? If you don't mind me asking.'

Shannon was aware of the soft strains of the Boyz II Men song 'I'll Make Love to You' on the radio. She'd have turned it up and sung along to the catchy tune if she'd been alone, but as it was, given her present company, the lyrics felt highly inappropriate. She tapped the steering wheel and toyed with her reply, unsure how much she wanted to tell James, then deciding she had nothing to hide, said, 'A relationship split and being left in a flat I couldn't afford.'

They were passing Maeve's cottage. 'Will you call in on Maeve later?' Shannon asked, glad of the diversion.

'I had planned to.'

An uncomfortable silence filled with unanswered questions floated between them. Shannon watched out of the corner of her eye as James turned his head to gaze out the window and decided now wasn't the right time to push for answers.

'Boston's steeped in history, but things like that blow me away. I can't imagine you'd ever take having a castle on your doorstep for granted.'

He was talking about the ruins of Kilticaneel Castle. The castle stood spectre-like, overseeing the waters of Emerald Bay as they slapped onto the shore. A few gulls soared around the castle's ramparts, and one hardy walker with a dog skipping ahead of them could be seen bundled up against the wind that always whipped along on the coastal path.

Shannon recalled the painting she'd been smitten with at Mermaids. Freya had informed her an American had bought it. 'James, did you buy a watercolour of the castle from Mermaids in the village?'

James looked surprised as he nodded. 'I did, yeah. Have you seen it then?'

'I saw it when I called in on Freya the night you...' She coughed. '...um, caught me in time before I connected with the pavement.' She didn't have to turn toward him to know his eyes would have crinkled at the corners. 'It's a wonderful painting, and I don't take the castle for granted. It's where my grandad died. Finbar Kelly.'

There was something about talking to a virtual stranger that made you feel you could open up. Shannon wondered how many hairdressers, beauticians and the like knew the intimate details of their clients' lives. They were sounding boards or, on the sidelines, counsellors. It was because they weren't linked to your life in a personal way. And this was why she found herself opening up about the awful day her grandad had passed away to James. 'I went into nursing because of Grandad. And I can remember feeling alone for a long time after he died, even though my family surrounded me.'

She kept her eyes on the well-travelled, winding road ahead, feeling James's sympathetic, or was it understanding, stare.

He cleared his throat. 'I'm sorry you went through that. It must have been hard. How old were you?'

'Fourteen.'

'A tough age.'

Shannon nodded as they bounced over a pothole.

'I became a vet because of Cocoa, our black lab. When I was about eight, he got hit by a car, and Mom rushed him to the vet. I remember sitting in the waiting room, promising myself that if the vet managed to save him, then that's what I'd be when I grew up. Cocoa survived, minus a leg, and lived to a ripe old age. And here I am.'

Shannon smiled. 'I'm glad Cocoa pulled through. But, what you said about not taking things like the castle for granted; I might not take Kilticaneel Castle for granted, but you stop seeing ruins and historic sights when you grow up around them. They're just part of the scenery, even though you're aware they're special.'

'I get that. It's the same at home. When I spend time with someone new to the city, I appreciate things like Beacon Hill or the Freedom Trail. But otherwise, I barely notice they're there.'

'I'd so love to walk the Freedom Trail,' Shannon enthused, not that she'd be purchasing a plane ticket to Boston in the near future.

'You should do it someday. And hey, maybe you'll see things through different eyes today.'

This time she glanced over at him and caught his smile.

'Where are we headed first?' James asked.

'We're going to head to Clifden town. It's about an hour's drive, and we could stretch our legs there if you like, and then we'll take the Sky Road and stop to wander up to Clifden Castle.'

'That sounds great. And, Shannon, I know your family put you on the spot, but I want you to know I appreciate you taking the time to show me around.'

'Ah, it's not a bother.' She dismissed the remark. 'Sure, you saved me from doing the big shop with Mam. She's terrible bossy when she's any sorta list in her hand.' A side-eyed glance revealed he had the slightest dimple in his right cheek when he smiled.

'I read about the Sky Road last night in my Lonely Planet. It's a sixteen-kilometre circular route, right?'

'It is, and the views are gorgeous. You can see the country-side as well as out to the islands. At the highest point, there's a parking area overlooking Connemara's coastline, and on a good day, you can see Mayo in the North and County Clare in the South. We could have lunch there. We'll not see that far today, but you'll get the idea.'

'A good plan.'

They sat in easy silence as Shannon drove the familiar road.

'Tell me about Finbar Kelly. What was he like? If he were married to Kitty, I'd imagine he was quite the character.'

The question came left of field. 'He was that, all right.' Her eyes danced as she talked about her grandad's love of his family, a good meal, a pipe and a pint. Then, glancing past James to where the mighty Atlantic thrashed against the rocks below them, she said, 'He used to tell me stories about the selkies.'

'Who're the selkies?'

'They're seals who can shed their skins and take on human form.'

James's eyes had taken on the same hue as the sea today, more grey than green, and his head was tilted ever so slightly toward her as she told him the stories she'd listened to at her grandad's knee. By the time she'd finished her tale, they'd rounded a bend and were greeted with the town of Clifden nestling in the valley below. Two church spires punctuated the vista of colourful buildings, framed by the Twelve Bens mountains' jagged outline.

'Wow,' James said, and Shannon felt inordinately proud, as though she were responsible for the sight spread out before them as she accelerated into the town.

25

Shannon and James wandered past the townsfolk laden down with bags as they embarked on their last-minute Christmas shopping. Rather than sitting in a cafe, they'd opted for take-away coffees from Walsh's bakery, content to stroll the town centre after sitting in the car for the last hour, and Shannon drained her frothy dregs. Now and again, she'd hear the word 'snow' being bandied about, and despite her initial lack of enthusiasm where Christmas was concerned this year, she'd found herself hoping they were in for a white one. There was something special about being with your family and friends on Christmas Day, far too full for your own good and with the snow falling outside, meaning you couldn't do anything other than sit around and eat and drink even more.

She tossed her takeaway cup in a bin, James doing the same, and as they carried on their meander, Shannon tested her feelings out where Julien was concerned. Suppose things had played out how she'd thought they would. In that case, she'd be in Paris now, waiting for a surprise proposal up the Eiffel Tower, not wandering around Clifden's town centre, feeling surprisingly relaxed around James. Had she had a lucky escape?

She couldn't recall ever having felt this at ease when she was with Julien. It dawned on her that she'd exhausted herself trying to keep him happy, and the yearning for the Frenchman and the future she'd thought they'd have was no longer there. She risked a sidelong glance at James and saw him enjoying the bustling atmosphere of Connemara's capital. It was all very confusing, and she decided the best thing she could do was focus on her surroundings.

'Look,' she breathed, moving toward a bright pink building with a turquoise door in Market Square. In the window was a jewel-like display of glassware. 'I don't have a crafty bone in my body. I'm in awe of people who do.' Freya sprang to mind.

They admired the artisanal works through the window and then carried on until James halted outside a two-storey yellow building. It had blue trim with matching awnings over the windows in which gifts were displayed on one side of the door, sweaters on the other. Shannon decided it was a mix between Isla Mullins' Irish Shop, and Eileen Carroll's Knitters Nook back in Emerald Bay.

'Shannon?'

Something in James's hesitancy made Shannon glance up at him curiously. 'What is it?'

'If I tell you something, do you promise not to laugh?'

Shannon thought he had a sheepish look about him, loitering there on the cobbles in his Gore-Tex gear. 'I'll do my very best not to. Although, from experience, it's usually hard not to when someone begins a conversation like that.' She waited with her hands thrust in the pockets of her puffa to hear what it was he'd say.

He flashed that hint of a dimple. 'I want to buy an Aran sweater.'

Shannon snorted.

'You promised not to laugh!' His mouth twitched.

'I said I'd do my best not to, and that wasn't a laugh, it was a snort. Is it a gift to take home for one of your brothers, like?'

'No. The Cabot brothers wouldn't appreciate the fine craftsmanship.'

'I hate to shatter the image you have of the fisherman's wives sitting in their stone cottages knitting the sweaters over on the Aran Islands, James, but I think they probably use machines to make them these days.'

'Very funny. They look so warm and...' He frowned, trying to find the right word.

'Snuggly?'

'That's it.'

'Sure, all that waterproof get-up you've on there would see you toasty on the side of Everest. So what do you need an Aran sweater for?'

James glanced over his wet weather gear. 'It's not the same. I keep getting sweater envy when I see all the Irish men in their thick wool. I want to buy an Aran sweater to wear on Christmas Day.'

Shannon was laughing properly now as she asked whether it was fisherman's cable-knit he was after or whether he'd prefer something with a reindeer on the front of it.

The light twinkling in his eyes told her he was enjoying stringing her along with his tale of sweater woe.

'So, will you help me choose one that doesn't make me look too much of an idiot?'

'Eejit,' she corrected. 'If you're going to wear an Aran sweater, you'll have to use the lingo. C'mon then.' She pushed open the door to the shop, which was doing a brisk trade in souvenirs and knitwear.

They found the corner dedicated to the fabled sweaters and began to see what was on offer.

'What size are you?'

'Medium, although if last night's meal was anything to go

by, I'll be in a large by the time Boxing Day rolls around,' James replied, only half-joking. 'What do you think of this one?' He held up a crew-necked, navy fisherman rib knit.

'Too plain.' Shannon said, rifling through a pile of greyish-green sweaters with the cable stitch that represented the fisherman's ropes. She fancied the shade was close to the in-between hue of his eyes, not that she'd tell him that. 'This colour would look well on you,' she said instead.

James, however, was pointing to a knitter's nightmare in cream on display. 'That looks traditional.'

'Sure, all you'd need to complete the look is a shepherd's crook.'

'Is that a no then?'

'Is the Pope Catholic?' Her eyes rested on the 'M' inside the label of the sweaters she'd been going through. 'Here, this is more the sorta thing.'

James took the sweater from her and held it up in front of him. 'Yes or no?'

'You should try it on,' Shannon confirmed. She'd been right about it. It matched his eyes.

She watched as he headed to the fitting rooms. A few others were also waiting to try on garments they'd slung over their arms, and Shannon picked up a pull-on hat in the exact hue of the sweater she'd just sent James off with. He'd be the only one on Christmas morning without a present to open, she thought, and without thinking about it, her feet carried her over to the counter.

She was stuffing the hat and the receipt in her shoulder bag, telling herself it had been a moment of madness because she didn't even know if he'd like the sweater, let alone a matching hat. A throat clearing saw her glance up to see James striking a pose. Shannon forgot about spending money she didn't have on a fella she wasn't interested in romantically, barely even knew for that matter, as she giggled at his silly hands-on-hips stance. If ever she decided to take a break from nursing, she could have a job as an Aran sweater consultant, she decided, giving herself a pat on the back. The colour was perfect, and the cable stitch gave him an air of ruggedness. He'd not be looking like he'd stepped off the set of a corny rom-com set in Ireland, not on her watch. 'It suits you, so it does. But is it snuggly?'

'It's very snuggly.'

'There you go then.'

James made for the counter, and Shannon told him she'd wait outside. There was a Spar shop across the way, and she nipped over to it, emerging in time to see James scanning the street for her. Then, waving out, she crossed back over.

'Here.' Shannon thrust a Lion bar at him. 'An Aran Sweater and a Lion chocolate bar. We'll make an Irishman of you yet.'

26

Shannon smiled, listening to James waxing lyrical about the Lion bar. Her hands were resting lightly on the steering wheel as BB thrummed along the beginning of the Sky Road. When James added that the gooey caramel, nougat and wafer biscuit wrapped in milk chocolate was an experience no visitor to Ireland should miss, she laughed. 'You should be on commission.'

He moved on to admire the views over the Atlantic, which today presented a wild scene of foam-topped waves. The sky and the sea blended into a leaden vista, and Shannon knew the panorama would be completely different on a settled summer's day. Come June, the sea would be a brilliant blue, the green countryside emerald-like and the sky full of cotton wool clouds. It was what she loved about her corner of the world. It was never the same from one day to the next. To her mind, on days like this, the moodiness only added to the majesty of Connemara.

Her headlights were on full beam, which was just as well, or she'd have missed Clifden Castle's gates, and after indicating, she parked a little way down from the arches.

'You can't go inside the castle, so it's all about the walk to it,' she informed James, who retrieved his guidebook from the glove box and looked up the site.

He found the page he was after. 'According to this, the castle was built in 1818 by James D'Arcy, the founder of Clifden.'

Shannon nodded. She'd known that at the back of her mind, probably having learned about the castle's history on a class trip. There was a memorial to him somewhere off the Sky Road too.

James had unbuckled his seat belt and was eager to get out of the car and snap a photo of the castle gates.

'It takes about fifteen minutes or so to walk to it.' Shannon said, following suit and locking BB behind her.

James held his phone up and, angling the camera for the best light, snapped a photo, then suggested Shannon go and stand in front of the gates.

'No, I'm only the tour guide, but I'll take one of you. It's your holiday.'

'But you're much prettier.'

Shannon laughed the compliment off, trying not to read anything into it as she held her hand out for his phone. He handed it to her reluctantly. 'You really should have your new sweater on for this,' she said, waiting as he went and stood to the side of the stone arches. Then at risk of sounding like her mam trying to organise a family photo, she ordered him to turn toward her a little more before clicking twice for good measure.

They set off down the unmade road framed on either side by wooden posts and barbed wire. A lone horse grazed on the hillside to their right, and on the left, waving grass gave way to an inlet with the body of water rippling as the wind gusted. 'Mind the ice,' James said, veering around a puddle that had a crunchy top. Their cheeks had reddened with the cold when the mist-shrouded castle came into their line of sight. Shannon might have seen it before but it still took her breath away.

James stopped and stared at it. 'Pinch me. That can't be real. It looks like a painting.' Then, 'You have got to get in this with me.' He held his phone up. 'Please. Otherwise, I'll go home with nothing to show my mom and brothers but pictures of me, castles and that random fellow American I met in Galway.'

Shannon conceded, moving to stand alongside him. She tried not to jump as he dropped an arm around her shoulder and pulled her close. She couldn't see the screen clearly as he held the phone out in front of them but hoped it wouldn't be a nostril shot as he said, 'Say cheese.'

'Cheese.' She broke away from him hastily. 'Let me see.' There was no way he'd be showing the photograph to anyone unless she approved it. She didn't want his family in Boston thinking he'd a tour guide showing him about the place with big nostrils.

It made her feel peculiar seeing herself and James looking for all the world like a couple enjoying a day's exploring. She swallowed hard and nodded her approval handing the phone back to him as though it had scalded her.

As they picked their way around the castle ruins, the baaing of the nearby sheep sounded mournful. The once-grand stone pile was crumbling in places and covered in rambling ivy. James whiled away a happy half hour capturing the D'Arcy's former home from every angle on his phone's camera. Shannon was frozen by the time they headed back to the car. Nor was she surprised to feel an icy drop followed by another landing on her head.

'It's snowing.' She laughed as James trudged alongside her, and by the time they reached the car, a hush had fallen over the countryside as the tiny ice crystals floated gently down.

'Should we turn back?' James asked, climbing in alongside Shannon as she turned the engine on, keen to warm BB up.

'Snow's not forecast, so it shouldn't get any heavier, and the road's gritted. If we get stuck, I can always phone Dad to come

and tow us out in his monster truck.' She smiled to show she
was kidding and turned the radio up to listen to the forecast just
in case as she reversed out and carried on down the scenic
route.

The windshield wipers swished the flurries away, and
Shannon pointed out the old coastguard station where the road
ahead split in two. 'That's been remodelled into holiday lets
now. It overlooks Clifden Bay.'

They took the upper Sky Road and listened in silence as the
news came on, waiting for the weather report. Snow flurries
were predicted, so Shannon drove on confidently to the viewing
point, listening to James tell her about the drifts in Boston, so
deep you couldn't see out the windows of his basement flat.
She'd be surprised if this flurry even settled.

The car park was deserted, and she chose a prime spot to
admire the rusted browns and green of the land as it undulated
into the fog. The surrounding counties, sea and islands were
barely visible through the mist, but James didn't seem disap-
pointed as he enthused, 'It's magical.'

It was, Shannon agreed as they sat in silence, until she broke
it by asking, 'Hungry?' She wondered how they'd go about
eating and drinking in such a confined space.

'Starving. Shall I plate up while you pour the tea?'

'Deal.'

Before he got out of the car, James suggested pushing the
seats back to give them some room to eat and began fumbling
around down the car door side for the lever. Shannon had
opened her mouth to say it was under his seat when he shot
back, finding himself gazing up at the ceiling. 'Wrong lever.' He
laughed as he returned to the upright position.

Not thinking, Shannon twisted in her seat and leaned over
to help him, immediately regretting her impulsiveness as her
hand brushed past his leg. He didn't appear to notice, and she
located the lever tucked under the seat, sending him scooting

backwards with a thank you. She busied herself sorting her seat, then opened the door.

The fresh air stinging her eyes and face was a welcome respite after the closeness in the front seats. BB glowed like a yellow beacon, she thought, stepping around to open the boot. Dad was right about the colour being visible. James appeared at her side and, sheltering under the hatch, opened the picnic basket, passing her two plastic mugs. Next, he fetched two plates and arranged the sandwiches and cake Nora had packed on them while Shannon poured steaming water from the thermos onto the two teabags she'd dropped into the mugs.

'I forgot the apples,' she realised.

'I don't think we're going to go hungry,' James said, holding up a plate filled with a fat sandwich, egg squishing out its side. A thick wedge of fruity buttered cake sat alongside it.

'You'd think Mam was feeding the five thousand,' Shannon muttered. 'Milk?' She held up the canister.

'And one,' James replied. She stirred in the milk and sugar then they began the delicate balancing manoeuvres of getting back inside the car.

They ate in hungry silence until James remarked how good the cake was.

'Barmbrack's a traditional Irish holiday cake.'

'My mom makes something similar, but she just calls it fruitcake.'

'Nan always makes brack this time of year, oh and you want to watch your teeth too because there's liable to be a coin buried in it. My sisters and I used to fight over it when we were younger.' Who was she kidding? It would still annoy her if one of the others wound up with it in their slice. She smiled, recalling what her nan used to recite when she pressed the surprises into the bottom of the cake. 'A coin for wealth. Ring: will marry within the year; a pea will not. A matchstick: unhappy marriage... um, bean: poverty... and there's one more...'

James paused with his cake halfway to his mouth, waiting.

'Got it! A thimble: single for life.'

His crooked grin rewarded her before he took a bite of the cake and mumbled something incoherent. Shannon watched, amused as he retrieved the offending item from his mouth.

'I warned you.'

He was busy brushing the crumbs off the object, and when he held it up, Shannon saw it wasn't a coin but rather a novelty ring. She'd be having words with Nan when she got home. It was too much of a coincidence, especially given Nan had taken to only putting a coin or two in the brack for tradition's sake these last few years. Remembering she was a nurse, she quickly asked, 'No broken teeth?' Not that she'd be much help if he did have any.

'Nope, all good.' He eyed the ring and then put it down on the dashboard. 'That will make my mom happy.' His laugh, though, sounded hollow.

Shannon studied his profile, but it was unreadable. 'Are you OK?'

He was staring straight ahead at the snowflakes dancing dizzily toward the windscreen. 'Most of the time I am, but now and again, it hits me afresh.' He turned toward her. 'My mom's sick. It's uterine cancer, and she's been fighting a good fight, but the prognosis isn't great.'

She could almost feel the weight of his words settling over them. 'James, I'm sorry.'

His smile was wan. 'People go through this stuff all the time, but you always think it won't touch your family.'

Shannon nodded. She'd heard the sentiment many times from family members of her palliative care patients.

'It's always been just me, my brothers and Mom. The Cabots against the world. It's been hard watching her go through treatment, but it's even harder to imagine life without her in it.'

Shannon knew from experience that when you didn't know what to say, the best thing to do was to listen, so she stayed silent. A question burned, though. Why was James in Ireland if his mother was sick? Given how close he clearly was to her, she'd have thought he'd want to spend every minute he could with her, especially what might be her last Christmas. But then again, she'd known patients whose family members couldn't cope with their illness and never came to see them. She also knew they regretted their choices after that person's passing too.

He read her mind. 'You're probably wondering why I'm here and not home with her.'

'I did wonder, but you don't have to tell me if you don't want to. It's none of my business.'

'No. I want to. I came to Ireland because of Mom. She wanted me to try and find out her birth history for her. She was adopted,' he explained. 'It was never a secret or anything like that. It just was.'

Shannon nodded as she connected the dots where Maeve and James were concerned.

'Mom never talked about it, so we didn't either, and I guess it would have felt disloyal to question where she came from, because we loved our gran and pops. She had a great upbringing, too, but when she got sick, I began to wonder. Mom used to call me Curious George when I was a kid. You know, after the monkey?' He looked at Shannon with a half-smile playing at the corner of his mouth.

She smiled back. 'I remember the book.'

'Anyway, I wanted to know whether she'd ever thought about finding out where she came from. All we knew was Gran and Pops had adopted her in Ireland when she was eight weeks old and brought her back to Boston with them.' James paused and sipped his tea. Shannon didn't move, wanting to hear the rest of his story.

'My brothers and I took turns being Mom's chemo buddy,

and if you've ever sat with someone while they're having treat-ment, you'll know there's not much else to do but talk. So, one afternoon I asked her about it. She told me she had thought about trying to find her birth mother, but after my dad died, she didn't have the money, time or energy to delve into it all. Ireland seemed a long way away, and it would be a difficult and prob-ably lengthy process, especially if her records were sealed. We were her priority. Then, she said, once we'd grown up, she felt she'd left it too long and wouldn't even know where to start looking.' The muscle in his jaw worked, and he stared straight ahead. 'And now that she was sick, it was too late. To find out where she came from would be a piece of the missing puzzle was how she worded it, but I think Mom was frightened to dig into her history because of what she might find out. We'd seen *Philomena* and heard the stories about the Magdalene laundries.'

They all had, and it made Shannon feel sad and ashamed that such places had existed in her country. The horrors and heartbreak endured by unmarried Irish girls and women sent to the Mother and Baby institutions were unimaginable.

'After talking to her, I felt this need to find out more. I kept thinking, what if her birth mom's been living in the hope her daughter will reach out to her? And how, when Mom passes, she won't even know.' He sighed. 'If I'm honest, I wanted to know for me too. I've always assumed I'll have chil-dren one day, and I'd like to be able to tell them about their biological history on my side. I told Mom all this, and she agreed to let me look into it for her. My brothers weren't so sure. They thought I was rocking the boat and that nothing good would come of it, but Mom was adamant I had her bless-ing. She gave me the paperwork Gran and Pops had passed on to her, and once I got the ball rolling, she was really enthused. So were my brothers. It's given her, all of us, something else to focus on.'

Her eyes were smarting with threatened tears, Shannon realised, batting them away with her lashes.

'The only information I had to go on initially was that the adoption took place at a Mother and Baby Home near Cork City. It was hopeless trying to get information over the telephone, so I decided to come here myself.' His sigh was heavy. 'I wish I could have brought her with me, but she's not well enough to travel. She'd have loved all this' – he gestured to the snowy vista – 'but I'm sending her pictures and updates every day, which she says make her feel like she's here with me.' He drained his mug. 'You've probably guessed the rest.'

'Maeve's your grandmother, your mother's birth mother.'

'Yeah, and I can't imagine how my phone call coming out of the blue as it did must have made her feel. I mean, I've read that the trauma of their time in those homes never leaves a lot of the women or girls sent to them. Some even suffer from PTSD years later.'

Shannon, too, had heard this. It was hard to imagine Ireland ever having been such a parochial society. Still, she'd listened to enough of her nan's and grandad's stories to know it had been a very different country once, and not that long ago.

'Understandably, Maeve was reluctant to meet me at first, but I told her I had all the documentation to prove I was who I said I was, and I left her my number. Then, a couple of days later, when what I'd told her had sunk in, she rang and asked me to come and see her.'

It explained so much, Shannon thought. She'd always felt there was something that haunted her friend. Once or twice she'd sensed Maeve was close to confiding in her, but she'd always clammed up.

'You've told your mam you've met her?'

'I rang her last night. She's got so many questions. I told Maeve I'd call in later this afternoon. I'm hoping she'll feel up to talking about the past. Will you come with me?' A lock of hair fell into his eyes as he turned to look at her, and Shannon would have liked to reach up to brush it away.

'Of course I will.' She held his gaze a moment too long before switching her attention to what was happening outside. 'Jaysus, that weather's closing in. I think we'd better head back.' So much for flurries, she thought, squinting into the gloom. It would be a long drive back to Emerald Bay.

27

The return journey was slow, and James, sensing Shannon's uneasiness at driving in such conditions, had offered to take over, but she knew the roads, and he didn't. The thing with snow, though, Shannon had thought, was everywhere looked the same when blanketed in white. Her hands had been white-knuckled on the steering wheel because the snowflakes spiralling toward them in the muted light were hypnotising. BB's windshield wipers were working overtime, and her frown was one of intense concentration on the road ahead. By the time she pulled over outside Maeve's cottage, a headache had started to nag.

'You did great, Shannon,' James said. He'd been silent for most of the trip, aware she didn't need any distraction. 'And thank you for today and this.' He looked toward the cottage from which light shone invitingly through the window.

Shannon reached into the back seat for her bag, unable to remember the last time she'd seen snow this heavy, and she didn't want him to see how much the drive had rattled her. It had been silly not to leave when the snow had begun falling in earnest, but she'd wanted to hear what James had to say.

Allowing her hair to fall across her face, she made herself busy looking for her phone. 'Ah, sure, it was no bother. You go on ahead if you like. Just leave the door off the latch, and I'll follow you in. I'd better call my dad to let him know we're back in Emerald Bay. He'll be worrying.' But then, locating her smartphone, saw she'd missed two calls already from him.

James left her to it, and she watched him trudge up the cottage path, his boots leaving prints in the fresh snow. He was a shadowy shape as he waited, and then the door swung open, illuminating him and Maeve briefly. As it closed, swallowing them up, Shannon counted rings, one, two, three—

'Shannon! It's Shannon, Nora.'

'We're grand, Dad. Don't be worrying. We're just calling in to see Maeve Doolin, and then we'll head home. I'd have turned back earlier if I'd known how heavy the snow would get. The forecast on the radio said "light flurries".'

'That's Irish weather for you. You think you're in for sun, but you get rain. Today we were supposed to get a dusting of the white stuff, and it turned into a complete white-out. I wouldn't be stopping too long, if I were you. It looks set to get heavier, and you don't want to wind up snowed in.'

Actually, Shannon thought a few seconds later as she disconnected the call, if Maeve had made a fresh batch of her shortbread, there were plenty worse places she could think of to be stranded at.

'All right, Dad, catch you later. Oh, and would you please ask one of the girls to feed Napoleon?'

'I will. And not too late, Shannon – are you listening?'

'I am. Bye, Dad.'

Shannon locked BB out of habit rather than necessity and made her way inside the cottage. 'It's only me,' she called out, expecting to find them in the kitchen.

Maeve was sitting in her chair, pink-cheeked from the warmth of the fire, but there was no sign of James.

'He's gone to fill the peat basket for me. You look pale, Shannon. Are you feeling poorly?'

How Maeve's son, Fergus, thought his poor mammy managed in the depths of winter, Shannon didn't know. She'd not seen any signs of life in the cottages on either side of Maeve's, and with her being a proud woman, it was doubtful she'd telephone anyone in the village, Shannon included, if she needed help. It was just as well they had called in this afternoon because it made her shudder to think of Maeve venturing outside to fill the peat basket. What if she slipped?

'I've got a headache, is all.' Shannon supposed she should start at the beginning. 'I was roped into being James's tour guide, and we just drove back from Clifden. I don't mind telling you, it was hairy.' Shannon moved toward the fire and rubbed her hands together in front of the dying flames, seeing it needed stoking.

'Who did the roping?'

'All of them conspired.'

Maeve smiled. She knew Shannon was talking about her family.

'And was it so bad?'

'Driving in that weather is not for the faint-hearted.'

'I wasn't talking about the driving, as well you know.'

'I know you weren't.' Shannon was saved from answering by the back door opening. They heard James stomping his feet on the doormat, and he appeared a moment later, bowed down with the weight of the full basket. He set it down fireside and tossed one of the peat bricks onto the fire. It hissed and spat in protest and then flamed into life, filling the room with its aromatic scent.

Maeve thanked James and made to get up from her seat, grimacing as she did so.

'What are you after, Maeve?' Shannon asked, gesturing for her to stay where she was.

'I was going to fetch us all a drop of the Sheridan. It's
Christmas, after all.' She sank back down gratefully.

'What's Sheridan?' James asked, moving to sit on the sofa.

'You don't know what Sheridan is?' Maeve asked, her eyes
twinkling. 'Well, now you're in for a treat, so you are. Shannon,
you'll find it in the cupboard over there, along with a tray of
glasses – and don't forget the ice.' She turned to James once
more. 'It'd be sacrilege to serve it without the ice.'

Shannon crossed the room to the sideboard and retrieved
the bottle filled with the dark chocolatey coffee and cream
liqueur and the glasses tray. She carried them over to the
worktop and found an ice tray on the freezer's top shelf. This
would go down well, she thought, pouring the liqueur over the
cubes of ice. The potent, sweet liqueur would settle her jangling
nerves, which weren't just down to the drive either, she realised.
There had been a connection between her and James as they'd
sat inside BB with a mystical Connemara spread out beneath
them. However, it was a connection she would not allow herself
to take further. She was too raw and not ready to risk her heart.

'Be generous, Shannon. No mean little pours.'

Shannon smiled and, not needing to be told twice, added
another splash before carrying the tray through to pass out.

'I'd like to make a toast.' Maeve raised her glass.

Shannon, who'd opted to kneel near the fire, raised hers too,
as did James, waiting expectantly.

'Lucky stars above you, Sunshine on your way, Many
friends to love you, Joy in work and play, Laughter to outweigh
each care, In your heart a song, And gladness waiting everywhere, All your whole life long.'

Shannon recognised the blessing for children, having heard
it at christenings. 'That's beautiful, Maeve.' And it was, but she
was unsure of its relevance.

'The last time I said those words out loud was to your
mother, James.' Maeve's eyes were glittering with unshed tears,

and her chin wobbled as she raised it to meet her grandson's gaze. 'The day she was born.'

There was no sound apart from the lapping flames. Shannon watched as a tear spilt forth, trekking slowly down Maeve's cheek. She wiped her own cheek with the back of her hand as James reached out for his grandmother's hand, and she took it, holding it tightly, drawing from him the strength she needed to tell her story.

28

'When I was fifteen, I went to work for the Leslie family up in the big house. You'd have seen it there, James. A big pile of stones perched on the hill with windows that look down on us all so.'

There was a bitterness to her words that was unlike Maeve, Shannon thought, her head tilted to one side. She could recall having counted Benmore House's windows once. There were twenty-eight of them, all facing the village. Now, sitting back on her haunches, waiting to hear what Maeve would reveal, she wondered if the tenant farmers had felt as though the house were sneering at them.

Benmore House had been in the Leslie family for as long as anyone could remember. Mrs Leslie Senior had been widowed before she was forty and had clung to the past and the old ways of them and us. Her three children growing up were never sighted in the village, and these days it was her eldest son, Matthew, and his younger Swedish wife with their two daughters who resided at Benmore.

Like his mother before him, Matthew Leslie and his family were rarely seen in the village, and when they did deign to visit any of the local shops, a Chinese whisper swept through Emerald Bay at the breaking news the Leslies had been sighted.

Shannon knew from word of mouth the daughters boarded at an exclusive school for girls in Dublin, and their parents split their time between Emerald Bay and Stockholm. Nobody was ever sure what Matthew Leslie did, but 'something or other in finance' was vaguely muttered when the question was raised.

She watched James nod in response to Maeve's question and take a tentative sip of his liqueur. His expression was composed, but there was a tremble in his hand as he raised his glass, signalling he was fearful of what Maeve would tell them. However, she could also see the determined set to Maeve's jaw and knew she needed to tell them her truth, no matter how harrowing it would be to hear.

'The times were hard and money scarce here in the late fifties. Then Mam got wind of a housemaid position up at Benmore House through her friend Mrs Eaton. She was employed as the Leslies' cook. With the chance of work, there was no question of me staying at school. It broke my heart leaving, so it did. I loved the learning, and I'd dreamed of breaking the mould where the women in our family were concerned. I wanted to go to university, because I had high hopes of studying the Arts, and there was talk of a possible scholarship for Trinity. Scholarships and studying were all well and good, but they wouldn't put food on the table was Mam's argument the day she marched me up to Benmore House.'

Shannon thought about how she and her sisters took their lives and the choices available to them for granted. It was hard to imagine having no say in your future. It was also hard to imagine worrying about there being enough to eat. She'd grown up in a home overflowing with equal measures of food, love, warmth and security. Her worries were trivial matters by comparison to past generations.

'The housekeeper, Mrs Mangan, was a dour old widow, and

she was in charge of the hiring. She fired off her questions about my suitability for the role, and Mam jumped in before I'd had a chance to open my mouth. It wasn't like it is now, where you're encouraged to speak up and say your piece.' Maeve shook her head. Her frown was angry. 'Do you know I hear people of my generation tutting about how bold the young wans are these days, and it makes my blood boil, so it does. 'Tis a good thing to have a voice and to be heard. 'Tis a good thing.'

James squeezed her hand, and her frown softened as she returned once more to the past.

'I was very sheltered, growing up in Emerald Bay. Sure, we all were. None of us children knew much of anything. But I soon accepted my lot and the work wasn't so bad. Mrs Mangan could sometimes be an auld wagon, but I didn't give her cause for complaint.' She gave them both a small smile. 'Mam used to roll her eyes when I'd come home at the end of the day bone tired from all the scrubbing and dubbing but full of stories about Benmore House. She thought I was getting notions above my station, which wouldn't do, but it was like stepping into another world each day. I enjoyed being privy to the beauty of all the Leslies' things, and I'd relieve the boredom of my chores by drifting off to the faraway places Mr Leslie had visited.'

Shannon pictured the young Maeve, wide-eyed and full of dreams that fate had already seen fit to quash.

'I remember there was a figurine in his study. I'd never seen the likes of it before. Wooden, it was, of a fierce, proud-looking black woman from the torso up.' She jabbed at her middle. 'The only statues and figures I'd seen before were religious deities, but she was naked and adorned with jewellery, for one thing. I called her Sheba – you know, after the Queen of Sheba – and then one day, Mr Leslie himself walked in on me having a one-sided conversation with her. I'd only caught glimpses of him up until then but thought him very distinguished. He was probably around the same age as my auld da, but oh so dapper. He put me in mind of Clark Gable. I was ever so flustered and expected a dressing-down as I stood there like I'd taken root, but none came. Instead, he looked amused as he sat down in the leather chair behind his desk and, after lighting a cigar, explained she was a princess, not a queen. A tribal princess from the Cameroon, no less. I couldn't study the Arts, but I learned about all the treasures he'd accumulated on his travels and the stories behind them because he took it upon himself to tutor me after that while I set about my duties. It made the long days much shorter.

'I'd been working for the family for nearly a year when everything changed. Mrs Leslie was away in London with the children, and Mr Leslie, for whatever reason, had stayed behind. He'd been drinking, and instead of speaking about Africa or Turkey as I did the dusting, he'd grown maudlin, telling me how cold his wife could be towards him. He'd never spoken to me about her before and it made me uncomfortable, but I continued with my work, not saying a word. He followed me from room to room, and then in the drawing room, he made advances. I tried to fend him off, but I'd no show, and I was too frightened to cry out. It was all over very quickly, and it only happened the once, but once was enough because I fell pregnant.'

'Oh, Maeve.' Shannon rocked forward on her knees and reached out for the little woman, who seemed to have shrunk into her seat with her words. Maeve patted her hand, and James squeezed the hand he was holding tighter.

'Now, now, you'll set me off, the pair of you, carrying on like so. It was all a long time ago but something like that, it never leaves you.' Her face reflected the pain of the past but her voice when she spoke was strong. 'Now let me finish. I need to finish.'

Shannon sat back down, and James withdrew his hand, letting Maeve compose herself with a sip of her liqueur. She closed her eyes, clasping her hands in her lap, and when she opened them, she was back in the 1950s once more.

'I told my mam what had happened, and she and Da went cap in hand to speak to the Leslies about it and to sort out what would happen next. Of course, Mr Leslie denied any wrongdoing, and Mrs Leslie implied I'd been overly friendly towards the young lad who helped the gardener. Mam, God rest her soul, was having none of it. The outcome was, in return for leaving my post quietly and Emerald Bay for the duration of my pregnancy, I was to be given a generous sum of money. I wanted nothing to do with them or their money, but Mam wasn't too proud to take it. It was enough to ensure our family didn't have to endure hardship again, and the rest was to be invested for my future. Blood money, it was.'

Maeve's nest egg, Shannon thought. So the rumours were true, but what a price she'd paid for it.

'Mam sent for the priest, and it all happened very quickly after that. I was packed off to a Mother and Baby Home in Cork.' Maeve's hands twisted and turned on her lap. 'It was a horror of a place, and when the door clanged shut behind you, you knew it was no home but rather a prison you'd been sent to. The nuns didn't allow us to use our real names, and I was told I was to be called Bridget for the duration of my stay. It's all true what's come to light. They used us as slave labour, scrubbing the never-ending corridors and clipping the lawn with scissors and the like. I only survived my time there because of my friend Hilary. She'd a little boy, Tom, born with a club foot. He was nearly four years old when I came to the home, and he lived in the nursery wing, along with the other children nobody wanted. She was allowed to see him once a week, but him being there meant she wouldn't leave the place. They were trapped with no place else to go. I don't know what happened to her or Tom.' A tear trickled down her cheek, but she was oblivious.

'The day your mam was born, James, I'd been working in

the kitchen, peeling endless sacks of potatoes when the pains started. I told the sister keeping an eye on us that I was in pain, and she told me it was God's way of punishing me and that I was to finish the work set to me. I could barely walk by the time she took me to the birthing room.'

Dear God, Shannon felt sick at the cruelty of it all, and as for James, he looked stricken.

'I called my baby daughter Hilary, after my friend. Her warmth in my arms made me forget about all that had come before. She was beautiful, and I never wanted to let her go, but the sister whisked her off to the nursery an hour later, and I was back at work within a few days. I was only allowed to see Hilary after that for the set breastfeeding times. Cows to the milk shed, we were.'

'I'm so sorry that happened to you.' James's voice cracked, and he held his head in his hands.

'Look at me now, James,' Maeve said sternly.

He raised his head slowly.

'It's not your fault. None of it is you or your mam's fault. It's not mine either. It took me the longest time to accept that.'

He gave a slight nod.

'The day the big car rolled up the driveway, I watched the smartly turned-out couple leave with a baby swaddled in a blanket, and I knew it was my Hilary they were after taking.'

'They were good people, my grandparents. It's important you know that, Maeve,' James urged as he sat forward in his seat.

'I'm glad. I wondered, and I hoped for that.'

'I don't think they had any idea what it was like for you and the other girls at the home. I can't imagine they'd have taken my mom if they had.'

'They were liars, those nuns, liars.' Maeve all but spat the words. 'They drummed it into us we were bad and left us girls feeling ashamed and lost, but sure they were the evil ones. I've had a long time to think about it all, James, and you can't change the past. But you have to let it go because, otherwise, they'd win, wouldn't they? And there was good, too, in what happened, because you and your brothers wouldn't be here if your mammy hadn't gone to America.'

'I hope there's some comfort in knowing she had a great upbringing, Maeve.'

She nodded slowly. 'There is.'

'Did Ivo know, Maeve?' Shannon asked, hoping she'd not had to shoulder all of what she'd told them alone.

She nodded again. 'I couldn't marry him with a secret that big between us. We tried to find out where Hilary had gone after we were wed. The nuns were a closed book, though, and there was no help to be found elsewhere because the State and the Church walked hand in hand.'

'Was it hard to stay here in Emerald Bay?' Shannon asked, unsure if she'd be able to if she were in Maeve's position. What must it have been like for her to have lived in the shadow of Benmore House?

Maeve thought for a moment before speaking. 'Mr Leslie had died while I was away. It was cancer. He faded quickly, but I hoped as he lay in his bed dying, he had time to think about what he'd done and to confess his sins. As for Mrs Leslie, she rarely showed her face in the village after he passed. But when I first came back to the bay, I did feel frightened each time I'd pass by the house. Then, after I met Ivo, the fear became anger, but it faded until eventually I felt nothing at all. The farm here had been in Ivo's family for generations, so there was never any question of us leaving. Ivo would say to me, if anyone should be ashamed of themselves, it was them lot up there. Eventually I decided he was right.'

'What was he like?' James asked.

Maeve's face lit up. 'He was a good man, my Ivo. We had our struggles over the years – it's hard to make a living off the land – but he wouldn't touch the Leslies' money. He said it was mine and Hilary's, no one else's.' Then her eyes flickered with sadness. 'We were only blessed with the one child in our marriage: Fergus.' She gestured to the photograph on the sideboard. 'He lives in London. He and his wife have two children.'

James got to his feet, crossing the room to study the picture.

'He takes after Ivo's mam with his colouring, and Ivo was the spit of his dad. It's funny the way the genes get divvied up.'

'It is,' James said softly, putting the photo carefully down.

'I'd like to see a photograph of her.' Maeve's voice was tremulous. 'If you have one with you. The only thing I was left with to remember her by was this.' She reached for the envelope on the side table next to the cross stitch she'd been working on. Inside it was a creased photograph, and Maeve stroked it for a moment before passing it to James.

'Hilary took it in the nursery with a camera one of the girls had sneaked in. She had more freedom than the rest of us, given how long she'd been there, and she got the film developed in the town. She gave the photograph to me not long after your mammy was taken away, and I've treasured it, so I have. You can't see, it being black and white, but her eyes were blue.'

James looked up from the picture. 'You're so young,' he said, and Shannon could hear the anguish at what Maeve had suffered in those three words.

She didn't appear to hear him as she said, 'Her eyes were the same blue as the Connemara sky in the sunshine. Are they still blue, James?'

His face softened. 'They are. They're just like yours. Here, look. Here...' He dug his phone out of his pocket and held it out for her to see. 'This is a recent picture of her.'

Maeve studied the picture of Hazel he'd pulled up with an expression of wonder.

Shannon was beginning to feel she was intruding on this deeply personal time and had made her mind up to slink off to the front room, not wanting to interrupt, when Maeve beckoned her over.

'Come and see my girl, Shannon. She's beautiful, so she is.'

'I'd love to see her, Maeve,' Shannon said, gently coming to kneel alongside her. Hazel Cabot was indeed beautiful, despite the weariness in her eyes that were the image of Maeve's.

'There's four of us boys,' James was saying. 'Brayden gets his brown eyes from our late dad, but Alex, Oliver and I all have the same in-between colour.'

'Sea glass,' Shannon murmured, looking up from the phone. 'Sorry?'

'The colour of your eyes is sea glass.'

'I've never been told that before, but I like it.'

'I want to hear about them all, James.' Maeve's gaze was greedy on him as he began to talk about his brothers and what life had been like for them growing up in Boston with a single mother. He flashed through photos on his phone with Maeve staring in disbelief at the grandsons she hadn't known existed, before passing the phone to Shannon. They were all different, yet you could tell they were brothers, she thought, smiling at a group shot of them with their arms draped around each other's shoulders, all laughing.

She handed the phone back to James. 'May I see that?' She gestured to the black-and-white snap resting on his lap, and he passed it to her while Maeve asked what his father had been like. She didn't hear a word as she soaked in the haunting image of a thin girl in ill-fitting clothes who was barely a woman. Her eyes were hollow, but her smile was proud, and in her arms, she cradled a baby whose face peeked from beneath a woollen hat. In the background, Shannon could see rows and rows of cots. Her chest tightened, thinking of all those lost babies and the women who would never get over the pain of the way they'd been treated. How could it have been allowed to happen? It was a question she knew was still waiting to be properly answered.

The lights flickered, and Shannon put the photograph back down on the side table, remembering her dad's words to her earlier. She got to her feet and padded through to the kitchen to peer outside. It was too dark now to see much, and they really should go, but they couldn't leave Maeve alone. She'd bring her back with them to stay at the pub, she decided, and was set to inform them both they needed to make tracks, but James was clearing his throat.

'There's something else I need to tell you about my mom, Maeve.'

Shannon didn't move from where she was standing in the doorway. This was not a moment she could interrupt. She wished things were different and that Maeve's story would have a happy ever after as James told his grandmother that the daughter she'd last seen from the grimy window of a Mother and Baby Home in Cork was terminally ill. He spoke of how his journey to Ireland was helping him, his brothers and Hazel, whom he knew desperately wanted to connect with her.

'Would you like to talk to her, Maeve?' He searched her face.

'I would.'

The emotions tugged, watching as Maeve, determined to be brave for her grandson, didn't take her eyes off James's phone. The sound of the app trying to connect with his mother in Boston filled the small kitchen.

Shannon exhaled, relieved and anxious as a woman's voice rang out.

'Hey Mom, I've someone here who'd like to say hello.'

He angled the phone so that Maeve could see, and for a moment, she appeared overwhelmed. Shannon was worried it was too much for her, but Maeve reached out and touched the screen.

'I've waited such a long time to see you again.'

29

The lights flickered once more as Maeve and James said their goodbyes to Hazel and promised to be in touch again tomorrow.

'She tires easy, Maeve,' James explained once the call had been disconnected.

'It's a lot for her to take in.' Maeve blew her nose for the umpteenth time. Her voice was beginning to grow hoarse from all the talking, tears and laughter as she and Hazel had tried to traverse the sixty-plus years since Maeve had last seen her. Shannon knew Maeve would need all the support she could get in the ensuing days, because once the euphoria of finding Hazel wore off, she'd have to face the reality she would soon lose her all over again.

It was a lot for all of them to take in, and Shannon's mind was fuzzy and her body leaden from the emotion of the afternoon. The pile of tissues on the side table was a small snow-white mountain from the amount of nose-blowing she and Maeve had done. She'd seen James furiously trying to keep his feelings in check, too, and had wanted to reach out to him. If she was overwhelmed by everything Maeve had told them, she could only imagine how he was feeling. Instead of offering comfort, though, she'd made sure the fire didn't die down and poured them each another nip of Sheridan, because sometimes it was a practical hand that was needed.

It had crossed her mind she should ring her dad once more, but she'd dismissed it. He knew where she and James were, and he'd only urge her to come home.

'Maeve,' Shannon said, now surprised as she saw the clock on the side table ticking into the evening, 'I think you should pack an overnight bag and come back to the pub with us tonight. I won't sleep a wink knowing you're here on your own in this weather.'

'That's kind of you to worry, Shannon, but I've weathered worse storms than this. I'll be grand. And besides, I'd never manage the stairs.' She fidgeted, suddenly anxious. 'Fergus! I need to talk to him. James, would you mind passing me the telephone?'

James glanced at Shannon and shrugged as he got up and retrieved the landline telephone from its charger.

Maeve tapped out her son's number, and Shannon could see she was apprehensive. Ringing him right that moment was a strike-while-the-iron-is-hot thing, because she might not have the courage to tell him he had a sister and nephews again. The news would come as a shock, and she hoped Fergus would go easy on his mam as she picked up the empty glasses and carried them over to the sink to give Maeve some privacy in which to talk to her son. James followed behind her.

'What an afternoon,' he said in a lowered voice, leaning against the worktop. 'I can't believe everything that's happened since I came to Ireland.' He ran a hand through his hair. 'It's been some journey.'

'I'll say it has.' Shannon ran the hot tap. 'I feel happy, sad. I can only imagine what it's like for you all,' she repeated her earlier thoughts.

James looked at her bemused. 'What do you mean happy-sad?'

'I mean, what happened to Maeve was terribly sad, but her having the peace of knowing where her baby went and that she had a good life with parents who loved her makes me happy. I always felt there was something. A sadness in her life. It must have haunted her, but now she's gained not just a daughter but four grandsons, and that's something to feel happy about. But then I'm sad that Hazel won't have much time to get to know her birth mam.' She was waffling, but her following sentence was concise. 'I'm sorry, James. It must be very hard for you.'

He kept his eyes focused on the back door, and she saw his Adam's apple bob as he swallowed hard before answering. 'Yeah. It's tough. But that sums up how I feel right now too. Happy-sad. It's a good analogy.' He stifled a yawn. 'Sorry.'

'Don't be. It's been a huge day.' The liqueur had eased the headache she'd been starting with earlier, but she was weary too and hungry. It was dinnertime.

'I'm tired, but I doubt I'll sleep tonight for thinking about everything Maeve told us. It's hard to understand the cruelty of those nuns and the nerve of the Leslie family treating her the way they did.'

Shannon agreed. 'I suppose there are some things that are inexplicable. What Maeve said, though, about not holding on to the past because that way they win – it made sense. You can't heal if you hold on to hate, but it must be hard to let go of it. You've done a good thing in finding Maeve, James.'

He smiled wearily as an eerie whistling whipped about the cottage's eaves.

Shannon peered out the kitchen window into the darkness. 'That wind's getting up. I'm worried about being snowed in.'

'You're right about not leaving Maeve here. I'll try and talk her around once she's made her call. If not, I'll stay the night.'

They both turned, hearing Maeve's agitated voice.

'Fecking Fergus,' Shannon muttered. 'I'm sorry to be the one to have to break it to you, James, but your uncle's an arse.'

'Shannon,' Maeve called tremulously. 'Fergus wants a word.'

Steeling herself, Shannon took the phone from Maeve, who was crumpled in her chair. 'Hello, Fergus, it's Shannon Kelly here,' she said, putting on the no-nonsense telephone voice she usually reserved for difficult patients. While Fergus might not be a patient, he was difficult.

'What's all this rubbish my mam's after spouting?' a voice barked down the line.

Shannon could picture him ballooning with indignation. 'I know it must be a shock, Fergus, but I can assure you it's not rubbish. Your mam has a daughter who was adopted and taken to America over sixty years ago. Her grandson, James, is with us now.'

'I can't believe you're taking this fly-by-nighter at his word – and you a nurse. You should be ashamed of yourself for letting him upset my mother.'

Shannon's nostrils flared, but before she could respond, he was spluttering on.

'It's her money he's after. He's taking advantage of an old woman who's not of sound mind.'

That was a step too far. 'Your mam's sharper than most,' Shannon snapped back. 'Listen, Fergus, would you like a word with James yourself? He can put your mind at ease that he is who he says he is.'

'Put him on, and I'll give him a piece of my mind, all right.'

But at that moment, the room was plunged into darkness, and the telephone line went dead.

30

James steered BB slowly through the darkened village, her lights sluicing through the whirling snow. Shannon, strapped into the front seat, had been happy to take him up on his offer to drive them back to the pub. She twisted in her seat so she could keep an eye on Maeve in the back of the car with her overnight bag on the seat to next to her. He chatted about the snow ploughs that ensured life in Boston carried on as usual in the winter months and how when a storm was coming, the roads were anti-iced by spraying a solution on them.

'Well, in Emerald Bay, the power goes out, life stops, and we all gather at the pub,' Shannon said, spying the candles flickering in the windows of the Shamrock Inn as a welcome sign.

Maeve, who'd been listening to the chatter, tutted her agreement. She hadn't taken much persuasion to let Shannon help her pack a bag for a few nights once they'd established it wasn't a fuse that had blown, but rather the power was out. Shannon had reassured her she wouldn't be putting anyone out by staying in the small room next to the family's living room so she wouldn't have to worry about the stairs.

James nosed BB into the spot she'd left early that morning,

and Shannon heaved a sigh of relief to be home safe and sound. She clambered out of the car and went around to the rear to drag Maeve's bag out, leaving James to help his grandmother from the car. Then, steering Maeve along, they navigated to the back door, pausing to stamp the snow from their feet on the mat. The conversational hum inside the warm and cosy pub was like bees around a hive as it washed over them. Hannah would have liked the analogy, Shannon thought.

It seemed like the entire village was here, although she couldn't spot Freya as she made out the faces of all the usual suspects dotted around the tables, supping and chatting by a mix of candle and firelight. The pub was a safe haven where everyone could gather. Mr and Mrs Sheedy were sitting alongside Mrs Tattersall and Mr Kenny. She wondered who'd picked Mr Kenny up, because he'd never have been able to get his motorised scooter along the snowy road. She still couldn't see Freya, and she made a mental note to text her. Her eyes flitted to Imogen, fully recovered and holding court by the fire like the queen returned from a crusade, while Ava cleared drinks at a nearby table. Before she could look to see where the rest of her family was, they were pinned in a beam of torchlight. Liam loomed large in front of them.

Shannon squinted into the light. 'Dad, you look as though you're about to burst into the seven dwarves' song. Is it off to the mines you go?'

'It was off to work the seven dwarves went, Shannon, and the head torch 'tis a handy tool for a publican in a power cut because it means my hands are free for pulling the pint.'

James laughed.

'Don't be encouraging him, James,' Nora said, her head peering around her husband's shoulder. 'Your dad's been like a cat on a hot tin roof, so he has, worrying about you.' She directed this at Shannon.

Shannon felt Maeve squeeze her arm. 'Ah, now that would

be my fault, Liam, Nora,' she piped up, looking from one to the other.

Liam waved his wife's comment away. 'Well, you're all here now, safe and sound. That's all that matters. Will you be stopping with us then, Maeve?'

'If it's no bother?'

'Of course, it's no bother, and I'm happy to hear it, so I am. There's always room at this inn.' Liam chuckled.

'I've a pot of stew warming on the Aga,' Nora announced. 'James, why don't you settle yourself and Maeve at that table just there to the left of the fire and warm yourselves up. Kitty will be glad of the diversion. Eileen Carroll's been bending her ear this last hour.'

Shannon knew her mam was curious about what she and James had been doing at Maeve's and would drill her as soon as the door to the kitchen closed behind them. But, as James had told her when she'd initially enquired about his relationship with Maeve, it wasn't her story to tell. It was up to Maeve whether she wished to share what had happened to her all those years ago and that James was her grandson. 'Just let me go and say hello to Napoleon first, Mam, and then I'll sort the dinner out.'

As her father returned to the bar, headlight illuminating the row of taps, she saw him elbow Grace aside as she attempted to pour a pint of Guinness. No sign of Hannah then, she thought, hoping she was making a fuss of Napoleon. He was happiest when he was on the receiving end of attention, and she'd been gone hours. So what difference would a few more minutes make? She made her way toward Imogen and perched on the arm of the chair her sister was sitting in.

'So, c'mon now and tell me what you're not saying about yer man, Nev,' Shannon whispered in Imogen's ear, butting in on her conversation.

Imogen flicked her hair back from her shoulders, her eyes glistening in the candlelight. 'I don't know what you mean.'

'I know there's something, Imo. Has he children? Is that it?'

For the briefest second, Shannon saw vulnerability flash across Imogen's face, but then her mouth settled in a flat line. 'No, for your information, he doesn't. You're imagining things. Haven't you got a cat to see to?'

Imogen was right, and Shannon could tell there'd be nothing forthcoming from her sister about whatever it was that wasn't so rosy where Nev was concerned. Giving up, Shannon got up and swept through from the pub to find the kitchen lit by a sputtering candle. She whipped out her phone, banging out a quick text to check Freya was all right on her own. She'd just pushed send when she heard a voice calling out upstairs. 'Here, Napoleon, kitty, kitty, kitty.'

'Hannah?' Shannon navigated to the bottom of the stairs as her sister appeared on the landing. She had a torch in hand.

'You're back.'

'I am.' It was too dark to read Hannah's expression.

'Feck, Shan, I've looked everywhere, but I can't find him.'

Shannon put a foot on the bottom stair. 'Have you checked under the beds and the wardrobes?'

'I've checked everywhere,' Hannah repeated. 'Well, everywhere, except James's room, obviously, but the door's closed anyway, so it's not as if he'll have got in there, and Imogen's all but bolted the door to our room shut. And I've made sure he wasn't stuck in any of the wardrobes.'

'What about down here? Could he have got shut in the cleaning cupboard?' Shannon cocked her ear, straining for tell-tale mewling but could hear nothing.

'Checked.'

Shannon felt a pinprick of fear. Napoleon liked attention, and Hannah was calling him. He'd come trotting out to see what all the fuss was about if he were here. 'When did you last see him?'

'He was curled up on your bed this afternoon when I ducked upstairs, and then I remember Ava putting his dinner out for him after you rang Dad.'

Shannon disappeared back into the kitchen, hearing Hannah thudding down the stairs. Napoleon's food hadn't been touched.

Hannah began flicking the torch into all the corners of the room.

'He's not here,' Shannon stated flatly, frightened to put her next sentence into words. 'He couldn't have got out. I told you all to be careful.'

'It's been mad here since the snow set in and then with the lights going out...' Hannah's voice trailed off. 'He could be hiding in the pub, Shan. C'mon. We'll check in there.'

Shannon heard her phone ping and checked it, relieved to see Freya was OK as she followed Hannah's lead.

'You haven't seen a small cat, have you?' Hannah spotlighted the first table, illuminating the Molloy family.

'No. Can't say we have.' Dermot looked to his wife, who shook her head. 'Kids, have you seen a cat about the place?'

Hannah flashed the light on the brood of Molloy children, who could have been arranged around the table in order of height, in time to see masticated crisps as they all chirped, 'No, Dad.'

'Silly question,' Dermot said to Shannon and Hannah. 'If they'd spotted a cat, he'd have been loved to death by now.'

Shannon gave a weak smile and trailed after Hannah. This was hopeless. 'Could I borrow your torch there, Carmel?' Shannon asked the owner of the Silver Spoon.

'Of course, you can. I haven't had a chance to catch up with you yet, Shannon. How're you?'

It wasn't the time for chit-chat. 'I'd be grand if I could find my cat, Carmel.'

'Your cat, you say?'

'Napoleon, he's a Persian. I don't suppose you've seen him?'

'No, I can't say I have, although you'd be forgiven for thinking that's a cat Mrs Rae's got wrapped around her neck. Jaysus wept, the fur stoles went out half a century ago. If yer woman were anywhere else in the country other than Emerald Bay, she'd get egged by the anti-fur brigade, so she would.'

Shannon shone the torch over in the direction Carmel was gesturing and received a wave from Father Seamus and Mrs Rae. A pair of glass eyes belonging to the fox draped over her shoulder gleamed back at her. She shuddered, grateful it wasn't Hannah shining her torch in that direction. She'd have had plenty to say about the stole. Then, thanking Carmel for the torch, she flashed it into the darkened corners of the pub with no luck.

'Shannon. Is everything OK?'

Shannon swung round. Realising she must look like a ghoul with the torch shining under her chin, she quickly dropped it to her side. 'I can't find Napoleon.'

'I'll help you look.'

'He's not in here, James. I can feel it. I'm going to check outside.' Shannon made to move away, but James put his hand on her forearm gently.

'I'll come with you.'

She nodded, and once they'd retrieved their jackets, they ventured outside. Shannon's boots sank into the snow, now settled like a thick shagpile carpet over the expanse of garden. She couldn't make out the fields beyond, and her insides twisted at the thought of her snuggly friend lost in the boggy beyond.

James, who'd hijacked a torch, suggested they check the bushes edging the beer garden. 'I'll go this way.'

Shannon nodded and shone her torch in the shrubbery as

he padded away. 'Napoleon,' she made kissing noises. 'Come on, boy. It's too cold for you out here. Come on, fella.' She checked the bushes he'd done his business in earlier, but there was no sign. Just then, James called out, 'Over here, Shannon.' Her heart began hammering as she forged her way across the lawn toward where James was now crouched down.

'What is it?'

James flashed the torch through the evergreen foliage, and Shannon saw two yellow eyes glowing.

'Napoleon!'

A mewling sounded, and then the little cat unfolded himself, and Shannon scooped him up, almost crying with relief as she opened her jacket and cuddled him to her chest. 'I was so worried about you.' The purring was overly loud, given the muffled silence of the snow.

'Thank you.' She smiled up at James in time to see his eyes had softened as he smiled back at her. This time when her heart began to thump, it was for an entirely different reason. He was going to kiss her. She wasn't being fanciful. Oh God, he was going to kiss her!

James reached out for her, his hands resting on her upper arms, his head dipped, and he pulled her gently toward him. Shannon nearly stumbled in her haste to break free by stepping backwards. 'No. James. I can't.' She shook her head, not waiting for a response, as she turned and hurried back to the pub. Her body was hot despite the freezing temperature.

ONE DAY UNTIL CHRISTMAS

May the songs of the season rise to greet you.
May the winter wind be always at your back.
May the frost shimmer soft upon your fields.
And, until we meet again,
May the love of God shine warm upon your
    home.

— *IRISH CHRISTMAS BLESSING*

31

The village of Emerald Bay awoke to a crystalline fairyland on the morning of Christmas Eve. The snow clouds had been blown away by the gusty wind whipping off the sea. In their wake, a blue sky had appeared, along with a winter's sun doing its valiant best to apologise for yesterday's storm. Children were making the most of the unexpected snow and had congregated in the park beside the church. Snowmen were being built, and snowballs lobbed. Meanwhile, in the kitchen of the Shamrock, Nora and Kitty were whipping up breakfast on the Aga's hotplates and singing the cooker's praises. There was a lot to be said for a coal-burning fire in a power cut, although it ran on gas these days.

It had been late when the last of the villagers, arms linked and singing 'Danny Boy', had trudged home in the snow. Shannon had successfully avoided the evening of storytelling, music and song by camping out upstairs with Napoleon. 'I can't possibly leave him, Mam,' had been her response to Nora trying to coax her downstairs to join in on the sing-song. Finally, her mam had given up, leaving her to write how grateful she was James had found her best boy in her journal. She'd snapped the notebook shut after that because she was not grateful he'd gone and made things awkward between them by trying to kiss her.

Despite the power still being down and the tired eyes around the Kelly table, there was an excited buzz of chatter about Christmas being one more sleep away.

Shannon swirled the remaining dregs of her teacup as she avoided eye contact with James, unaware Maeve's sharp blue eyes were on her. She decided that she would have to keep a low profile today. Although how she was going to manage that, given she would be dressed like an elf later on, she didn't know.

Grace asked their dad whether he'd be dressing up in his Father Christmas outfit to hand out sweets to the youngsters in the village, and Shannon tuned back in. A smile played on her lips at the memory of the first year he'd donned the fabled costume. Ava and Grace hadn't twigged it was their daddy behind the big beard doing the ho-ho-hoing. Then, the following year, when they'd discovered the truth, their noses had been put right out of joint over not having received special treatment where the handing out of the sweets quota was concerned.

'If he can get into it, Grace,' Nora said as she began dishing up the silken eggs scrambled with a knob of butter. 'And if he does manage to, he won't be needing any extra padding, that's for sure.'

'Excuse me, missus, I've lost a kilo, I'll have you know.' Liam sounded put out as he made them all laugh by visibly sucking his tummy in.

Kitty elbowed her daughter-in-law out the way. 'Here we are, son. You get this down you before you fade away.' Much to his wife's chagrin, a heaped plateful was placed in front of him.

Nora informed her daughters it was a blessing they'd got the big shop in before the snow had rendered heading over to Kilticaneel foolhardy yesterday through pursed lips. She'd all the veg in, and the turkey was thawing as she spoke. The sisters knew she'd be assigning tasks for the prep work needing to be done today before breakfast was finished. The Christmas dinner feast the Kellys presented each year to share with those in the village who'd otherwise spend the day on their own would be served up, power cut or no power cut.

Shannon thought it would be a relief to be kept busy, rubbing at eyes itchy from lack of sleep. The memory of James's expression in that split second before he'd attempted to kiss her in the snow last night had kept her awake into the small hours.

Ava, who'd stumbled into bed shortly after 1 a.m., had known something was up from the huffy sighs emanating from her older sister's side of the room. She'd pulled the pillow over her ears, determined to go to sleep until a particularly loud huff had seen her sit up and ask Shannon what the problem was. Of her sisters, Ava was the one who could keep a confidence. So Shannon whispered what had transpired between her and James across the darkened bedroom.

As Shannon pushed the eggs around her plate, she replayed the conversation.

'Move on from Julien, Shan. I know he hurt you, but that doesn't mean you should close yourself off to new possibilities. Stop analysing whatever it is that's going on between you and James, and go with it. It was a kiss he was after, not your hand in marriage. You've only known him a few days.'

Shannon had stared up at the ceiling in the dark, comforted by the warm weight curled up by her feet. She wondered when her baby sister had become this wise young woman lying in bed opposite her. She was right, she'd realised, but still, she'd said, 'I know that, Ava, but it's not that easy.'

Ava had given a huffy sigh herself then, and they'd dropped back into silence, nodding off at some point.

'Earth to Shannon.'

Shannon realised Imogen was speaking to her. 'Sorry?'

'I said pass the salt, please.' Imogen, who somehow managed

to look as though she'd stepped out of the pages of a fashion magazine while the rest of them wore the late night like a crumpled badge of honour, frowned at her sister. Then, her eyes flicked across the table to James, and she met Hannah's knowing gaze with a nod of understanding.

Shannon was oblivious to the unspoken dialogue between the sisters as she dutifully passed the condiment before tapping her teacup with her spoon. However, she had something important she needed to make clear.

Everybody stopped eating and looked toward her in surprise.

'Do we need to charge our teacups?' Liam asked.

Shannon ignored him, clearing her throat. 'Um, as you know, Napoleon got out last night, and if James hadn't found him, he could have frozen to death out there.' She waved her spoon toward the door studiously, avoiding eye contact with James. 'Napoleon is an indoor cat. So please be careful when heading outside that he doesn't try and sneak out with you.'

There was debate around the table as to who had let the cat escape in the first place, with accusatory fingers pointed at the obvious suspect, Imogen, who denied any deliberate wrongdoing. There was murmuring about an indoor cat being a ridiculous state of affairs. And Shannon pinpointed the source of dissent. Her dad. She shut him down with a fierce stare. 'Just promise me you'll keep an eye out.'

'All right, all right,' Liam consented, not wishing to upset his daughter. 'But I'm telling you, Honey, that cat of yours gives me the willies, so he does. I can feel his eyes boring into me every time my back's turned, and when I look back over my shoulder, there he is with his squashed-in little face peeping around the doorway. Sure, lookit! There he is now.' Liam had swivelled in his seat to where Napoleon was lurking in the doorway to the kitchen.

'Dad, you're paranoid. He's curious, that's all. Hello, my

lovely boy.' Shannon tried to entice him over, but he wasn't moving. She could sense James had raised a questioning brow at her dad's use of her pet name, Honey, but she'd not be elaborating.

'He's probably keen to bond with another male, 'tis all, Dad,' Hannah offered. 'How're things, Napoleon?'

'And sure, you've both got an impressive head of hair on you.' Grace sniggered. 'It's a kindred spirit he sees in you.'

She had a point, Shannon thought. Both her dad and Napoleon were looking exceptionally wild and woolly today. She'd have to give him a good comb-through later – Napoleon, that was.

Liam spluttered indignation at the comparison, smoothing his hair down with his hand.

'Your father's sandy,' Nora appeased.

'Like a younger Robert Redford,' Liam announced.

'Whereas Napoleon's more Bryan Adams with highlights, Grace. I fail to see any similarity between them, apart from around the middle. You're feeding that cat too much, Shannon,' Nora said, fixing Kitty in her line of sight.

'My son's got the Kelly family nose on him. He looks nothing like Napoleon there.'

Maeve and James tried to keep track of the banter around the table.

'That reminds me. You owe me for another packet of anti-histamines, Shannon,' Imogen tossed at her sister. 'I had to stock up because Heneghan's will be closed over Christmas.'

'Well, I think he's gorgeous,' Ava stated loyally, receiving a grateful smile from her eldest sister. 'Napoleon, I mean.'

'Thanks a million,' Liam muttered.

Napoleon raised his furry face haughtily before stalking off, and normal conversation resumed. Shannon, who wasn't hungry, forced the rest of her food down. This loss of appetite was most unlike her, she thought, grateful for the mouthful of tea to wash it down with. The rest of the chatter flowed over her until she heard Nora asking James what he'd planned for the day, given it wouldn't be wise to go far until they'd listened to an update as to the state of the roads.

'I've some calls home to be making,' he said, smiling at Maeve. The exchange was largely unnoticed, and if anyone was curious to know what it was between the pair of them, then they kept it to themselves. Nora's attention was diverted away from their guests by the clatter of knives and forks being put down on plates. She wanted to allocate the chores that needed doing before her girls could disappear upstairs and began reeling off who was in charge of peeling what.

'Ah, Mam, can't I make the stuffing for a change?' Imogen whined. 'The potato peeling's the worst.'

'And I could make the mulled wine,' Grace offered, optimistic about avoiding trimming the Brussel sprouts.

Shannon, told she was on parsnips, excused herself, leaving them to bicker it out.

By 11 a.m., the Christmas tree in the square was suddenly illuminated once more. Electric lights lit the candlelit spaces in the cottages scattered about the village while televisions and radios sprang into life. It was a Christmas miracle.

By 11.15 a.m., Shannon was fed up with staring at the four walls of her bedroom. Opening the door just a crack, she poked her head out. Satisfied she could make it downstairs without being collared by either James or her siblings, she crept down to the kitchen. It was deserted. She'd heard her sisters fleeing not long after breakfast with cries of 'I'll do it later!' Shannon surmised they'd all headed out to catch up with old school pals in the area who'd also returned home for Christmas. Mam and Dad would be manning the bar, and she'd hazard a guess that

Kitty was sipping tea at the Silver Spoon with one of her crafting cohorts.

It was just as well everybody was otherwise engaged, because she wasn't in the mood for chit-chat. Tilting her head to one side, she listened out but couldn't hear anyone talking in the living room. So perhaps James and Maeve were in the pub too. Either way, it was a reprieve from the effort of not looking directly at James when he was speaking, and she was grateful for it.

Her mam had left the veg to be peeled in a box on the table. The pile of buckets stacked by the sink were to be filled with icy water and a squeeze of lemon to stop the peeled vegetables from browning. She dutifully filled a bucket and then scraped the parsnips over the sink. Her mind drifted off to the elf outfit she would don later, and she decided, once she'd got through this lot, she would change into her costume and call in on Freya. If the roads weren't open and she couldn't get to Westport, her friend would need a laugh. And, if Freya was going ahead with her travel plans, then Shannon could do with a giggle at her own expense. An unfamiliar plunking sound saw her spin round to see the source of the noise was Maeve's walking stick on the lino.

'I thought I heard someone in here.'

'I thought you and James were in the pub. Would you like to keep me company while I peel this lot?' She angled the vegetable peeler toward the bag of parsnips. 'I could make you a cup of tea.'

'No. I'm awash with the stuff, so I am, Shannon, and I'll not sit there with idle hands. Fetch me another peeler, and we'll make short work of that lot.'

'Ah, now I can't be having that, not when you're a guest under our roof, Maeve. Mam would go mad if she thought I'd set you to work.' Shannon smiled.

'Nonsense. I'm rattling about surplus to requirements while

James is upstairs talking to his brothers. He's trying to organise one of those Zoom things. You know where you can all talk to one another over the computer. I'm at sixes and sevens with it all, Shannon, I don't mind telling you. What if the rest of the boys think I'm a terrible woman for giving their mammy up? And the thought of Hazel so poorly is breaking my heart. Then there's Fergus...' Her voice trembled, and she leaned heavily on her stick.

'It will be all right, Maeve, you'll see. Now come on, sit down, and I'll fetch you that peeler.'

Maeve sank into the seat she'd occupied over breakfast, and Shannon set her up with a pile of the root vegetables, a peeler and a bowl for the skins. She left her to roll up her sleeves as she set to work once again up at the sink.

'Have you spoken to Fergus this morning, Maeve?'

'No. I thought it best to leave it until later on Christmas Day to let it sink in.'

Shannon could hear the uncertainty in her voice. She hoped for Maeve's sake that once Fergus had had a chance to mull over the news that he was no longer an only child, he'd be curious to find out more about his American family. 'Fair play. And James's brothers won't hate you, Maeve. They'll understand it was a different time. Besides, they wouldn't be here if things hadn't worked out the way they had.'

'That's true enough. But what of Hazel, Shannon? What am I going to do? It's not the natural order of things.' Maeve's voice faltered.

Shannon couldn't fathom the pain Maeve must be feeling after discovering that she only had a short time to get to know her daughter. The parsnips could wait, and she wiped her hands dry abandoning her chore. There weren't the right words, and all she could do was offer comfort. 'Maeve, you're right. It's not the natural order, and no mother should have to say goodbye to a child, and to have to do so twice is unthinkable, but you're doing the only thing you can do by giving your daughter the answers she needs.' She wrapped her arms around her friend's frail frame.

Maeve leaned into Shannon for a moment before gently pushing her away. 'C'mon now, sentiment won't peel these parsnips.'

They settled back into their work in silence, apart from the mewling Napoleon, who'd padded downstairs to see what was happening.

'Oh, it's you, is it?' Maeve said. 'I hope you know you caused Shannon there a lot of bother last night.'

Shannon turned in time to see Napoleon leap onto Maeve's lap, and she smiled, watching him lap up the fuss she was giving him before turning her attention back to the parsnip in her hand.

'James and I were talking earlier,' Maeve dropped in conversationally.

'Oh yes?' Shannon, grateful she had her back to the sink, fished the vegetable she'd dropped at the mention of James's name out of the pile of peelings.

'Yes. He was telling me about the woman he thought he would marry.'

'Feck!'

'What was that?'

'Sorry, Maeve. I nicked myself, that's all.' Shannon held her thumb where she'd scraped it with the blade to her mouth for a moment.

'Are you sure you're all right?'

'Grand. I'm grand.' She'd live, but she was not grand. Maeve's words had thrown her into a spin, but still, she wanted to hear the rest of what she had to say.

'Well, his fiancée broke their engagement off not long after Hazel underwent her first chemotherapy session. Her reason was James wasn't there for her. Billie, her name was. So the poor lad went through a terrible time with his mammy, and this selfish mare complains he's not there for her! I could tell he was shattered when it all happened, but reading between the lines, he had a lucky escape, if you ask me. Oh yes, it was a lucky escape he's after having. A bit like you with that French fella of yours, really.'

Shannon turned around, sure there was a subtext to what Maeve was saying, but she was the picture of innocence as she blithely carried on petting Napoleon.

32

Shannon tiptoed out of the room Imogen was now sharing with Grace and Hannah, closing the door behind her before Napoleon could slip in. He was desperate to enter the bedroom purely because it was out of bounds. When Shannon had ventured upstairs earlier, having finished the parsnips, she'd found him outside her sisters' door, scrabbling at the carpet as though trying to dig a tunnel through to the other side. Mam would go mad if she caught him at it, and picking him up, she carried him back to her room, hoping he'd settle down for a snooze while she was out.

'I'm on a mission, Napoleon, and I'm beginning to feel I missed my calling with all this skulking about I'm after doing. I'd have made a superb MI5 operative, so I would.' She deposited him at the foot of her bed. 'Stay there and be good. I'm off to see Freya, and the reason I look like a flasher is because I don't want anyone catching me in the stupid fecking elf outfit I'm wearing underneath this coat.' She tickled behind his ears. 'I don't want Imogen catching me in her coat either. She's a slave to fashion, your Aunty Imo, because this get-up might be on trend but I feel like poor old Paddy in his mac.'

The little cat jumped off the bed and trotted out the door. 'And you don't give a toss that I'm to be humiliated in front of the whole village later, do you?' She followed behind him, watching as Napoleon took up his pew outside her sisters' room, eyeballing the door as though he could open it with mind-power. Shannon sighed and told him to leave the carpet alone if he knew what was good for him before taking to the stairs. A door opened overhead, and she froze midway down the stairs.

'Shannon, have you got a minute?'

It was James. Her hand resting on the rail, she didn't turn to face him as she called back, 'Um, no, sorry. In a rush. Catch you later.' She shot down the remaining stairs, only pausing to catch her breath once she'd made it safely outside.

'You're behaving like a child, so you are, Shannon Kelly,' she muttered into the crisp air, giving the poor fella the cold shoulder. It was too late now, though. She could hardly go back inside and ask him what he was after. 'Ah, Grandad, what's got into me?' Her eyes roamed the sky overhead, seeking one of his colourful signs, but there were none to be seen. Shoving her hands in the pockets of Imogen's coat, she set off intending to call in at Heneghan's for an update on the great perfume heist.

The road was clear as she crossed to the other side, but the pavements were still thick with snow, and people were out and about. In the distance, Shannon could hear children squealing. She smiled, thinking a snow fight was taking place on the reserve beside the church. A cluster of tourists captured the postcard prettiness of Main Street with their phones. The roads must be open then, Shannon deduced.

She was glad of her boots as she trudged along, berating herself for not brazening it out with James. All he'd done was try to kiss her. It wasn't a big deal, and Ava was right: she was overanalysing it. The next time she saw him, she'd act as if nothing had happened. They were just two people who'd shared a highly emotional couple of days and carried the

weighty baggage of having been left behind in their relation-
ships. She hadn't gone far at all when her father's hearty voice
boomed behind her, causing her to jump.

'Where are you off to, Shannon Kelly?'

She spun around, her hand on her chest.

'Jaysus, Dad! Where did you spring from?'

'Well, there you go. Now you know what it's like with that
cat always sneaking up behind me. And to answer your question: the Bus Stop.' He rattled the newspaper he'd tucked under
his arm. 'Some of us still prefer to read our news in print. I want
to see how the rest of the country is faring after the wild
weather. And, if you were to read the paper now and again,
Shannon, you'd know all about the scandal that's broken here in
Emerald Bay.'

Shannon's ears pricked up at the juicy word. 'What
scandal?'

He waved the paper under her nose. 'Page two.' Then he
made a show of flapping it open to the article he was talking
about.

Shannon's skimmed over the news story incredulously, a
smile twitching as she read:

Emerald Bay Youth Left Red-Faced
By Martin Deveraux

*Kyle Hogan, a fifteen-year-old youth from Emerald Bay, was
left red-faced when his girlfriend inadvertently handed him in
to the very business he'd shoplifted her birthday gift from.*

*Ella Final, who turned fifteen on 23 December, also from
Emerald Bay, took the large bottle of perfume she'd received
from Hogan back to Heneghan's Pharmacy, Main Street,
Emerald Bay, to ask for a replacement based on the fragrance
having no scent. Her boyfriend no longer had the receipt, Ms
Finlan informed pharmacy assistant Nuala McCarthy, who*

instantly recognised the perfume bottle as being the display-only bottle stolen from the pharmacy's front window a day earlier.

'The bottle was filled with coloured water,' Ms McCarthy informed Sergeant Badger of the Kilticaneel Garda.

Heneghan's Pharmacy proprietor Niall Heneghan opted not to press formal charges against the teen. Instead, in a private arrangement made with Kyle Hogan's parents, the teenager is to donate his savings to the Emerald Bay community park upgrade, where he will also be in charge of mowing the lawns every Saturday for the next year.

Shannon shook her head, recalling how she'd seen Kyle and Ella with their friends here on Main Street just the other day. She'd thought the backpack Kyle had been toting looked heavy and wondered if he'd had the faux perfume stashed in it then. Ah well, he'd been named and shamed and the punishment fit the crime. No doubt young Ella had given him the flick too. She folded the newspaper and handed it back. Her dad's gaze travelled from her green tights to the belted red coat, then he looked beyond her and shook his head.

'Sure, you and Paddy are peas in a pod today. Twinning, are you?'

Shannon tracked his gaze to where Paddy was swaying outside Heneghan's. She caught a few words and realised he was serenading Bridget in the window. He also had on a pair of green trousers protruding from the bottom of his mac, the only point of difference being Paddy's mac was muddy brown and Shannon's fire engine red. With a scowl at her dad for thinking he was a comedian, she told him she'd see him later at the carolling and then got on her way. At least she wouldn't be the only one dressed like an eejit come four o'clock.

33

Shannon cheerily greeted Paddy as she drew level with the pharmacy. He was in full song now. His joy at the return of Bridget's perfume was evident. However, curiosity got the better of her, and she pushed open the door to Heneghan's. 'I hear the mystery of the perfume bottle theft has been solved, Nuala,' she said, closing the door swiftly on Paddy's caterwauling. 'Dad's after showing me the newspaper just now.'

Nuala glanced up from where she was curling a ribbon with a scissor blade on a gift-wrapped package for Nessie Doyle. 'Don't I know it.' She inclined her head to the window where Paddy was swaying about. 'He's been at it all morning. Sergeant Badger's after suggesting we put a security camera in.'

Niall Heneghan looked up from the dispensary. 'It'll be a sad day when we have to resort to that. Sure, Kyle Hogan's learned his lesson, and an example's been made of him in the local rag. It will be a long time before he lives this latest escapade of his down. I'm sure that will be deterrent enough.'

Shannon agreed, then, remembering her manners, greeted her old nemesis, Emerald Bay's hairdresser. 'How're you,

Nessie? Merry Christmas.' *Good God, what had she done to her hair? The last time she'd seen her, it was blonde, but she'd gone for choppy red layers, making her look like she'd had a nasty fight with the lawnmower.*

'Merry Christmas to you, Shannon. I've been run off my feet, so I have. I only popped out of the salon to pick up a gift for young Tara to take home with her today. Of course, she's already had her Christmas bonus, but it's always nice to have something to open, isn't it?'

Nessie didn't wait to hear Shannon's response as she stepped toward her. 'Jaysus, yer spilt ends are hurting my eyes there. It's a trim you're needing, Shannon Kelly, and you're in luck because my three o'clock has just been cancelled.'

Over my dead body will you come near my hair with a pair of scissors ever again, Shannon thought. Smiling sweetly, she replied, 'Ah no. Thanks a million, but I've somewhere to be this afternoon, Nessie.'

Nessie made a clucking sound, and with the red hair, her beaklike nose and jewel-bright, teal sweater with a ruffled collar, she reminded Shannon of a bossy rooster. 'Well, be sure to book in early come the new year. We'll be busy so, but I pride myself on always managing to slot those with hair emergencies, Shannon.'

'I will, Nessie.' *I will not.*

'Will we be seeing you later at the carolling?' Nuala asked. 'Niall, don't forget Father Christmas will be giving the sweeties out for the children at three thirty.'

Niall gave Nuala a grateful smile, and Shannon watched as she basked in it.

'Sure, what would I do without you, Nuala?' He tipped the pills he'd been counting into a container. 'I'll have Mrs Mooney bring them down to the square.' He addressed Nessie and Shannon. 'It's a three-thirty closing for us today and all the busi-

nesses on Main Street. I don't think we've seen the last of the
snow either.'

'It's a white Christmas we're in for, either way,' Nessie
agreed. 'That dumping out there won't melt in a hurry.'

'We can go straight from here for the carol singing, Niall,'
Nuala suggested.

Niall nodded his agreement and went back to dispensing
tablets for the villagers of Emerald Bay.

They were like a married couple, Shannon thought, fighting
a strong urge to march into the dispensary there and then to tell
Niall to take his blinkers off to see what was under his nose. It
was high time the pharmacist paid as much attention to his
right-hand woman as he did the pills he was so intent on counting, she thought. Then, remembering Nuala's question, she
replied, 'I'll be there with bells on. Or a pom-pom at the very
least,' she added cryptically, thinking of the hat she was to wear.

'Help yourself to a spray there, Shannon,' Nuala said,
dipping her head toward the tester bottle of Seduce Me on the
counter before giving the ribbon one last upward stroke with
the scissors.

'I don't mind if I do. Thanks, Nuala.' She gave herself a
generous squirt. Then, with a 'catch you later,' she left Nessie
coughing in a haze of perfume drops, pausing only to say a
quick hello to the sultry, silent Bridget at Paddy's insistence.

Then, as she crossed over the road, she was in time to see
Enda ambling toward her.

'Good afternoon there, young Grace. I'm on my way to see
if I can get a smile from Kitty today. How's that ferret of yours?'

'It's Shannon, Enda. And Napoleon's a cat. He's very well,
thank you. Nan's out at the moment. I've a feeling she's at the
Silver Spoon.' She smiled, knowing Nan wouldn't thank her for
divulging her whereabouts, but it was payback for putting her
name forward to Isla Mullins for this year's carolling.

Raising a hand to shade her eyes against the snowy glare,

she scanned the path ahead to where Shep was stationed outside Dermot Molloy's Quality Meats attacking something.

Enda glanced back over his shoulder. 'That's one of Dermot's finest pork sausages he's after snaffling, thanks to Mrs Riordan. I've a juicy bone in here for him come Christmas morning.' He raised the bag he was toting. 'I might just call in and say hello to Kitty.'

Shannon grinned, and they set off companionably, given they were headed in the same direction. 'And we'll be seeing you for your Christmas dinner, Enda?'

'I'm looking forward to it, Hannah. You're smelling lovely today, if you don't mind me saying.'

Shannon didn't bother correcting him this time as she made him blush by telling him the perfume was Seduce Me. As they drew level with the cafe, she saw she'd been right. Her nan was busy chatting to the group of women she was sitting with and didn't see Shannon as she said cheerio to Enda. Today the millionaire's shortbread, iced ginger snaps and wedges of apple and tea cake arranged in the cabinet didn't call to her. Her appetite was definitely on the blink, and she didn't linger to see her nan's expression when Enda waltzed into the cafe.

A few last-minute Christmas shoppers were browsing the shelves of Quigley's Quill, and as she drew level with the Knitters Nook, Shannon bowed her head but risked a sidewise glance in the window. A relieved exhale whistled through her teeth. Eileen Carroll had her back to her, in conversation with a customer. She was nearly home and dry, the sign to Mermaids in her line of sight, when Isla burst out of her Irish shop. Today she'd donned a Christmas hat and a *Kiss Me I'm Irish* sweater, and twin miniature reindeer dangled from her ears. Shannon wondered if anyone had obliged where the sweater was concerned.

'I thought it was you under that coat, there. Don't forget the

Emerald Bay Elves congregate by the big tree at four o'clock sharp, Shannon.'

'I haven't forgotten, Isla. I'm all prepared, see.' She kicked up a green leg. 'And I have the hat in my bag here.'

'Excuse me, are the snow globes on sale?' a guttural accent called from inside the shop.

'I thought we'd be dead quiet today after yesterday's snow, but there's a shuttle bus full of Germans on the loose in the village.' Isla excused herself with a reminder for Shannon not to be late.

Shannon rolled her eyes as the door to the shop banged shut and, taking the last few steps to Mermaids, she paused to peer in the window to see how busy Freya was. She had no plans of flashing her elf outfit at German tourists, but instead of European travellers, she saw an American in deep conversation with her friend. Her mouth parted slightly, and she frowned, wrong-footed by seeing him there. So much for avoiding him. He must have jogged up the road to have got here so fast.

In his hand was a cardboard tube, and she guessed he'd called in to collect the painting she'd coveted of Kilticaneel Castle. She thought they were looking very secret squirrel, watching the exchange through the pane of glass, wondering what they were discussing.

Freya spotted her in the window first, and James turned to see what had caught Freya's attention. Shannon registered their startled and then amused expressions, realising what she must look like loitering outside the shop in Imogen's flasher coat. She hastily moved toward the door, opening it to go inside and face the music.

'What were you up to, you eejit?' Freya asked, laughter dancing in her eyes as, toying with the silver pendant around her neck, she checked out Shannon's strange attire. 'You smell nice.'

'Thanks, it's um, never mind.' She couldn't bring herself to say the perfume was called Seduce Me while wearing what was likely Imogen's booty-call coat.

James nodded a greeting, and Shannon, remembering how she'd informed him she couldn't stop when he'd asked her if she had a minute earlier, felt her cheeks go pink.

'I, um, I wasn't sure if you were open or not, so I was looking for signs of life.'

'Did you not see the sign spinning around with "open" in capital letters?'

If James hadn't been standing there listening to their conversation, she'd have told her friend to feck off away with herself. She was feeling ridiculous enough in her coat and tights as it was.

'I came to pick up the painting I bought,' James said. 'And I bought my mom a hand-crafted Claddagh ring. You've a talented friend.' He barely looked at Shannon as he said this. 'Thanks, Freya.'

Shannon could have sworn Freya winked at him as she replied, '*Go n-éirí leat.*'

Freya might be fluent in Irish, but Shannon remembered enough of what she'd learned at school to wonder why she'd just wished him good luck.

The two women held their hands up in goodbye, and then as he grasped the door handle, Shannon blurted, 'James?'

'Yeah?'

'I was talking to Maeve earlier, and she's scared, you know, how your brothers will take to her. I think the phone call with Fergus upset her too. I just thought you should know.'

James's expression softened. 'I'm heading back to the pub now to hook up online with them, and it's OK, Shannon. I'll be right there next to her. My brothers can't wait to meet her, and they might be idiots at times, but they're not assholes.'

'Sorry. I worry about her, that's all. Maeve comes across as a strong woman, and she's had to be with all she's gone through in her past, but it's not been that long since she lost Ivo.'

'I promise I'll look after her.' James held her gaze for a moment, giving her his lopsided smile in reassurance. Then, opening the door, he was gone.

'Jaysus wept, the tension between the pair of you. Your pupils have dilated to twice their size.' Freya's messy blue bun wobbled as she shook her head. 'That was like watching one of those reality TV shows where you scream at the television, "G'won get it on, why don't you!"'

Shannon eyed her friend. 'Hannah's been in your ear. And don't you dare mention baboons.'

'I wouldn't dream of it. Shan?'

'What?'

'Why are you dressed like a stripper in green tights? I mean, that coat. What've you got underneath it? Something, I hope.'

Shannon had nearly forgotten what she'd come here to do. 'It's Imo's, and of course I do. I called in to see if you're still going to Westport.'

Freya's face lit up. 'The roads are open, so I'll be going.'

Shannon pulled her friend into an embrace. 'Have a grand Christmas.'

'I will. I can't wait to see Oisin. It feels like forever since I last saw him. As for you, make sure you eat and drink way too much.'

'It's a Kelly family Christmas, isn't it.' Shannon smiled at her friend. 'Oh, and there's something I came to show you. Close your eyes.'

'Ooh, a surprise. I love surprises.' Freya placed her be-ringed fingers over her eyes, grinning all the while.

Shannon dug out the hat, pulling it down low, so the pointy little elf ears sat level with her own. Then, fiddling with the belt, she whipped open her coat. 'OK, you can open them. Ta-dah!' The door burst open, and the bell jingled madly on her hat as she twirled around to see who it was.

'Nice outfit.' James grinned. 'I forgot my mom's ring.' He crossed the shop floor to the counter and pocketed the prettily wrapped box still sitting beside the till, and then with a wave, he was gone, leaving a mortified Shannon staring after him.

34

The glorious blue skies over Emerald Bay were short-lived, and by early afternoon the clouds overhead grew heavy once more. It was almost dark, and light snow had begun to sprinkle down on the village by 4 p.m. The fairy lights on the enormous Christmas tree behind Shannon winked at the villagers starting to gather in earnest in the square for the carolling. If you were after a last-minute container of milk or loaf of bread, packet of headache pills, whatever, you were out of luck now. The businesses on the main road were officially closed for Christmas.

Shannon thought it was like a scene from one of Isla's snow globes, making her way toward the elves. Annoyingly her hat kept slipping down over one eye and, adjusting it, she saw the small crowd was filled with faces she knew, along with a handful of people she'd yet to meet. The German tourists who'd filed into town, she suspected. All that was missing was a leprechaun or two to complete the scene.

She took her place in the middle of the front row, squeezing in between Mrs Tattersall and Mrs Bradigan, grateful for their shared body heat and the fact Dr Fairlie's wife, Helena, was two rows back. There was solidarity in numbers, she thought, tugging the tunic down. She didn't feel so ridiculous in her get-up now that she was part of the group. A surreptitious glance at Mrs Tattersall's knobbly knees and Mrs Bradigan's dimpled ones visible through their green stockings confirmed this. Although Freya and James, who'd left his present sitting on the counter, had found her costume hilarious.

A tap on her shoulder saw Shannon twist around.

'That antacid you recommended worked a treat on my indigestion, Shannon,' Mrs Greene informed her. 'Thanks a million.'

'Glad to hear it.' Shannon smiled and, turning back, she glanced up at the late afternoon sky. The bell on her hat tinkled, and an icy, wet flake landed on her nose. She swiped it off, hoping Freya had kept her promise to drive to Westport at 10 mph. She wondered whether James and Maeve had connected with his brothers, her grandsons, yet.

Maeve, she could see, was sitting on a chair in the row of seats carted outside from the pub for the village's older residents. She was chatting amicably to Mr Kenny, who'd driven up alongside her on his motorised scooter.

As Mrs Brady wandered past with a mug of mulled wine, Shannon's nostrils flared. The drink was being doled out with a soup ladle from crockpots inside the Shamrock for the princely sum of two euros. It was a BYO mug, and all proceeds would go toward a long-overdue upgrade to the children's playground in the park beside the church. Rita Quigley had organised the fundraiser, and Eileen Carroll, not to be outdone, had arranged for the mass baking of mince pies which were being passed around gratis to the huddled crowd by members of her knitting group. Shannon hoped there'd be some icing sugar-dusted pies and mugs of the warming wine going spare after they'd finished their song set. She and the rest of the Emerald Bay Elves were going to need it.

The younger children who'd been shrieking their excitement over Father Christmas coming to visit them half an hour ago were now silent because their teeth were stuck together by toffees. The man in the red suit had generously handed out the sweets once he'd heard whether each child had been behaving themselves and what they were hoping he'd drop down the chimney for them.

Shannon knew the sweets were a dentist's dream because she'd helped herself to a toffee from the bag by the kitchen's back door upon her return earlier. By the time she'd completed mission impossible, returning Imogen's coat to the wardrobe without getting caught, it was almost a case of lockjaw. But at least she'd not stuffed two in her mouth like she usually would.

Isla passed a lit candle to Shannon, who took the saucer from her, careful to hold it steady lest the flame go out before they'd even started singing. She hoped Mrs Shea didn't singe her hair with her candle behind her.

'Smile, Shannon!' Grace shouted, holding her phone up.

'Say cheese!' Ava called out.

The flash flared.

'Loving the ears!' Hannah put her fingers in her mouth and emitted a piercing wolf whistle, which earned her a cuff from her mam, who'd left her mulled wine station to see how the proceedings were coming along.

'Did you take my coat out without asking? It reeks of that perfume you were after spraying on yourself,' Imogen roared.

'Feck off with youse all,' Shannon muttered, receiving the sharp end of Mrs Tattersall's elbow.

A hush descended on the crowd, and the villagers and visitors to Emerald Bay parted to make way, for what? Shannon squinted into the encroaching darkness at the shape moving toward the Christmas tree. Her mouth opened, and her phone simultaneously signalled the arrival of a text message. Walking towards her with a leprechaun hat jammed on his head and giving her a lopsided grin was James.

Isla lit one last candle addressing the elves. 'James here is a fine baritone, and he's joining us all the way from Boston. Shift over there, Agnes, and make some room for him.'

Mrs Tattersall did so with an audible murmur of discontent at the tardiness of this interloper.

James slotted in beside Shannon.

'What are you doing?' she hissed out the corner of her mouth.

'Mrs Mullins made me an honorary elf after auditioning for her this afternoon.'

'But you're wearing one of the leprechaun hats Isla sells in her shop.'

'It was the best she could do at short notice, and I sweetened the deal by buying three more of the hats. One for each of my brothers.'

'But you won't know the words to some of the carols. We have a whole repertoire of Irish carols like "Curoo Curoo" and the "Wexford Carol".' They'd plenty of family-friendly jingle bells songs, but James being here now was too much. She'd forget all the words.

Ignoring Mrs Tattersall, who was shushing them, James said, 'I'll lip-sync if I get lost.' He threw in a cheeky wink, and Shannon remembered Freya's wink earlier. She pulled her phone from the tunic pocket and quickly scanned the new message.

If u catch a Leprechaun, Shan, u might find love instead of gold at the rainbow's end.

Freya was behind this! There was no time to think about what she and James thought they were playing at because Isla held three fingers in the air, then two, then one.

The Emerald Bay Elves and their honorary leprechaun launched into 'Hark! The Herald Angels Sing'. Shannon's brown eyes turned to gaze up at James in surprise. His voice was rich, deep and smooth like melting chocolate, she thought, trying not to lick her lips.

35

'I don't understand why it's called Midnight Mass if most parishes in Ireland hold the service earlier in the evening nowadays.' Hannah's voice was muffled as she double-wrapped her brightly striped scarf around her neck, half-covering her mouth. She had a matching beanie on her head, and her dreadlocks hung long down her back.

'Channelling Bob Marley tonight, are we?' Imogen enquired, belting her red coat. She had opted for a matching red version of the beanie.

Hannah scowled at her sister. 'At least I don't look like I should have a feather boa around my neck.'

'Imogen, your sister has a point. It's the parish church you're off to. Not the Moulin Rouge.' Liam frowned at his second eldest daughter.

'Given you look like a geriatric member of Westlife in that polo neck and coat you've on there, Dad, you're in no position to lecture me on my fashion choices.'

'I chose that coat for your father.' Nora was put out. 'I thought the polo neck made him look distinguished.'

'Mam, you didn't answer my question,' Hannah whined.

'It's tradition. That's why, Hannah.' Nora turned to Maeve and James, who were also readying themselves to venture forth into the night, although James had announced he would drive Maeve and Kitty and anyone else who didn't fancy walking the short distance to church. He'd looked at Shannon, but she'd made no move to accept the offer of a ride. Imogen opted to take the spare seat, which was probably wise given the size of the heels on her boots. 'She's never been any different,' Nora continued with an apologetic shrug. 'She always has to question everything.'

'A questioning man is halfway to being wise.' Maeve smiled at Hannah as she slipped an arm into the coat James was proffering. 'Thank you, James.'

'Curiosity killed the cat, more like,' Nora muttered.

'No, Mam. If it were tradition, Midnight Mass would be held at midnight.' Hannah was a dog with a bone.

Nora sighed exasperatedly. 'Sure, now listen to me, would you. If I were to say, "We're off to the nine o'clock Mass, Hannah," it wouldn't have the same ring.' She made a noise that sounded like *phftt*. 'And you university-educated.' Then, pulling on the mulberry-coloured beret she'd chosen to tone in with her smart new winter jacket, she tilted it just so.

'Ooh-la-lah,' Liam said, waggling his eyebrows at his wife, making them all laugh.

'And you're to behave yourself in the church and all.' Nora wagged a finger at him playfully.

Grace and Ava sniggered. James, too, who'd swapped his Gore-Tex and leprechaun hat for appropriate church attire, watched the bickering banter with amusement and something else, Shannon saw. His absorption in the family scene gave her the chance to study him, and with a burst of clarity, she understood what it was she'd seen flicker across his face. Wistfulness. He'd lost his father when he was young and hadn't grown up privy to the easy way between two people who'd been married for over half their lives. She took her mam and dad's relationship for granted, while he missed what he'd never had. The realisation made her want to hug him.

Of course, she didn't act on it. Instead, she thought back on the last few hours as the fingers of her left hand worked the thread that had come loose inside the pocket of her puffa.

Once she'd recovered from her surprise at James gatecrashing the carolling and the fact that he could sing, she'd employed diversionary tactics. She'd had to because her senses had suddenly sharpened as though someone had turned the volume up as he squeezed himself in between her and Mrs Tattersall. There was the faint mix of the herbal shampoo and aftershave she knew he used. Then there was the awareness of her shoulder pressing against his arm. She knew she was in danger of doing something silly like stretching her fingers out to entwine them with his, not to mention fluffing the words to 'Rudolph, the Red-Nosed Reindeer'. What with Helena Fairlie giving it her all in the back row, she owed it to the villagers of Emerald Bay to stay on track, and she'd managed it by focusing on all the things she'd text Freya later.

As they'd wound into 'Good King Wenceslas', Shannon had realised it was no good pretending she wasn't physically attracted to James because she was. She really, really was in a wanting to rest her hands on his shoulders, stand on tiptoes and kiss him way. But that didn't mean it was a good idea to act on it. He'd be heading back to America soon enough, and she would forget all about him. Sure, hadn't she found Chris Hemsworth very attractive in that Thor movie Julien had dragged her to? And she'd forgotten all about him, eventually. Besides, the thought of copping off in that Laura Ashley wonderland her mam let out as a guest room was just wrong.

So when the festivities in the square were over, Shannon had slunk back to the pub, opting to hide in her bedroom, and the first thing she'd done was text Freya. Instead of telling her friend off for plotting with James, her fingers tapped out how he made her think of Lion bars. Freya knew how Shannon felt about Lion bars. She'd get it. Her friend had been quick to text back, and Shannon read how happy Oisin was to see her. There were too many yellow circle emojis with love heart eyes following this to convince Shannon, though. Her heart hurt for Freya, but there was nothing she could do about it. She'd learn the hard way, as Shannon had with Julien. However, there was one thing she could do concerning her self-preservation, and that was to make sure she wasn't left on her own with James.

Nor had she been in the hours since.

It seemed her mam wasn't finished with the Midnight Mass topic yet, for she heard her say, 'And I can't speak for other parishes, but Father Seamus is getting on, and you can't expect the poor man to be sitting up until midnight these days.' She was fanning herself as she spoke, then stopped and began to flap her coat instead.

'He manages to stay up until midnight in a lock-in when you keep topping up his whiskey for him right enough,' Liam stated.

Nora gave him a look that said he was bordering on blasphemy before addressing Hannah again: 'Don't be going on about the poor bees to all and sundry when we get to church, either, Hannah. You're to be on your best behaviour. That goes for all of you.'

Shannon nodded, feeling like she was four instead of thirty-four as her mam looked from Hannah to her for assurance before moving down the line to Imogen, Grace, and Ava. She'd said the same thing to them every Christmas Eve for as long as Shannon could remember. She'd be spitting on a handkerchief and wiping their faces next.

Seeing Maeve buttoning her coat, Nora added, 'Obviously, I'm not pointing the finger at you and James, Maeve.'

'Are you all right there, Nora?' Maeve asked, looking up.

'You're not sickening for something, are you? You've gone very red in the face all of a sudden.'

'It's a power surge, is all, Maeve. Nothing to worry about.'

Kitty, also rugged up in a coat and hat, was prodding at the ham she'd set to boil earlier for the sandwiches on their return from church. 'It can rest while we're at the service,' she said half to herself as she draped a tea towel over the top of it.

A comforting glow settled over Shannon. The ham sandwiches on soft white bread had always been the perfect end to Christmas Eve. That and ensuring Father Christmas had a plate of biscuits and a glass of ale to enjoy after he slipped down the chimney with a sackful of presents.

'Right, well, we should be off,' Liam announced with a clap of his hands. Then, shuddering, he added, 'Jaysus, Shannon, would you have a word with that cat of yours?'

They all looked to where Napoleon had appeared in the doorway to eye them all disdainfully.

Father Seamus welcomed his flock and handed out the order of service at the entrance to the village church while Mrs Rae banged out 'Oh Come, All Ye Faithful' on the organ. Shannon slid along the wooden pew next to Maeve. She was seated next to James, her arm firmly linked through his. Just who this American man was to Maeve Doolin would be a hot topic among the congregation slowly filing in, Shannon knew. She breathed in the heady muskiness of incense and women's perfumes, wondering how many women had popped into Heneghan's for a squirt of Seduce Me earlier. The combination of the two made her eyes water and her nose tingled with a threatened sneeze. A baby was crying a few rows up from where they were sitting, and Mrs Molloy called out for one of her sons to sit down and stop running about the place like a heathen.

Ruby McGinn, directly in front of Shannon, made her

flinch by flicking her long hair back off her shoulders, nearly whipping her with it. The speed with which Ruby's thumbs were working her phone was mesmerising, and Shannon blinked as the device was abruptly snatched off the teenager by Mrs McGinn. 'Ella's only sitting over there. You can talk to her after Mass,' she scolded, tucking it away in her handbag. Ruby slumped down in her seat, arms folded over her chest mutinously.

Families greeted one another as though it had been months instead of days since they'd seen each other, and those that had fallen out patched things up, shaking hands on their differences because it was Christmas after all.

Shannon, her head tilted to one side, listened to Maeve chattering about the wonders of modern technology with a smile.

'Would you believe it, Shannon? I've four grandsons. Four strapping, handsome grandsons,' she was saying now.

Several heads swivelled in Maeve's direction upon hearing this, but she was forgotten as the doors Father Seamus had just closed opened, and Matthew Leslie, his wife and two daughters swept in.

Shannon knew she was gawping, but she couldn't help it. Mrs Leslie and her two daughters were like Nordic clones of the Cambridges, while Matthew Leslie was more Prince Harry-ish Next to her, Maeve stiffened, and as the family glided past, it occurred to Shannon how strange it must be for her. The posture of Matthew Leslie was that of a self-assured and entitled man. He had no idea the American sitting to the left of little Maeve Doolin, who used to clean his grandparent's house, was his nephew. Her hand automatically grasped Maeve's and, catching James's questioning gaze, she replied with a shrug. Now wasn't the right time to lean over and whisper who the Leslies were.

Shannon craned her neck to see where they'd sat down.

The Molloys had bunched up to make room for the family whose housekeeper placed a regular meat order with their butcher's shop. It was funny, Shannon thought, watching the deference on the villagers' faces. The days of the big house overseeing the village were gone, but the legacy remained. What must it have been like for Maeve all these years, living in the shadow of the house on the hill?

Father Seamus made his way to the front of the church, and as he took his place, he reminded his flock it was Jesus, not the Leslies, who was the star of this show.

'It was a grand service.'

'Father Seamus did us proud.'

'Mam, what if we walk in on Father Christmas delivering our presents?'

'Merry Christmas!'

The voices mingled loud and cheerful on the silent night as the residents of Emerald Bay exited their church. An SUV's headlights illuminated the inky night. Shannon had seen the Leslie family, who'd paused only to thank Father Seamus for his service, climb into it. They'd not conversed with any of the gathered villagers, and as the shiny, oversized vehicle rumbled past, she saw the windows were tinted.

'Shannon, can I have a word?' James interrupted her thoughts. Maeve and Kitty were chatting with Rita Quigley and Brenda Gallagher a short distance away. As for the rest of her family, they would shake hands and wish their friends and neighbours a happy Christmas. She'd been about to do the same, but she nodded, looking at him expectantly, her breath juddering at the sudden current the touch of his hand on her elbow had sent tingling up her arm. He steered her gently away from the crowd around the side of the church. His sea-green eyes were black as they held hers with an intensity that made Shannon part her lips in expectation.

'Shannon, there's something I need to say, so I'm just going to say it.'

The trance broke as a horde of overexcited kids playing tag raced past. What was she doing? If it was merely a physical pull toward him, she felt she might be able to throw caution to the wind, but it was more than that. She liked him, and she wouldn't risk taking the next step because he would be leaving. The emotional fallout of Julien's leaving was still too raw.

'Don't, James, just don't.' Shannon broke away and hurried back to the others.

CHRISTMAS DAY

*May the good saints protect you and bless you
    today.
And may trouble ignore you each step of
    the way.
Christmas joy to you!*

— *IRISH CHRISTMAS BLESSING*

36

'You're an honorary Irishman in that sweater and apron, so you are, James,' Liam boomed overtop of Grace doing Bono's melody in 'Do They Know It's Christmas?' playing on the radio. He'd bustled back into the kitchen full of the spirit of Christmas with his Santa hat on. 'Hurry up with those serviettes there, girls. Your nan and Maeve are after setting the table. Half an hour and our guests will be knocking on the door.' He rubbed his hands together as the aroma of roasting meats filled the kitchen. With her snowman earrings dangling, Nora closed the cooker door on the enormous turkey surrounded by onions and carrots.

'It's coming along a treat,' she said, pleased. 'And I'll give the roast beef another minute before resting it.'

How any of them were going to find room to eat after the enormous breakfast they'd consumed earlier was a mystery, Shannon thought, but the outcome was the same every year. Room was always found, especially when it came to the Christmas pudding and trifle Mam had assembled earlier that morning.

'Why couldn't we just roll the napkins up and bend them in

half to go in the glasses like usual?' Grace griped as she tried to fold the green paper into the complicated Christmas tree shape Kitty had tasked them with.

'Because Nan's mad about the origami at the moment. You know that, Grace, and it's not that hard once you've done the first couple,' Ava informed her twin, who didn't look convinced. Napoleon was curled up, happy to be in the hub of things upon her lap.

Shannon, folding the last corner of her napkin, glanced over at James. He'd been put in charge of parboiling the potatoes for the roasties. His back was leaning against the worktop as he watched the intricacies of paper-napkin folding while waiting for the water to come to a rolling boil so he could drop the spuds into the pan. Shannon dropped her gaze as his eyes locked on hers, and she was all fingers and thumbs as she moved on to the next serviette.

He wore the Aran knit better than any Irishman she knew. And the fact he was wearing her nan's favourite *I don't need a recipe, I'm Irish* pinny didn't just cement his look – it let them know he'd won Kitty over with his insistence of being put to work straight after they'd cleared away the last of the Christmas wrapping paper. He'd started by giving their dad a hand to push three tables together in the pub.

It was a shame he wouldn't get the hat she'd purchased on impulse in Clifden. But she couldn't very well give it to him now, not after shutting him down last night. It would send out a mixed message, and she was clear in her mind she'd done the right thing. Infatuations passed. Getting involved with James for the rest of his stay in Emerald Bay was pointless and would leave her right back where she'd started when she first arrived home. Besides, he needed to concentrate on getting to know his grandmother.

At least Mam had ensured he and Maeve both had something to open on behalf of the Kelly family as they'd all gathered around the tree in the pub where presents had appeared overnight. A book of Irish poetry that wouldn't take up room in his backpack for James and a gift set from Heneghan's for Maeve. Nora was big on supporting the village's businesses and shopping local, except when it came to the groceries!

Shannon had received, among other things, the book she'd been after and a bottle of Seduce Me eau de toilette.

Hannah, however, excelled herself on the gift-giving front with packets of bee-attracting wildflower seed mix for her sisters and a beehive smoker for her parents.

There'd been a gift Shannon hadn't been expecting too.

As things got underway in the kitchen for dinner, she'd nipped upstairs to check on Napoleon. She wanted to make sure he was getting mileage out of the ball with the bell inside it she'd bought as his present, and while winning him over with the cat treats she'd splurged on, there'd been a tap on the door. She'd opened it to see James standing there in all his Aran knit glory and must have looked wary because the first words out of his mouth were, 'It's OK, I got the message last night.'

'James, I didn't mean—' What didn't she mean? She dug around, trying to articulate her feelings. 'I just don't think it's a good idea.'

'I get it. I do. You had a messy break-up. You don't want to get involved with anyone.'

He didn't get it, because Shannon *did* want to get involved but the timing was wrong.

'I've got something I wanted to give you in private. And I promise, there are no strings attached.' He produced a cardboard canister from behind his back. Shannon took it, unsure what it meant.

'Open it,' James said softly.

She prised the plastic seal off and slid the rolled-up contents out, nipping her bottom lip with uncertainty as she unfurled the pulpy paper, having guessed what it was.

The painting of Kilticaneel Castle she'd been drawn to at Mermaids.

'I know it makes you think of your grandad.'

Shannon nodded recalling their conversation in Clifden. 'It does, and it's very generous of you, but I can't accept it.' She really would be having a word with Freya when she returned from Westport.

'I want you to have it, Shannon.' And this time, it was James that shut down the conversation by leaving her there holding the painting as he disappeared back down the stairs.

When she returned to the kitchen, she found her mam fawning over James as they got down to the serious business of ensuring their guests would be fed.

'I can make a mean omelette,' Liam had thrown in, not wishing to be outshone by their American guest in the kitchen. Nora slapped his hand dipping into the tin of Quality Street chocolates open on the table.

The big hand on the clock had moved five minutes when steam filled the kitchen as James drained the potatoes before sprinkling flour over them. Nora was at the ready with the baking tray of hot goose fat, and there was a satisfying sizzle as he carefully put the potatoes in it.

'Right, James, it's on to the salmon starters,' Nora announced once the potatoes were in the oven. Kitty had appeared in the interim, demanding the Christmas tree serviettes. Piling them into the basket in the middle of the table, Shannon picked it up and trailed through to the pub after her nan.

Maeve was seated at a table polishing the last of the silver. Kitty had tossed two white sheets over the tables they were to eat at, and a red gingham table runner and matching placemats added colour. The holly and pinecone centrepiece Kitty insisted was a family heirloom was in pride of place. 'How many place settings are there, Kitty?' Maeve asked, ready to tackle counting the knives, forks and spoons.

'Fifteen, Maeve.'

Shannon set the serviettes down next to each gleaming wine glass, frowning at a napkin that resembled a shrub rather than a tree. Grace's effort, no doubt.

At one o'clock sharp, Enda Dunne rapped on the door to the pub. He'd fallen out with his only son over his refusal to sell the family farm and move to a retirement complex in Galway. Paddy McNamara staggered forth next, reeking of whiskey and full of apologies because his Bridget was otherwise engaged. They were swiftly followed by Silé Twomey, whose husband had vanished in the sixties. The consensus had been he'd started a new life in Australia. Mrs Twomey had said good riddance and had remained happily footloose and fancy-free ever since. She'd state that the only time she felt his absence was Christmas, but sure hadn't the Kellys fixed that problem for her with their generous offer of dinner on the day itself? Then there was Adella Garcia, a Spanish teacher who taught at the high school in Kilticaneel. She rented a flat above the Knitters Nook and had, for reasons unknown, opted not to return to Spain for the holidays. Then, finally, Piaras Fennelly arrived, a widower whose family had emigrated to Canada.

Kitty and Finbar's tradition of ensuring no one in Emerald Bay spent Christmas day alone by inviting them to dine at the pub with their family was one Nora and Liam had proudly continued. The Kelly girls had grown up used to pulling their weight while various villagers were seated at the table for Christmas dinner, and as a result, throughout the meal, the kitchen ran as smoothly as a Michelin-starred restaurant. Kitty, Nora, Shannon, Imogen, Hannah, Grace and Ava were a well-oiled machine when it came to serving the food. Liam, too was in his element, playing his role of the convivial host. He kept the glasses topped up and the fire crackling throughout their meal.

Enda picked up the first cracker once the dinner plates had been cleared away. 'Would you pull it with me, Kitty?'

Kitty conceded – it was Christmas, after all – and tugging the red-and-gold cracker, her competitive streak flared. Then, with a pop, she was left holding the cracker. Donning her hat and showing everybody her prize, a plastic keyring, she unfolded the slip of paper and cleared her throat.

'Why was the turkey in a pop group?'

'I don't know,' echoed around the table.

'Because he was the only one with drumsticks.'

The punchline was met with groaning and laughter, more crackers were pulled, and paper crowns donned. Nora wondered whether she should fetch the trifle and Christmas pudding when the door to the pub was flung open, startling them all.

A man whose hat was pulled low and scarf wound high banged it shut behind him, and it was only when he'd unwound the scarf Shannon recognised the ruddy face beneath the hat. It was Maeve's son, Fergus. She glanced toward Maeve, who'd gone pale with shock, but he began jabbing a finger toward the seated group before she or anyone could acknowledge him.

'Which one of you is the American come to part my mam from her money?'

James looked baffled for a moment, and then Shannon watched it dawn on him as to who this man must be, and he made to stand up, but Maeve placed a restraining hand on his forearm. 'No, this isn't your corner to fight, James.' She eased herself upright.

'Fergus. It's a Merry Christmas to you too, son.'

'Mam! I've been worried sick. You've not been answering your phone.'

'Because the power was out, and the Kellys graciously offered to put me up for a few days. I'd have telephoned you from here, but I thought it wouldn't do you any harm to digest what I'd told you for a day or two. I planned on ringing you this evening to wish you and the family a Merry Christmas.'

His chest puffed up beneath his coat. 'It's thanks to him, I take it,' he glowered at James, 'that I've been robbed of spending Christmas with my wife and children. You've no idea what it was like trying to book a last-minute flight to Dublin, not to mention hire a car.'

'Well, you needn't have worried yourself coming. Unless you were desperate to spend Christmas with your auld mam.' Maeve's keen blue eyes studied her son.

Fergus tugged at the collar of his coat, his face growing redder by the minute. 'Never mind all that. I'm here now.' He strode to the head of the table and looked at all the faces, most of whom he knew, except Adella. 'Do you know who that scam artist sidling up to my poor mam says he is?'

Shannon could tell he was enjoying playing to the crowd.

'Only her grandson.' The open-mouthed 'Oh's' murmured were all the ammunition Fergus needed. 'Oh, indeed. I got some convoluted story about Mam having had a baby before marrying my dad. You've lived here forever and a day' – he pointed rudely at Kitty – 'did you know anything about this so-called baby?'

Maeve banged her hand down on the table, causing the cutlery to rattle, and all eyes swivelled toward the little woman who usually wouldn't say boo to a fly. 'Fergus Doolin, that's enough out of you. Sit down this minute, and don't be pointing at your elders like a heathen. Your father and I raised you better than that.'

Fergus blinked. It was plain to see that he was taken aback at his mam shouting at him; pulling out a chair at a nearby table, he did as he'd been told.

'I'd like to apologise for my son barging in and shouting the odds.' Maeve addressed the table. 'As for James here. It's true. He's my grandson.'

Fergus snorted, but as Maeve shot him a warning glance, he seemed to shrink inside his coat, his expression one of confusion as to where his meek and mild mam had disappeared to.

Maeve laid both her hands down on the table. 'I've been silent long enough, and I won't be bullied anymore. Not by the Leslie family, the nuns, and certainly not by you.' She stared hard at her son, but all the bluster had gone out of him. 'I've realised in the last few days since my grandson James came to find me that life is short, and I won't be wasting any more precious time.'

Shannon could see her family and their guests trying to figure out the connection between Maeve, the Leslies and the nuns. That Fergus was and always had been a bully was a given and a mystery because he didn't get his aggressive demeanour from either of his parents, who were both gentle, loving souls.

James put his hand over the top of Maeve's. 'You don't have to explain to everyone,' he said quietly.

'No, you don't,' Kitty reiterated.

'But I want to. I've nothing to be ashamed of.'

The only sound in the room was the splintering wood on the fire as Maeve told her story, and when she was finished, eyes were being dabbed at with crumpled Christmas tree napkins. Kitty got up to embrace Maeve, and Shannon heard her murmur, 'You're a brave woman, Maeve Doolin. And I'm sorry for what you went through. The Leslies and the Church have a lot to answer for.'

It was a sentiment agreed upon around the table.

'And I'll tell you something else,' Maeve directed at Fergus. 'The money my mam took from the Leslies on my behalf will be used to buy myself and James here first-class tickets to Boston to meet your sister before it's too late.'

Shannon almost felt sorry for Fergus as he took off his hat and rubbed at his temples, trying to make sense of all his mother had said. He had a sister who didn't have long to live and four nephews. Liam got up from the table without fanfare and fetched him a stiff drink.

She watched as Maeve sat back in her seat and James looked at his grandmother with pride. What she had said about life being short and time precious replayed in Shannon's head. *You only get one shot at it*, she thought, knocking back her wine. Maeve had been brave. So would she.

37

'You were right,' James said to Shannon as she shut the back door behind them, and they stepped onto the snow-covered ground. The flakes that were still falling were softer now and powdery like talcum. 'Fergus is an arse. The way he blundered in...' He shook his head at the memory of Fergus Doolin bursting in the door as if he were Poirot about to point the finger at the murderer. 'I hope Maeve doesn't live to regret her outburst. Emerald Bay's small, and it's her that has to live here, not me. It was never my intention to upend her life.'

'Oh, I think that had been a long time coming on Maeve's part, and it was therapeutic. I mean, can you imagine carrying all that hurt and loss around inside you all these years the way she's done and keeping such a huge secret from your son? But, as she said, it wasn't her that did anything wrong. And sure, it will be gossip fodder for a week or two, and then something else will happen. Emerald Bay might be small, but there are always shenanigans afoot. And, who knows, perhaps it will wake Fergus up, because you only get one mother, and he should look after his better.'

'I'd have to disagree with you there. My mom has two mothers.'

Shannon glanced up at him. It would generally be dark at 5 p.m. this time of year, but she could see his profile beneath the hood of his jacket clearly in the strangely luminous light. 'You're right.'

James turned to look at her, seeming to read her mind as he said, 'It's called the scattering of light. I did a school project on why the night sky seems so bright when it snows. The snow on the ground reflects light up into the atmosphere, and the snowflakes falling keep it trapped there.'

'The scattering of the light,' Shannon murmured. 'That's lovely. It sounds like the title to a poem.'

James agreed with her as they walked in no hurry across the car park onto the lane beyond, breathing in the smoky bite of the fires burning in the village. Illicit peat mingling with timber.

'That's a smell I won't forget,' James said, inhaling deeply. Shannon was leading him, and while he might be clueless as to what direction they'd take, she knew where they were going because she, Shannon Marie Kelly, was taking a leaf out of Maeve's book by being brave. She'd bided her time until the furore over Fergus's unexpected arrival and Maeve's resulting revelation had settled down, then quietly asked James if he would come for a walk with her later. The quizzical look he'd greeted her request with was only to be expected, but he'd agreed anyway, and once their guests had drifted home and they'd all pitched in clearing the table, they'd slipped into their jackets.

Fergus and Maeve were talking fireside in the empty pub while Nora had suggested trying to find a Christmas movie on the television to watch while their meal went down. 'The washing-up can wait,' she announced. Nobody argued, and Shannon and James had made their escape while the Kelly family arranged themselves on the sofa in the living room.

'I can hear the sea,' James said, stopping alongside the hedgerow. He pushed his hood back to listen.

Shannon smiled. It wasn't often the mighty Atlantic was silent. Their breath and footsteps crunching on the snow and the distant crash of waves were the only sounds to be heard. The villagers who'd opted to rug up and walk their Christmas dinner off were long since home, and it felt as if a wand had been waved over the village, sending it to sleep for a hundred years. Eyeing James as he put his hood back on, Shannon remembered what she'd stuffed in the pocket of her puffa before they'd left.

'I bought you something for Christmas,' she said, having made her mind up to be bold.

'You did?' James sounded surprised.

'I did.' Shannon reached into her pocket to produce a bag. She thrust it at him, frightened her nerve might falter.

Bemused, James opened it as Shannon held her breath, waiting to see what he'd say. He examined the hat.

'It matches your Aran sweater. Sea green, like your eyes.'

He pulled the beanie on down over his ears and gave her a lopsided grin. 'I feel complete.'

'Aran Man.' Shannon giggled, both from nerves and because he looked so darn cute. 'C'mon.' She set off at a faster pace now, impatient to get to where they were going.

The church was in darkness as they passed it, and Shannon imagined Father Seamus would be snoozing in front of the fire in the presbytery while Mrs Rae busied herself washing up the remnants of their dinner. As for the adjacent park, apart from the plump snowman with a scarf, hat and carrot nose who was guarding it, there was no sign of life there either. Their feet sank into the deeper snow, and as they passed the swings, her shins grew damp.

Shannon's palms felt clammy inside her mittens, and her heart had begun to beat faster, but she carried on toward the furthest corner where her teenage self had once hung out, hidden from view.

To not take risks would be to lead a half-life, she thought. If, as she suspected she would, she fell hard for this American who possessed a grin that made her feel like her insides had turned to marshmallow, and he broke her heart, then so be it. She repeated Maeve's earlier sentiment: life is short, and time's precious. So, stop wasting it being frightened, she told herself determinedly, putting one foot in front of the other until she reached the bushes where she knew the holly bush was hiding.

'What are you doing?' James asked as, holding her phone as a torch, she began swiping the white blanket from the shrubs almost flattened under the weight of the snow. Shannon didn't answer. She was intent on finding a clue, and there it was, she thought as she spied a cluster of red berries. She snapped a piece of the prickly holly off and turned to face James. 'When I was a teenager, it was a thing among the village girls to hold a sprig of holly over the head of a boy you liked, to steal a kiss.'

James was quiet, and Shannon wondered if she'd been a fool bringing him here. Her breath shortened as she forced herself to look into his eyes, knowing she'd find the answer to whether she'd misread things there. The moment she'd seen him beside the Christmas tree as she drove into Emerald Bay, his eyes had caught and held her attention, and now she felt herself falling into them as James reached out and took the holly from her. He held it above his head and, feeling as though she were in a dream, Shannon reached up and rested her mitten-clad hands on his shoulders. She paused, relishing his nearness as she breathed in his familiar citrus and spice scent. It filled her with delicious anticipation of what was to come.

James, however, was impatient and, placing his index finger under Shannon's chin, he tilted her head upward. They searched one another's eyes fleetingly in the pale light and their eyes fluttered shut as they leaned in, their noses bumping as their lips met, making them laugh at their clumsiness.

'Shall we try that again?' James asked, surprising her by brushing her mouth with the briefest peck as he hit his mark this time. It was enough for Shannon to feel the roughness of his chapped lips.

'A stolen kiss, so you know I like you,' he said, smiling as he tossed the holly aside to free up his hands. 'A lot.'

'I like you too,' Shannon murmured, that lopsided grin flooding her body with warmth. One day she'd tell him what that smile of his did to her. She might even tell him how his eyes turned her insides molten. For now, though, all that mattered was the sensation of his hands settling around her waist. He pulled her toward him, and she could feel their strength but knew too they were healing hands.

This time their lips met tentatively, then tenderly and as their mouths began to bruise one another's, thrillingly. Shannon could taste sweet sherry, and her toes curled inside her boots as she understood that she was exactly where she was supposed to be.

She was home.

A LETTER FROM MICHELLE VERNAL

Dear reader,

I want to say a huge thank you for choosing to read *Christmas in the Little Irish Village*. If you did enjoy it, and want to keep up to date with all my latest releases, just sign up at the following link. Your email address will never be shared and you can unsubscribe at any time.

www.bookouture.com/michelle-vernal

I had so much fun writing about the Kelly family of Emerald Bay and I hope you enjoyed getting to know them and the characters who live in the village. I can't wait to return to the bay in book 2 of this new series and to share what happens next with you!

Ireland is a place dear to my heart as I turned twenty-one there on my first visit. I returned seven years later and got engaged to my now husband, Paul, and brought my wedding dress, bought from a colleague in my legal secretary days second-hand, home to New Zealand with me.

It's a country that draws you back and I feel fortunate to spend so much time there in my head writing and bringing to life colourful characters I very much hope feel like family and friends to you.

I hope you loved *Christmas in the Little Irish Village* and if you did I would be very grateful if you could write a review. I'd love to hear what you think, and it makes such a difference helping new readers to discover one of my books for the first time.

I love hearing from my readers – you can get in touch on my Facebook page, through Twitter, Goodreads or my website.

Thanks,

Michelle Vernal

www.michellevernalbooks.com

 facebook.com/michellevernalnovelist
twitter.com/MichelleVernal

ACKNOWLEDGEMENTS

I'd like to thank my editor, Natasha, for her faith in me and helping me bring this story to life. Also to Kim and Noelle and the wonderful Bookouture team. It's so exciting to have *Christmas in the Little Irish Village* published by such a vibrant and forward-moving publisher like Bookouture.

I also want to say a huge thank you to my husband, Paul, for his support and hard work ensuring everything at home runs smoothly while I'm writing. I love you and our boys to the moon and back.